GRACE AT THE GATE

A Troubled Journey

GARY L. FISHER

Best Wishes –

Gary L. Fisher

DocUmeant *Publishing*
244 5th Avenue
Suite G-200
NY, NY 10001
646-233-4366
www.DocUmeantPublishing.com

GRACE AT THE GATE: A troubled journey

Published by
DocUmeant Publishing
244 5th Avenue, Suite G-200
NY, NY 10001
Phone: 646-233-4366

Disclaimer: This is a work of fiction. Names, characters, businesses, places, events and incidents are either the products of the author's imagination or used in a fictitious manner. Any resemblance to real persons, living or dead is purely coincidental with the exception of a few famous individuals and locations mentioned briefly. Celebrities or locations mentioned in this work do not represent endorsements by them, their heirs, or any business mentioned in this work of fiction.

Permission should be addressed in writing to:

garmarsa@bellsouth.net

Copy Editor, Philip S Marks

Cover Design & Layout, DocUmeant Designs

Library of Congress Control Number: 2016943779

ISBN13: 978-1-937801-70-0
ISBN10: 1-937801-70-5

In Loving Memory of
Scott Michael Fisher

Dedicated to my wonderful daughter
Sarah Sullivan Fisher

Contents

Dedication iii

List of Characters ix

   Historical Characters.................................... ix

   Fictional Characters..................................... x

Prologue.. xiii

Acknowledgments xv

Introduction xvii

Chapter 1: Grace 1

Chapter 2: Aaron & Hannah 5

Chapter 3: James 10

Chapter 4: Charlie.............................. 14

Chapter 5: Hannah 18

Chapter 6: Grace 22

Chapter 7: Charlie.............................. 33

Chapter 8: Charlie.............................. 40

Chapter 9: Lucinda 47

Chapter 10: Hannah, 1884 52

Chapter 11: Charlie, 1902....................... 58

Chapter 12: Buffalo Bill........................ 61

Chapter 13: Charlie............................. 65

Chapter 14: John L.............................. 77

Chapter 15: Charlie............................. 92

Chapter 16: Charlie............................. 96

Chapter 17: Grace 100

Chapter 18: Charlie 108

Gracie at the Gate 111

Chapter 19: Charlie 112

Chapter 20: Grace 116

Chapter 21: Charlie 122

Chapter 22: Aaron 127

Chapter 23: Charlie 139

Chapter 24: Grace 144

Chapter 25: Lucinda 147

Chapter 26: Charlie 151

Chapter 27: Grace 160

Chapter 28: Aaron 165

Chapter 29: Charlie 167

Altoona Mirror 171

Chapter 30: Charlie 172

Chapter 31: Grace 177

Chapter 32: Charlie 189

Chapter 33: Aaron 203

Chapter 34: Grace 208

Chapter 35: Charlie 222

Chapter 36: Hattie 226

Chapter 37: Charlie 232

Chapter 38: Grace 235

Chapter 39: Charlie 237

Chapter 40: Isaac 250

Chapter 41: Charlie 256

Chapter 42: Isaac 261

Chapter 43: Charlie 262

Chapter 44: Grace 269

Chapter 45: Charlie 275
Chapter 46: Grace 280
Chapter 47: Charlie 284
Chapter 48: Aaron 287
Chapter 49: Charlie 292
Chapter 50: Aaron 300
Chapter 51: Charlie 303
Chapter 52: Grace 309
Chapter 53: Charlie 317
Chapter 54: Hattie 325
Chapter 55: Charlie and Vern 334
Chapter 56: Grace 342
Chapter 57: Charlie 347
Epilogue 352

List of Characters

HISTORICAL CHARACTERS

Grace May Reynolds, daughter of Aaron and Hannah Reynolds, born 1890, Port Byron, Illinois

Charles Henry Fisher, IV, son of James and Mary Alice Fisher, born 1887, Fayette, Iowa

James Henry Fisher, father of Charles, born 1856, Harrisburg, Pennsylvania

Mary Alice Joyner, mother of Charles, born 1862, Wisconsin

Aaron Reynolds, father of Grace, born 1862, Rock Island, Illinois

Hannah Rebecca Courtney Reynolds, mother of Grace, born 1870, Scott County, Iowa

Henrietta Reynolds, sister of Grace, born 1887, Port Byron, Illinois

Isaiah Reynolds, paternal grandfather of Grace, born 1824, Ohio

Lucinda Buzzard, paternal grandmother of Grace, born 1832, Ohio (?)

Walter Courtney, maternal grandfather of Grace, born 1846, Iowa

Mary Jane Day, maternal grandmother of Grace, born 1850, Greene, Pennsylvania

Pearl, Alta, James, Jr., William and John Leonard, sisters and brothers of Charles

Harmon Lovell, beau of Henrietta (Hattie)

Vern Marshall, friend of Charlie

Bertha Marshall, wife of Vern

Other Historical Figures

Thomas C. Williams, Sheriff of Henry County, Illinois

William F. Cody, frontiersman, Army scout, Indian fighter, showman

Nate Salsbury, Show Manager for *Buffalo Bill's Wild West and Congress of Rough Riders of the World*

John L. Sullivan, Heavyweight Champion of the World, grand-uncle of Grace

Samuel Clemens aka Mark Twain, author, traveler

Orville and Wilbur Wright, inventors

Captain Van Schaick, Captain of the *General Slocum,* New York City

Theodore Roosevelt, President of the United States

Carrie Nation, temperance crusader

FICTIONAL CHARACTERS

Skunk Pete, friend of Charles, fiddler and musician

Duggie Hayes, friend/foe of Charles

Sarah May Hayes, sister of Duggie

Priscilla Donnelly, school teacher

John O'Dea, President of Colonna City Bank

Ratface, a river man who befriended Charlie

Skillet, Scar, Lone Cat, Bear, Two-Shot, Whiskers, and Goliath, hobos

Clyde Rollins, Unskilled Laborer

Isaac Harmony, beau of Grace

Archibald Anvil, Farmer

Annie Anvil, Archibald's wife

Clementine Constantine, a teen-aged girl

Prologue

As America approached the start of the twentieth century, many historical figures each worked separately to forge the nation into a modern society. New ideas, new inventions, and exceptional men and women propelled the culture into a technical revolution.

But, these innovators were not the only people doing their part in making life better. Pioneers had migrated west and settled states from Ohio to California. Life was improving through railroads, new cities, and better modes of transportation. Electric power lines were erected, the telephone was making inroads on communications, and the automobile was beginning to look like it might replace the horse. Politics, the economy, technology, and cultures were all evolving into the new way of life.

Farmers continued to toil, working the land, growing crops, feeding not only their families but the families of the innovators, the inventors, the politicians, the automakers.

One such family lived on the banks of a small hamlet of the Mississippi River, itself an instrument of the changing environment. This story concentrates on two of these citizens.

Acknowledgments

My special thanks to my wife, Marilyn W. Fisher, for her proofreading and support. Very special thanks to my sister, Sheryl Hickman Peterson, for the love she constantly gives and her sweet nature, as well as reminding me of incidents in the Fisher family.

Introduction

This fictional narrative of Charles Henry Fisher and Grace May Reynolds touches the lives of people who lived at the turn of the 20th Century. Some of the events I have listed actually happened and others I have added to give interest to their story. I will list fact from fiction at the end of the tale.

1

Grace

With her red pigtails dancing behind her, Grace May Reynolds raced down to the river to see the *Queen Mary Belle* steamboat steering its way towards the shore of a little settlement on the Illinois side of the wide Mississippi River. Her older sister, Hattie, followed with equal anticipation of spying a handsome ship's captain, or maybe a muscular sailor pulling on the towlines to tie it off the dock.

Port Byron was little more than a string of homes and a few stores, a blacksmith, and saloons along the shore of the swiftly moving river, but the ship held a cargo of supplies destined for the town's General Mercantile.

"Gracie, don't run so fast," panted Hattie. "You know I can't keep up with you." Hattie might have been older by three years but found it hard to keep up with her lively sister.

Grace stopped beside the railroad tracks that ran parallel to the river and waited for Hattie. It was May 8, 1901, just a month past Grace's 11th birthday.

A couple of boys, sitting on the bank fishing, turned to see what was going on behind them.

"Come on, Hat, the *Mary Belle* doesn't come by here that often, and I want to see the paddle wheels."

"Mother told you not to call me that. My name is Henrietta. She said it was Okay to call me Hattie but *never* call me 'Hat'. It sounds like I'm a derby."

"Hattie the Derby, Hattie the Derby," taunted Grace. She hopped across the tracks to the bank leading down to the Mississippi.

"Gracie, Mother said to never go across the tracks. You could get your leg or something caught right when a train was a comin'."

"Oh, phoo! 'Mother said! Mother said!' She ain't gonna know iffen you don't tell her."

"I might, I just might . . . unless . . .," she said leaving her sentence unfinished.

"Lest what?" She pulled at her long red braid, eyeing her sister suspiciously.

"Lest you promise to fetch the water from the well for the next *month!*"

"Okay," said Grace, knowing full well that their mother would make The Hat fetch the water when it was her turn. She turned and started down the bank but lost her footing and tumbled the last eight feet to the river's edge. She tried to catch herself, but her momentum carried her right into the swirling water. She came up sputtering with clumps of mud on her red gingham dress and in her red hair.

Hattie took one look and started laughing. "Oh, look . . . it's the catfish that ate Port Byron."

Grace's temper matched her bright red hair. "Oh, you!" she stomped in the water which only resulted in getting her even wetter.

One of the boys laid down his fishing pole and went over to Grace as she tried wringing her dress out. "Here, let me help you out." She looked up into the face of a boy dressed in overalls and no shirt. Standing just a shade north of five feet, ten inches, his shoulders and arms revealed a body that was used to hard work.

"Don' need no help, Charlie Fisher! I got down here on my own and I'll get out on my own." She started out of the water, but the Mississippi mud sucked the moccasin off her foot. She started cursing like the sailors she'd heard as they off-loaded heavy bales of cotton from their barge. Some of the words she didn't even know their meaning.

Hattie's face blanched as she heard her sister using such strong language. She turned, running back towards town to escape the swearing and to hide her face in shame.

Charlie just laughed and folded his arms across his chest. "Got to admit you sure do make a purty catfish alright. But I'm a thinking you're too skinny. Iffen I caught sumpthin' like you, I'd just throw you back into the river. Or mebbe I would use you for bait for sumpthin' a bit bigger." He scratched his stomach. "Hey, I think that's a good name for you, Gracie. From now on I'm going to call ya 'The Red-Headed Little Bit'. "

Grace's temper had now reached its limit, and she let loose with another string of blue sailor words. She pulled her moccasin out of the mud and threw it at Charlie. It hit his arm and bounced back into the water. It floated for a few seconds and then sank under the waves.

"Look what you did to my shoe!" she screamed at Charlie. She pulled herself up as tall as she could and pushed her face right into Charlie's. "My name is Grace May Reynolds, and you better remember that, Charlie Fisher, or *my* daddy will come down and whup *your* daddy."

She turned on her heel, crossed the tracks and followed in Hattie's footsteps, with a bare muddy foot and the other still wearing a soggy moccasin as she left a wet track across the road.

Charlie yelled after her, "Ain't no big deal, Little Bit, cuz my own mama could whup my daddy!"

He turned to his friend Duggie Hayes, who was admiring the wisp of a girl. He noted she was starting to fill out some under that ragged gingham dress she was wearing.

"Duggie, I think I jest mite marry that little gal someday!"

Duggie turned a bright shade of crimson because he was thinking the same thing. He whispered to himself, "We'll jest see about that, Charlie. We'll jest see about that."

2

Aaron & Hannah

Aaron Reynolds folded his months-old newspaper, stood up, and crossed the kitchen to drop it into the kindling box.

"Looks like old Queen Victoria finally passed on."

"I swear, Aaron, you carry on more about the queen of England than the next fifteen people I know." His wife, Hannah, had just come in the house from outside where she was making a new pot of lye soap. "What she die of? A royal bug?"

Aaron grinned sheepishly. He was just a common day laborer, sometime farmer, that worked on the lime kilns down on the river but he admitted it was probably odd for him to know so much about the royalty from a foreign land. He'd followed the Queen's accomplishments for several years and admired her spunk.

"Mebbe so," he said as he tamped his pipe with fresh tobacco, "but a man's gotta stay in the know if he's gonna make somethin' of himself." The irony of his statement was not entirely lost on him.

Aaron was always the oddball of the Reynolds' family. His daddy, Isaiah, who had lived just over the hill with his second wife, Lucinda, would just smile and shake his head at his son's obsessions. He always took the notion that education was a needful thing. He read Shakespeare, Keats, and Shelly but had never made it past sixth grade himself. Aaron spent many an evening before the fire as his father read poetry to the family.

Isaiah had passed on in '93, leaving his Cindy with the remaining seven children to raise on her own. He had wished Aaron could have made more of himself than just working the kiln near the river and shooting at the raccoon-sized rats that seemed to have a large population along the shore of the town.

Producing white lime was the major industry of Port Byron and had been for twenty-five years. Port Byron Limestone was noted for its whiteness and good quality. Many areas near the river were pock marked with shallow basins where ancient seas had once covered the area, creating massive blocks of limestone and coral. Limestone was then placed in a large kiln and heated with lumber taken from the forests close-by. Once boiled off, the resulting powder was used in farming as fertilizer, painting as whitewash, and making mortar.

Aaron's job was cutting the trees. It was back breaking work and he had to use his own horses to move the trees to the kiln over roads that were often muddy, causing his wagon to break down or become mired at least once every couple of trips. If a horse died from overwork or a wagon lost a wheel, it was on Aaron to shoulder the expense.

His labor was hard and toilsome, so he often spoke his memorized poems to the horses.

Isaiah's first wife passed away when he lived in Ohio, but in 1856 he met a pretty Lakota Indian princess, Lucinda Buzzard.

Lucinda's father was a chieftain of a Sioux/Lakota tribe near Cincinnati and had forbidden his daughter from seeing Isaiah. But Lucinda was smitten with the tall, red-bearded man who picked flowers for her and recited poetry as they sat under a sycamore tree on the bank of the Ohio River. He convinced her she would have a good life in Illinois and finally one night managed to sneak her out under a moonless sky, he on a mule, she on a pinto pony. The chief chased them for several miles but lost their tracks and had to abandon his hunt. Isaiah always prided himself that he could "out-track an Injun and disappear into the tree leaves while the Injun was lookin' right at me."

Isaiah was always an outdoorsman, an expert tracker, a crack shot with a rifle and could live off the land for months if need be. He explored Pennsylvania, New York, and West Virginia before finally settling near the bend where the Scioto River met the Ohio. He found the deep forests to his liking with its abundance of deer, turkey, bear, and plenty of beaver. Isaiah trapped the water animals, skinned them for their pelts, and traded them for maize and the occasional horse with the Sioux.

Isaiah and Lucinda ended their journey in Rock Island County, Illinois, taking up residence in a two room cabin he built from the cottonwoods in a nearby grove. They soon had several children and Aaron, born in 1862, had been the light in his daddy's eyes. He knew his first born son was smart but he was never able to make more than a few dollars a week to keep his growing family in food and shelter. Education was valuable, he knew, but lack of funds kept his family living a scratch-dirt existence. Lucinda stood beside him right up to the day he died of consumption, knowing her husband could never give her the life he had promised when they were courting back in Ohio. Her love for the man was noted by many in the area.

Aaron grew up on the shores of the Mississippi River and the handsome boy's hardened body from the arduous work of the kiln caught the eye of many of the girls in town. The only one who seemed to have no interest in him was the one girl he knew he wanted for his own. The auburn-tressed Hannah Rebecca Courtney could have her pick of any of the young men who came calling, but it was the chance meeting of Aaron that won her heart. He often cited poetry to her as they sat on a bluff overlooking the Mississippi and it was those tender moments that made her say "Yes" to marriage in 1885. The newly married couple found a home not far from his parents' farm.

Hannah wiped her hands on the stained apron wrapped around her waist and pushed a strand of her hair back from her face. "Well, get your royal arse out here and help me pour some of that soap into the molds. I ain't got time for your foolishness, Aaron. Where's the girls?"

Grace had the unfortunate timing of rounding the house and running right into her mother. "Grace May Reynolds, why in the name of Sam's Hill are you so muddy? Land sakes, child, where's your other shoe?"

Grace knew better than lie to her mama because she had been caught too many times at it. Her mama always seemed to know exactly what had happened and today wasn't any different.

"Sorry, mama. I fell inta the river. This big ole catfish jumped out of the water and snatched that moccasin right offen my foot." She figured a *little* lie wouldn't do any harm.

"How many times I told you about staying away from the water? Henrietta, you're supposed to be looking after her."

Hattie had just turned the corner. "I'm suh, sorry, mama. I tole her not to, but she done it anyway."

"Grace, fetch the switch. You're gonna mind me when I say to mind me. Catfish, indeed!"

"Now, Becky, leave the girl be," said Aaron. "She's goin' to go ahead and do it anyways." Aaron always opted to call his wife Becky, using her middle name of Rebecca. "One shade the more, one ray the less, had half impair'd your daughter Grace, which waves in every auburn tress, or softly lightens o'er her face".

Aaron's attempt at adapting a Lord Byron poem only managed to further infuriate Hannah.

"Now don't go quoting poetry to me, Aaron Reynolds. That girl has got to mind her elders."

"Thanks, Papa," said Grace taking that moment to hustle into the house before Hannah could say anything but turn and give Aaron one of her death-kill-looks.

"Henrietta, get over here and help me with this lye. Your daddy's going out back to chop some wood now 'fore I lose my temper."

3
James

Charles Henry Fisher IV had been born in Fayette County, Iowa, in 1887, but his father James and mother Mary Alice Joyner moved to Rock Island, Illinois, in the winter months of 1900. Charlie came from a long line of Fishers named Charles. His family had roots in Harrisburg, Pennsylvania, but his grandfather, Charles Fisher, III, had moved to Iowa because he heard the fields of Iowa were rich, and crops practically grew themselves.

James was a farmer but managed to get a job as brakeman for the Atkinson, Topeka, and Santa Fe Railroad. He met a man in the town's tavern who said he was a representative for the railroad and for just five dollars, the job would be his. The agent said James could make up to ten dollars a week with a promise of promotion if he did a good job. James could not believe his good fortune . . . to run into someone that could change his life and in a bar of all places.

They shook hands, money was passed that represented a third of James' savings, a document was signed guaranteeing him a position, and he excitedly ran home to tell Mary Alice they were about to move. They put all their meager furniture and five children into a wagon pulled by two tired mules and headed to Rock Island, nearly 75 miles northeast. James tied their milk cow to the end of the wagon, but made his children walk because he was afraid the extra weight would kill the mules by the end of their trip. He wasn't so sure about the wagon either.

Mary Alice did not want to make the move until warmer weather set in, but James was insistent. He couldn't afford to maintain two households and he just couldn't take the chance on the railroad job not waiting for him. He knew that if he was to help his family survive, they would have to make the trip. As a sharecropper on a farm with few possessions, he had no choice.

It was a grueling journey to make in December 1898. The Canadian winds blew across the Minnesota prairies into Iowa and the snow was already five inches deep. Lillie Pearl was the eldest at thirteen and Charlie was just ten. They took turns with their mother keeping their siblings warm. The other children were Alta, six, Little Jim, five, and Billie, three.

They were fortunate in their trip because they often found a family willing to take them in for a night and give them a warm supper. The next morning, they would take offerings of a few biscuits and maybe a fresh barrel of water before they would set out again, fighting new drifts of snow that had fallen overnight. On those nights when they couldn't find shelter, they built a campfire near the wagon and huddled together for warmth. They spent their Christmas camped out near a frozen creek. Nobody mentioned the holiday because they all knew no one could afford to buy anything, even for the children.

As they listened to the howling of a wolf pack, they pulled their threadbare blankets over their heads and fell into a fitful sleep, wondering if they would freeze to death during the night. Alta hugged a wooden horse that Charlie had carved for her and almost threw it into the fire to stay warm just a few minutes longer. She couldn't do it. She loved her big brother because he was always looking out for her. As she slept, she had dreams of a house with a huge fireplace and a roaring fire as a Christmas tree stood in the corner, laden with presents just for her.

When they pulled into Moline after two weeks on the trail from Fayette County, the family was feeling the effects of frostbite. James found a shanty town near the outskirts where an empty shack could house his clan while he went to the railroad to claim his job.

Once there, he couldn't find the railroad office and finally found a telegraph operator who told him that the ATSF didn't come through Moline but was much further to the south near Dubuque. James had been hoodwinked. He dejectedly went home and told Mary Alice they had made the trip for nothing. He knew that the family could never make it back to their old home. Besides, being a sharecropper, he eked out a meager existence and as soon as James and the family moved out, someone else moved in.

James searched the Moline and Rock Island area for a month. His funds were quickly dwindling to the point where he knew he would have to find something soon or his family would starve. He happened into one of the many saloons that lined the Mississippi River banks and serving the sailors and others who made the river their home. He met a farmer, James Ledley, who said he needed someone to help on his ranch just twenty miles up the road, near Port Byron.

Once again the Fishers loaded up the wagon and had to do with just one mule since the other had died after the two-week winter trip from Iowa. The cow had stopped giving milk and James butchered it to give his family enough food to survive until he found work. The trip was made in a day and a half.

Ledley offered James a small shed behind the barn to live in while he helped work the fields. Charlie soon found himself baling hay, hoeing weeds, and corralling the rancher's herd of thirty hogs. The only pay he received was food on the table at the end of the day and a dry corner of the shed to rest until the next morning when he would start all over again.

Mary Alice announced she was pregnant, again.

4
Charlie

C harlie had long since given up school because he knew his father depended on him to help sustain their lives. His only source of entertainment was in Port Byron every couple of weeks to attend a barn dance. Charlie watched as the fiddler would rosin his bow and laid it across the strings of his instrument. He was fascinated at the sweet music that would come out of the fiddle and longed to make that sound himself.

The fiddler was an old codger named Skunk Pete. He'd gotten the name because of an unfortunate meeting with a polecat during the Civil War. Of course, it didn't help that he rarely took a bath and when he played his music at the barn dance, everyone would give him a wide berth.

Private First Class Peter McKinley had been a Confederate soldier and served under Brigadier General P.T. Beauregard fighting in the First Manassas, known as the First Battle of Bull Run in 1861.

Richmond, Virginia, had been established as the Confederate capital and was to be the target of an inexperienced army, camped near Manassas Junction. A poorly executed ambush against the Confederate left flank led to a rout by the Rebels with reinforcements from Brigadier General Joseph Johnston.

The battle was heated and Beauregard ordered his troops to pursue the retreating Union Army. Private McKinley had gotten separated from his squad and found himself surrounded by a small group of Yankees. Bullets were flying from different directions and Pete fell behind a natural earthen berm. He came face to face with a skunk that was already frightened by the noises coming from behind and in front of him. The skunk turned tail and let loose with a blinding stream into Pete's eyes. As he lay crying in the pain of his encounter, a Union soldier rushed up to the top of the berm ready to shoot the Reb.

Seeing his enemy writhing on the ground and repelled by the smell, he just backed away. "Mister, I'm supposed to show no mercy. That's 'zactly what I'm gonna do. Shootin' ya would just put you outta your misery. You owe that skunk your life."

He turned and shouted to his comrades. "Back away, boys, 'lessen you wanna shot of polecat juice."

Pete heard the men's shouts fading into the distance as he frantically tried to wipe the skunk's spray from his eyes. Groping his way to a stream he had stepped over earlier, he washed his face. He stripped his clothes and wrung them out in the water but it did nothing to neutralize the odor.

When he finally caught up with his squad, his fellow soldiers told him to stay away from them until he could get fresh clothes. "That's a skunk, Pete, you tain't nevah gonna forget."

From that point forward, Private First Class Peter M. McKinley became known as Skunk Pete. It was a name he even adopted for himself as a tribute to the striped polecat that saved his life.

As the years rolled by he turned to his fiddle to fill his lonely hours, never marrying because most women he met kept their distance as well.

Skunk Pete noticed the way Charlie seemed enraptured with his playing and soon made his acquaintance. He promised the young boy he would teach him to play the fiddle if he could carry a tune and sing at the dances. Charlie didn't mind Skunk Pete's odor. After wrestling with hogs all day he was immune to smells less offensive.

Charlie said he knew nothing about singing but was sure willing to give it a try. He listened to the songs and learned their words. When he first tried singing a song, Skunk Pete said he was amazed that someone could pick it up so quickly.

Soon Charlie was the featured singer and crowds would often stop their dancing just to hear him. Skunk Pete stayed true to his word and spent an hour every Saturday evening, after the last dancer had left, teaching Charlie how to draw the rosin across the bow of the fiddle, where to hold his fingers on the frets, and make the strings sing.

One Saturday evening, Skunk Pete was in the middle of *Skip to my Lou* when he pitched over to the ground, nearly smashing the fiddle in his fall. Charlie ran to his side but knew the lifeless eyes staring back told him that Skunk Pete had played his last barn dance.

Nobody knew if Skunk Pete had a family, even where he lived. Charlie helped some other men carry him out to the buckboard to be carted over to the undertaker for burial. He was the only one who showed up for the funeral. Pete was buried in a pauper's grave in Port Byron, no tombstone to mark where he lay. Charlie made up a wooden cross to place on the grave. He never knew the fiddlers real name, so he had written on it with a stub of a pencil: *Skunk Pete—playin' fer the angels.*

Charlie had picked up the fiddle and bow and taken it home. He would put it to his shoulder every evening after supper and entertained his family with reels, jigs, and the occasional waltz. Mary Alice held her newborn son, John Leonard, as she rocked to the music. She said it was her favorite part of the day.

5
Hannah

Hannah was a no-nonsense woman and once she set her mind to something, not even a team of horses and a three-inch wide Mississippi tow line rope could make her change it.

She inherited her name from her grandmother, Hannah Hayden who married Robert Day in Pennsylvania in 1850. The younger Hannah's mother was Mary Jane, married to Walter Courtney. Mary Jane had been born with a crippled spine and found it difficult to walk. Walter was a ne'er do-well, absent from the home more often than he was there. They lived not too far from Port Byron just south a couple of miles in the small coal mining town of Rapids City.

Walter never knew his father and barely remembered his mother. She'd died of the sleeping sickness in '71. Walter had been a Confederate soldier in the War Between the States and was much older than his teenage bride. He still harbored a dark nature, seething the loss to the Union. He spent his days brewing moonshine and drank more of his hooch than he sold to his neighbors.

He became friendly with Robert Day and supplied him with the drink just so he could go to their farm and ogle the young Mary Jane, a quite pretty girl in spite of her crippled spine. He convinced Robert that he would make a good husband and sealed the deal with a gallon of his product. Hannah's objections meant nothing to Robert.

"I'm the man of this here house and you know that little gal will never get herself a husband on her own. She goes with Walter and that's that!"

The sobbing Mary Jane had to be pried from her mother's arms as Robert picked her up and put her onto Walter's wagon. Hannah never saw her daughter again.

Walter's drinking binges went on for days and whenever he came home, he beat Mary Jane for no other reason than she was there. Often his violence turned to his children. In his drunken stupor he somehow blamed Hannah for Mary Jane's affliction, not stopping to think she had been born that way and had to have help standing up even when they got married. Mary Jane always managed to position her body between him and the child, taking the brunt of his rage against her husband's blows so they did as little damage as possible. The results always ended with black eyes, bruises that ached for weeks, and the occasional broken arm or jaw.

One day Walter came home drunk after a two-week bender and started in on Hannah.

"Git outta my way, you twisted old hag!" Walter had a bottle in one hand and used the other to prop himself against the table.

Mary Jane got up from her rocking chair and painfully made her way between him and her daughter.

Walter stared into his wife's eyes, breathing his foul breath in her face.

"Woman, you are the most worthless piece of rat crap this world has ever seed. What I ever seed in you is beyond me."

Walter backed Mary Jane up against the kitchen's butcher block and cracked her across the jaw, dislocating it. Falling back, she tried to catch her balance and her hand landed on a meat cleaver she had been using to cut up a chicken. Just as he raised his hand to strike her again, she swung the cleaver at his hand, severing his right forefinger.

As blood spurted from his wound, he stood unbelievingly, staring at the dismembered digit lying on the floor. It was still twitching from the severed nerves, making it point back at him, as if accusing him for being a drunk. Mary Jane raised the cleaver again and swung at his throat but he saw the blow coming and ducked under it. He grabbed his finger with his good hand and tried to put it back in its rightful place. He ran from the house screaming, "I'm gonna kill you, woman, I'm gonna kill you."

Mary Jane didn't wait to find out if he was ever going to come back and make good on his promise. She hoisted up her daughter and son Frank onto a buckboard and fled to live with her brother Asel in Colonna, just east of Moline. It was 1878 and Mary Jane had not a penny to her name.

Some folks say they heard of a man a couple of towns over with only three fingers on his right hand, drawing on a bottle of cheap whiskey and muttering about someone he was going to kill.

The young Hannah's resolve came from her mother. Even as crippled as Mary Jane was, she was a tough woman and Hannah's love for her was deep. She often thought of that day when her mother protected her from a brute of a father. She swore to herself she would take care of her protector until her dying day.

It was an oath that almost got her killed a few years later.

6

Grace

H annah awoke with a start as the sun shining in her eyes
came through a dirty pane of glass in the bedroom she
shared with Aaron. It was a shock to her as she never slept this
late, always getting up before the new dawn broke the day over
the hill behind their cabin. She got out of bed as the aroma from
a fresh pot of coffee hit her nose. Wrapping a thin robe around
herself, she walked into the kitchen to find Aaron standing over a
pan of fried mush.

"Well, good morning to you, sleepy head." He took pride in the
notion that he had actually gotten up before his wife.

"Land sakes Aaron, why didn't you wake me up? I have to get
the children off to school."

"Now, Becky, you needed your sleep. Gracie's down collectin'
eggs and Henrietta is bringin' in some wood for the stove." He
ran a spoon through the mush. "Sit down and have a cup before
you start your day."

"I'll do no such thing," she countered as she took the spoon
from his hand and pushed him out of the way. "I fix the meals

around here. You go tend to Blossom and bring me in some fresh milk."

He sighed and went to the door, knowing there was no use in arguing with her. He grabbed a bucket hanging on a wooden peg on the wall beside the door and turned to look back at her.

"Pillow'd upon my fair love's ripening breast to feel for ever its soft fall and swell, awake forever in a sweet unrest."

Hannah gave him a knowing smile at his quote of Keats and shushed him out. He left just as Grace came in carrying a basket of eggs. Aaron stooped down and whispered in her ear. "Watch out, Gracie, she's frightful mad that I let her sleep in this morning."

"Good morning, Mama," she said gaily. "I done brung in the eggs for breakfast."

"I *brought* in the eggs, Gracie," she said, correcting her.

"No you didden, Mama. I got 'em right here."

Hannah started to say something but just smiled and went back to her stove. She looked back over her shoulder at her daughter.

"Well, look at you; you've even combed your hair real nice, Grace." Grace's hair was a source of pride to the woman. Her mama, Mary Jane, had the reddest hair she had ever seen and Grace was almost a spitting image of her. She had never allowed the hair to be cut and it hung almost down to her waist. Every night Grace would sit on the floor in front of the fireplace while Hannah combed it out, counting out one hundred times, the wooden comb's teeth passing through the locks.

"I measured it last night, Mama. It's growed another two inches since Christmas."

"*Grown,* not *growed,* Grace."

"That's what I said, Mama. I'm gonna let it grow all the way down past my bum. I'll be the prettiest girl in the whole school."

"Yes, I believe you will be child. I do believe you will."

Henrietta walked in carrying an armful of wood.

"Good morning, Mama."

"Good morning, Henrietta. Now you girls call in your pa and sit down to breakfast. You can't be going to school on an empty stomach."

After breakfast was finished and the dishes cleared off the table, Hattie and Grace picked up their books and started to school.

At the end of the dirt path leading from the house was a gate that could swing both ways. Grace always had a habit of getting on the gate, swinging to and fro. When she wasn't doing chores, she sometimes went to the gate and swung back and forth for up to an hour at a time, day dreaming and singing softly to herself. On either side of the gate was a make-shift picket fence that Aaron had put up so that Hannah could plant flowers and add some color to an otherwise dirt yard.

Today was no exception, and Grace got on the gate pushing herself back and forth, much to the annoyance of Hattie.

"Come on, Gracie. We're gonna be late to school. And today is your turn to ring the bell."

Grace had forgotten that and she jumped off the gate, pulling it shut behind her, she fell in behind Hattie for the half mile walk.

Their school was a one room log cabin put together by some of the men in Port Byron. Their teacher, Priscilla Donnelly, wasn't really a teacher in the sense that she had a college education, but seemed to know how to teach arithmetic, reading from the Good Book, and had a flair for writing poetry. For that, she received a dollar a week from the Port Byron aldermen. Uncharacteristically for them, they voted to pay her 50 cents a week for days when school wasn't in session, even the summers. Luckily, she lived with her parents and was able to scrape by.

Miss Donnelly taught all the grades up to the sixth. After that, most of the children would stay home and work on the farms. Those who lived in town were merchants, the preacher, and saloon keepers. If they could afford it, they sent their children into Rock Island to continue from the seventh grade.

Grace was in the fifth grade and even though Hattie was three years older, she was doing the sixth grade over. Hattie had been terribly ill with the croup the past winter and had missed several weeks. The year before that she'd had the measles, followed by the mumps, and a bout with the ague. It took her a month before she regained her strength to return to school.

Grace and Hattie entered the dusty school yard and looked for their friends. Grace spotted Duggie Hayes and turned away to avoid his attention. He sat right behind Grace at the worn desks in the school room and was always pestering her. One time he dipped one of her long pigtails into his ink well and it took her four washings before she could get it out.

Duggie was vying for her attention and was giving the kind that was unwanted. He made the mistake of telling Charlie that *he* was the one who was going to be sweet on Gracie and *he* was the one who was going to marry her. Charlie told him that Grace was *his* girl and just better back off before blood was drawn. Grace had no idea they had developed a feud between themselves just over her. Their friendship had pretty much ended when they both declared Grace was to be their intended.

Ever since, Duggie had seethed and did what he could to vent his frustration.

"Oh, dang a mule's tail, there's Duggie," Grace whispered. "Stand in front me, Hattie, so he can't see me. He is one of the meanest boys I ever knowed."

"Just ignore him, Grace. He's not worth his salt and maybe sooner or later, he will get the message and lay off." She looked at her sister with a grin. "'Sides, I heard that Charlie Fisher was saying he wuz gonna marry you. He's cute and *I'm* jealous."

Grace turned red, pulling on a long braid. "I don't know what you're talkin' 'bout," she said, but secretly hoping it was so. She tugged on Hattie's arm leading her into the school room door.

"Good morning, Mizz Donnelly," they chimed in together.

"Good morning, Hattie. Good morning, Grace." She finished erasing the chalk board and picked up the school bell on her desk. "Grace, would you please ring the bell, and call everyone one into class?"

Grace and Hattie always took turns ringing the bell and they considered it a source of pride to be picked to do this morning chore.

Grace grabbed the bell by its wooden handle and ran to the door. She flipped her wrist a half dozen times and it rang across the school yard. "School time . . . school time!" she called.

The children all ran to the door, chattering about what they were going to do for Thanksgiving the following week. They'd learned just yesterday that President Lincoln had declared the last

Thursday of November as a Day of Thanks before that awful John Booth gunned him down.

Duggie shoved past Grace. "Outta my way, Red!" He turned to the boy following him. "My pa says we's gonna go out and shoot a big ole turkey on Sattiday. I'm gonna pull the trigger myself. Pa says I could."

"Duggie," Grace said, "you couldn't hit the back end of a mule iffen it was sittin' on your face."

He turned to give her a retort but was interrupted by the teacher.

"Come on in, children," called out Miss Donnelly. "Take your seats and turn to page twenty in your McGuffey's."

Grace settled into her chair next to Hattie. Duggie plopped down and grabbed one of Grace's pigtails giving it a yank.

"Owww!!! Miss Donnelly, he did it again."

"Duggie Hayes! Corner! *Now!*"

"Aw, horse nuggets," he pouted. He got up from his desk and leaned down to whisper in Grace's ear. "You're gonna pay in spades for this, Reynolds." He just couldn't seem to get the knack for sweet talk.

Grace just smiled up at him sweetly and said, "You just run along to the corner now, MR. Hayes."

"Mr. Hayes, what have I told you about using that kind of language in my classroom?" She picked up a ruler on the side of her desk. "Hold out your hand."

Duggie blanched and knew he was about to get a rapping.

"Ah, Miz Donnelly, I ain't meant nothin' by it," he cried. He squeezed his eyes shut and held out his left hand.

Miss Donnelly slapped the ruler across his knuckles drawing a howl of pain. The children behind him broke into a fit of giggles.

He turned and stomped up to the stool sitting in the corner of the classroom. Miss Donnelly made her misbehaving students face the corner for half an hour before she would let them return to their seat.

After lunch, the children returned to their desks. Duggie glared at Grace as he sat down behind her. He had been thinking up ways of getting even and had finally settled on the one thing he knew would be the worst possible revenge.

Half way through their arithmetic lesson, Duggie reached into his pocket for his jack knife. He kept it honed to a razor thin blade. He gently held one of Grace's long pigtails on his desk and started sawing a couple of hairs at a time. It took him nearly ten minutes but he finally worked his way through. Grace never felt a thing as she was intensely trying to pay attention to the times tables that Miss Donnelly was taking them through. Since they were seated at the rear of the room, no other students had noticed what was going on and Grace had no inkling as to what was happening behind her.

Duggie took the pig tail and placed it under his desk. He wanted to wait until just the right moment to spring his surprise.

When Miss Donnelly rang the bell for the end of the school day the students all started gathering up what they needed to take home.

Duggie got up before Grace did and as he passed her desk, he laid the severed pigtail on top of her books and ran out the door.

At first, Grace didn't know what had just happened. A bright red pigtail was lying on the books in front of her. As she slowly realized what it might be, she reached her hand behind her head only to grab a fistful of air.

A wail that grew from deep within her washed across the classroom. Duggie had paused just outside the door so he could enjoy the sounds of her cries. He let out a big laugh and skipped down the steps. That was just about the most fun he'd had in a long time. "I bet ole Charlie Fisher will ditch her now since she be so ugly," he chuckled to himself.

Duggie whistled as he walked the path back through the woods towards his father's farm, taking the time to stop and try to grab some crawdads in a brook he had to cross over. He relived the moment over and over in his head. He laid the pigtail down. He stood outside the door. He could hear Grace's wail. He was so wrapped up in his happiness, that he didn't hear the sound of running feet behind him just as he turned up the muddy track to his daddy's farm.

He caught just a glimpse of someone coming up and whirled around just as one-hundred and twenty-five pounds of a raging Charlie Fisher barreled into him, madder than a gunny sack full of wildcats.

Duggie outweighed the younger Charlie by at least thirty pounds but the momentum carried the two down into a deep muddy puddle and the only fists flying were those of Grace's angry beau. Duggie was taken completely by surprise. Charlie flipped him over onto his back and pummeled his face, knocking out a tooth, blackening both eyes, and opening up three or four gashes that started streaming blood.

"You sum-bitch, I came by to walk Gracie home when I heard what you'd done." He pulled Duggie's head up by the hair and socked him again.

Duggie's soft body couldn't brace itself against the wiry Charlie. "Stop, Stop, Stop!" he cried.

"I'll stop after I've beaten you to within an inch of your life, you sum-bitch. You ever show your face up in that school again, the next time, I'll kill you! You understand?"

He walloped him again just as Duggie's father came out of the house and started running towards the two wallowing in the mud.

"I said, *Do you understand?*"

"*I understand, I . . . I understand.* Don't hit me again!"

Charlie raised his fist for one final blow but his wrist was caught by Jeremy Hayes.

"Get up offen my boy, Fisher!" he screamed as he picked up Charlie by the straps of his overalls and threw him back across the fence lining the road. "I don't know what this is about but you git before I lose my temper."

Charlie picked himself up off the ground and pointed his finger at Duggie. "You don't forget what I said. We used to be friends but that's over now." He turned and stalked back down the road. He wanted to find Gracie and express his sorrow.

Jeremy turned to Duggie and cuffed him on the side of his head. "I doan know what that was all about and I doan care. But you let that skinny bag 'o bones best you and you're cryin' like a girl. Now get up to the barn and see to yore chores." He kicked Duggie in the rear for extra emphasis.

By the time Charlie had returned to the school, Grace and all the children had left. Only Miss Donnelly was there, busy picking up books off the desks.

"Miz Donnelly, you don't have to ever worry about that horse dung ever botherin' Gracie again," he declared. He turned on his heel and stomped out of the school door, leaving the teacher bewildered by what he had said.

Grace ran home completely distraught. When she got to the gate, she hit it full force nearly tearing it off its hinges. She stumbled and fell down, skinning her knee. Picking herself up, she limped up to the house. The pain she was feeling was not of her knee, but the one in her heart. She had to leave it to Hattie to tell her mama what had happened to her pigtail. When Hannah saw the butchered hair she sat down in her rocker with Grace curled up in her lap and they both had a good cry. She tried to console her daughter but was finding it hard to find the words that would soothe her own feelings as well.

"Grace, I know you are sad now but you're going to have to let me cut the other pigtail off because your hair won't look right if we just leave one side."

"Oh, mama, noooo!" she cried.

"I know, I know, child. I'm sad, too. But I'll tell you what I'm going to do." She pulled Grace up to face her and wiped off her tears. "Let's you and me take that red hair and weave it into a nice tail for Miss Petunia." Grace's one and only rag doll that she had gotten for Christmas when she was four years old was her best friend. It actually had no hair, but Grace loved that doll with all her heart.

"Really," she said in wonder. "You can do that?"

"Yes, darling! And whenever you hold Miss Petunia close to your heart, you can sing to her and tell her how beautiful she is because you gave her the one thing you loved most . . . your own hair. Think how sweet that would be."

"Oh, mama," Grace cried in a new set of emotional tears. "That would be wonderful. Let's go do it right now."

She jumped off her mother's lap and ran to get her doll, excited she was going to make Miss Petunia the most beautiful doll in the world.

Hannah smiled and dried her own tears.

Aaron stood in the doorway and found himself wiping a tear from his own eye. He dearly loved both his daughters, but Gracie was more like him as Hattie favored her mother. He turned, picked up his tool box from inside the doorway and went down to repair the gate, softly crying to himself as he worked.

Duggie Hayes returned to the school that evening, knowing it was never kept locked. He looked under Grace's desk and found the severed pigtail. He clutched it to his chest and ran back out. It would serve as his very own trophy and a reminder of the revenge he had served up. His hatred of Charlie and Grace only deepened.

7

Charlie

C harlie had just turned 15 in 1902. He was growing weary of tending the farm day in and day out, week after week, month after month. He was getting restless and feeling an itch that he couldn't scratch. He yearned to see what the world had to offer and he couldn't do that working on a farm that could barely grow a potato. His father had three other sons. Little Jim and Billy were getting to the age where they could help out on the farm. John Leonard was still in the crib, just learning to walk. The two girls, Lillie Pearl and Alta did their best to keep up with their brothers.

He had only two enjoyments that gave him any respite from his daily toil. One was when he was standing in front of a crowd at the barn dance, singing a song or playing his fiddle. The other was when he went calling on Grace who had turned thirteen that spring. Whenever he sang a love song he always imagined Grace's face in his mind. He was even growing to love the shorter hairdo. Grace had returned to school after a week of mourning for her severed pigtail and was fearful of running into Duggie Hayes.

She'd heard from Hattie what happened between him and Charlie Fisher. She secretly savored the thoughts of Charlie's fists coming down hard on Duggie. Every night as she closed her eyes after her evening prayers, clutching Miss Petunia, she visualized each blow and chuckled at the blood she imagined pouring from his face. Revenge was sweet!

Charlie's hard fists had permanently damaged a nerve near Duggie's left eye, leaving it to sag with a hang-dog expression. The eye would constantly water up making him use his shirt sleeve every couple of minutes to wipe away the tears that had formed. It was something he would have to live with for the rest of his life.

She saw him occasionally after that down by the river as he was fishing but he had never returned to school. His daddy needed help anyway on their farm. "I ain't never had no use for schoolin' and you doan need it either," he grumbled to his son.

One Saturday at the barn dance, Charlie saw a circular nailed to the side of the barn door advertising *Buffalo Bill's Wild West and Congress of Rough Riders of the World*. He knew of the name, William Cody, who acquired his nickname supplying workers for the Kansas Pacific Railroad with buffalo meat.

The extravaganza was going to appear for one day only in Buffalo Bill's hometown of Le Claire, Iowa, just across the river from Port Byron.

Charlie went to ask Aaron and Hannah Reynolds if they would allow him to escort Miss Grace to the show and promised to have her back by early evening.

Aaron and Hannah were not sure that was such a good idea. Grace was thirteen years old and a girl should never be out alone with a boy for several hours, even if it was daylight.

"Mama," Grace pleaded, "I'll be a good girl. I won't even let him hold my hand, or nothing." She gave a sideways glance at Charlie that said he could hold her hand all he wanted. "'Sides, he's always been most proper when he comes acallin' on me."

Charlie stood twisting his hat in his hands, nervously working around the brim several times.

Hannah turned and looked at Aaron, who gave her a very slight nod. He liked the young Fisher boy. Charlie always engaged him in conversation and seemed to enjoy the times in the evening when he quoted poetry to the family while seated in front of the fireplace. He always addressed him as Mr. Reynolds and was genuinely interested in his youngest daughter. He also knew of the incident with Duggie Hayes and was proud that Charlie had done something that he himself would have done if he'd been there.

"Okay, Grace," said Hannah, "but you must be back in time for your evening chores. Now go make yourself a tongue sandwich for your lunch . . . and one for Charlie, too. Aaron, go saddle up Champion for her."

Grace and Charlie walked their horses down through the gate and then paused to climb aboard. Charlie interlaced his fingers and hoisted Grace onto Champion's saddle. They rode to the river's edge where they would take the ferry over to the Iowa side of the river.

Charlie gave the ferryman four pennies to pay their passage and led the horses onto the flatboat.

Grace was excited about the prospect of spending the day beside the handsome boy who had defended her honor. As soon as they pushed off from Rapids City and she knew her parents couldn't see her, she placed her hand in Charlie's, and they stood like that all the way across the river. Charlie kept glancing at her hand holding his, and his heart swelled with an emotion that he couldn't quite understand.

Arriving in Le Claire, they led the horses off the boat and made their way to the fairgrounds where Buffalo Bill had set up his performance. Grace had never seen so many people in her life as they were going in all directions. The smell of horses and their by-products, the vendors selling their meats as they roasted over open campfires and the fresh sawdust that had been spread over the arena floor made it barely able for her to take it all in.

As they slipped onto one of the hard benches that encircled the arena, Charlie's eyes were likewise bulging but for different reasons. As they watched the performance, he marveled at the precision riding, the sharp-shooting Annie Oakley, and the bravado of whooping Indians circling the soldiers crouched in their midst. It was intoxicating to him. He had never imagined that people could lead such lives.

What excited him the most, however, was the music. Cody had managed to get one of the most popular band conductors of the era for a one-time only performance. He listed him on the flyers that covered the area as *"The World's Greatest March King—John Philip Sousa."*

Sousa's music filled the air with a rousing excitement that lent an added dimension to the spectacular. *Stars and Stripes Forever, Yankee Doodle Dandy,* and *The Invincible Eagle March* had the crowd standing on its feet, screaming as cowboys wrestled calves to the ground, Indians went into a whooping war dance, and Annie Oakley who hit her mark with every shot.

For the finale Buffalo Bill and his troupe of entertainers came out of the far gate in a full gallop to the pounding of *The William Tell Overture* as they rode to the futile rescue of General Custer. As they surrounded the tribe of Indians, shooting their blanks until every last one of them fell to the ground, the swelling of sound from the brass section of Sousa's band made Charlie's heart pound so hard, he placed his mind into that of the famous conductor. He swirled his arms to match those of the musician as he conducted the trumpets, the trombones and the booming tubas. Charlie had never felt such emotions in his life. At the end of the finale he continued cheering and thought for a minute he might pass out from the exhilaration he felt.

When the show finally ended, the gunpowder smells still wafted over the crowds as Buffalo Bill and Annie Oakley took three turns around the ring, waving at the cheering crowds, finally making their way into a corral. The sights and sounds left Charlie and Grace breathless as they made their way out.

A commotion was drawing in a crowd of people near the corral where the performers had exited. Charlie held tightly onto Grace's hand as he pulled her into the melee so he could see what was going on. He walked right into Buffalo Bill himself who was scribbling his name on pieces of paper that were thrust at him from autograph seekers.

"Whoa, hold on there, young fella. You'll get your turn," Bill said.

"I'm sorry, Mr. Cody. I don't want your autograph, I want a job with your show," he blurted out.

Even over the noise of the crowd, Grace heard what Charlie had said and turned to look at him in wonder.

"Well, let me take a look at you, son." Bill looked him over as he continued writing autographs. "You know how to handle horses, boy?"

"Yes, sir," Charlie replied, "been around them all my life. And I can ride, too."

"Tell you what, son. I like your demeanor and I like your boldness. Nobody's ever asked me for a job before in the middle of all this." He put his arm around Charlie's shoulders. "You see that fella over there with the big handle-bar moustache? His name's Montana. You go tell him that I just gave you a job. He's not gonna believe you until you tell him Bill said he knows his real name and he's gonna tell the next newspaper reporter he sees what it might be iffen you don't get hired. That's a might pretty little gal you got there. What did you say your name was?"

"Charlie . . . Charlie Fisher," he stammered. "And this here is my girl, Grace."

Grace gave a little curtsy. "How do you do, Mr. Bill?"

Buffalo Bill laughed with a deep bass sound that seemed to come from inside a rain barrel. "Well, Charlie Fisher, go over and see Montana." He tipped his hat to Grace and said, "Ma'am."

Bill turned and grabbed the next piece of paper to sign his name. Charlie, still holding onto Grace's hand, led her out of the crowd.

"What are you doing, Charlie? Are you gonna leave just when you wuz gettin' sweet on me?"

"I can't explain it, Little Bit. I just know I have to go see some of the world before I settle down. Will you wait for me, Grace? Will you wait for me, knowing I'm gonna come back and marry you?"

Grace dropped his hand and stood back, dumbfounded. Had Charlie just asked her to *marry* him?

Charlie grinned at her before she could answer. "Wait here." He ran over to the man Buffalo Bill had pointed out leaving Grace with her mouth agape. Her heart started to soar, and it was not until that moment that she knew she loved him.

"You bet I'll wait for you, Charlie Fisher," she whispered to herself. "You can just bet your life on it."

8
Charlie

Charlie was torn.

He knew he was in love with Grace and wanted her for his wife. She would be a fine woman to be at his side for the rest of his life. But he had an unexplainable itch that was pulling him away from Port Byron. He was barely fifteen and wanted to see some of the world before he settled down.

Buffalo Bill Cody had pulled in his entire entourage earlier that year and explained to them he was about to embark on a European tour with his show. The famous showman stood in the bright sunlight, running his calloused hands through his white goatee. He explained how they would fulfill their engagements booked for the rest of the year but by December he was taking everything to London, Paris, and other cities overseas. Each and every one of them would be welcome to join him. A rumbling, excited chatter erupted from his 200 some employees. Indians who didn't understand the white man's language had to wait for an interpreter to explain to them what had been said.

The next day Charlie said his goodbyes to James and to his mother, Mary Alice. His father was not happy at losing the help of his strong son, but was very envious that his son had made a difficult decision. He realized Charlie was no longer a boy, but a man who needed to find his own way in the world. Mary Alice wiped away her own tears as she watched her oldest boy make his way down the path, not knowing if she would ever see him again.

Charlie knew the hardest part was yet to come as he turned his horse through the gate and into the yard leading up to the Reynolds' home. Grace was waiting for him on the porch and promised herself she would not cry. Inside, she felt a hole had been punched into the middle of her heart.

"Hello, Little Bit," Charlie said as he got down off his horse.

Grace's resolve not to cry lasted no longer than it did for him to greet her as she burst into tears.

Charlie wrapped his arms around the slight girl. "Now, now, Gracie, let's have none of that." He lifted her face up by the chin and looked into her green eyes. "You're making this too hard on me."

"Oh, Charlie," she moaned, "I ain't gonna ever see you agin. I jest know it." She clutched him tightly, hoping . . . no, praying . . . he would see how he was breaking her heart and change his mind.

"You're going to see me again. I'll be back afore you know it. That's a promise! I'll make a lot of money with Mr. Cody and I'll come back and drop it all into your lap."

He looked over at Hannah standing in the doorway of the house. "I promise I'll be back, Miz Reynolds. I love your daughter and I promise you I'll be back."

Hannah used her apron to wipe away her own tear. "I know you will, Charlie. We're going to hold you to that."

Charlie gave Grace one more hug and kissed her on her lips. The warmth and emotion in that one kiss bound them together as one loving force. He released her and turned back to mount his horse.

A weeping Grace held onto Charlie's stirrup as they passed back through the yard to the gate.

"Love you, Gracie," he said as he turned the horse south. He swore to himself he would not look back because he knew he might change his mind. But he couldn't stand it and turned to get one more glimpse of the girl.

Grace was hanging on the gate, slowly swinging it back and forth, her heart breaking.

Charlie sighed, turned around and continued riding, the sobs from Grace ebbing as he passed a grove of trees.

Charlie was to meet up with the Wild West Show in Moline. From there they were to travel by steamer to New Orleans with stops in St. Louis and Memphis to finish out their U.S. engagements. Towns and cities all along the Mississippi heard that the famous Buffalo Bill Cody would be steaming south and they lined the shores, hoping to catch a glimpse of the heroic showman. Many were not disappointed as he strode the decks of the boat, moving from one side to the other to wave at the cheering throngs.

It was a magnificent sight to see the string of steamers making its way down the mighty Mississippi River towards the delta where the entourage would load onto a ship that would carry them to the White Cliffs of Dover. Bill had more than 150 horses, several buffalo and an entourage of two hundred people that were necessary for his performances. He had drovers, vendors, barkers, seventy-five riders, and a company of almost fifty Indians in the show. He even hired a veterinarian to provide doctoring to his menagerie. Added to that were wagons, saddles, bridles, an arsenal of more than two hundred guns and other equipment, tools, and trunks that had to be loaded onto the seven steamers making up the flotilla of ships carrying it all.

Charlie often stood beside Bill, drawn by his magnetism and excited by the prospect of seeing Europe. Bill had taken a real shine to the young man, Charlie Fisher. He gave him jobs that would keep him nearby. Charlie did, indeed, know horses. Bill, on some warm evenings would make his rounds on the steamers, often changing from one to another whenever they made port. He more often than not would find Charlie with the horses, checking their feet for sores, currying their manes, brushing their tails and making sure saddles and bridles were kept in shape.

One evening he came upon Charlie who had sat on a downturned wooden pail and was plucking out a tune on his fiddle. He put himself into his instrument and was trying to emulate Sousa's *Stars and Stripes Forever.* Cody stood in the doorway listening to Charlie's music, an idea formulating in his mind. The river was carrying them past Cape Girardeau as gas lights flickered in the dusk and the chorus of bullfrogs on the banks almost made it seem as if they were singing in tune with Charlie.

"Good evening. Charlie," he said pulling out a cigar. Charlie jumped up, startled and embarrassed that his employer caught him not working.

"I . . . I'm sorry, sir. Didn't know you were standing there. I'll get back to work, sir. Sorry."

"Charlie," said the showman, "you've got to relax sometime, else you'll end up baying at that moon up there." He touched a match to the end and the flame flickered in the evening breeze as he sucked on the stick of tobacco. He pulled out another and handed it to the young man at the railing. Charlie had never smoked before but here was the famous Buffalo Bill Cody offering him a cigar. He could hardly refuse and hoped he wouldn't look foolish as he tried to light it.

The first draw of smoke into Charlie's lungs sent him into a spasm of coughing. He felt about two inches tall, but Bill just smiled and took another puff on his own. "Your first, son?"

"Yes, (cough) yes, sir. Sorry."

"Don't be sorry, Charlie. Never apologize . . . sign of weakness. You'll get used to it."

"Yes, sir. Sorry." He turned red. "I mean, 'Yes, sir.'"

"That is the sign of progress." Bill said, pointing at the distant lights. "That is the sign of big things to come. I wish I was your age again, Charlie. You've got a future that is going to see some great things."

"Yes, sir."

"You ever hear of Henry Ford?"

"No, sir."

"Well, Mr. Ford has developed a horseless carriage."

"A what, sir?"

"They call it a motoring car. Imagine a wagon being driven without a team of horses."

"Are you funning me, Mr. Cody?"

"No, Charlie, I'm not. The motoring car, I predict, will be the greatest invention of all time, surpassing Mr. Edison's electric light."

Charlie tried braving another draw from his cigar. He was starting to get the hang of the smoke by not drawing it into his lungs but by just blowing it back out. "I've heard of that. Some of the stores in Port Byron have been talking about putting them in, tho' none of them done it yet."

"Look up ahead. See that bend?" Charlie nodded.

"Do you know what is beyond that bend, Charlie?"

"No, sir."

"I don't either and that touches something deep inside of me. I have to know what is around that bend. All for I know, I'll see a herd of wild elephants or a man walking a tightrope across the river. I gotta *see*, Charlie. I have to *know* what is beyond that bend."

Charlie looked up at Bill and sensed the fever that seemed to be gripping the showman. He was experiencing the exact same feelings.

"The world is changing, Charlie. It's spinning so fast that I feel I have to see as much of it as I can and live it as much as I can before I meet my Maker."

"Yes, sir."

"That's why I wanted you to come along with me on this tour across the ocean. I want you to see it with me."

"I'm looking forward to it, too, sir."

"Seems you play a pretty mean fiddle, Charlie."

"I try my best, sir."

"I'm going to promote you. I want you to be part of the program, not just taking care of my horses. Mr. Sousa declined my invitation to accompany us on the trip to Europe. I want you to work up a music program that will keep the excitement going while people are watching my show."

Charlie couldn't believe what he was hearing. Bill Cody wanted him as a musician? He was suddenly excited, but scared to death at the same moment. He was now asking him to be a John Philip Sousa for the extravaganza in the arena?

"I don't know what to say, sir." He could barely even take a breath at the prospect of doing what he loved the most . . . and for Buffalo Bill Cody.

"I think you and I are going to make a real splash, Charlie. *Buffalo Bill's Wild West and Congress of Rough Riders of the World* is going to be known around the world."

Charlie swallowed hard and said, "Sir, I can think of nothing that would give me more pleasure," Charlie said. He turned to look at the fading lights of Cape Girardeau. *Well, there is mebbe one other thing,* he thought to himself as he pictured a small wisp of a red-haired girl hundreds of miles to the north, swinging on a gate. *But I have to do this one thing first.*

Charlie had no way of knowing he would never make it to Europe.

9

Lucinda

Lucinda Buzzard was a full-blooded Lakota Native American. She married Isaiah Reynolds in 1856 after they both fled Ohio to escape her father, Long Bow. Upon settling near Coe, a small township north of Port Byron, they raised a family of seven children. She especially loved her granddaughter Grace because the child seemed to be possessed of a free spirit. She felt that of all her grandchildren, but Grace came the closest to being true to her heritage.

After Isaiah died from consumption, she often asked her son Aaron to let Grace and Hattie come visit as often as they could. During the summers it was not unusual for them to spend a couple of weeks with her. Her favorite times would be when she tended her garden with Grace and would tell stories of her life among the Lakotas.

"Granny," Grace asked one morning when she was six years old, "how come people don't like you and call you 'squaw'?"

Lucinda pulled a weed from her strawberry patch, got up, and took Grace by the hand, leading her to an old iron stool propped up next to an oak tree.

She pulled Grace up onto her lap. "Let me tell you a story, little one." Grace looked up into the gray eyes of the old woman, drawing in deep the smell of jasmine that seemed to seep from her pores.

"Many, many years ago I was *wikȟóškalaka,* a young woman. My *atkuku,* father, was the chief of our tribe on the Ohio River and he loved his family and his people. But the white man was pushing him off the land that had belonged to his people for a very long time. These foreigners were having many *hoksiyopa,* children, and they needed more and more land to feed them so they came and took ours."

"Was my grandpa a mean white man who took your land?"

"No, dear one, my Isaiah hated what was happening and sometimes would fight these men. When they found out he was sweet on me, they would beat him horribly."

"Did your daddy help grandpa?"

"No, he didn't." She took a sweet strawberry from her basket and put it into Grace's mouth. The taste of the berry made Grace's face crunch up as she sucked on the sweet fruit. "He didn't help your grandpa because he hated all white men. He forbade me to ever see him again."

"But you didn't obey your pa, did you? If I didn't do what my pa says, he would lay the switch to me."

"Your pa wouldn't lay the switch to you, my Grace, but he would be very disappointed in you."

"So what happened?"

"I loved your grandpa very much and if we couldn't be together out in the open, we decided to run away together so we could love each other forever."

"But you weren't a squaw, granny. You was a princess!"

"Sometimes white men don't distinguish differences from people that aren't like them. They were *ŏhitiká*, furious, with *ŋitûŋkasila*, and called him 'squaw man'. Their hearts were black as the moonless night and vented their rage with their insults and their fists."

"I love you, Granny."

"And I, you, Grace. With all my *căŋţe*, my heart." She hugged Grace tightly as a mist clouded her gray eyes.

That conversation stayed with Grace, and she often sought out her advice. This day was no exception as she stepped into the small, neat yard of her grandmother's home. She saw her granny sitting in her usual spot, on a rocking chair of a porch that was held up by a stack of mismatched rocks at each corner. Grace was amazed at how the old cabin still stood but her daddy often came by to help maintain his mother's home.

Even with her dimming eyes, Lucinda knew something was amiss as her granddaughter ran up the path, giving her a big hug, tears flowing down her face.

"Now, now, child. Nothing can ever be as bad as all that. Tell *ŋikuŋiki* what's wrong."

"Granny, my Charlie ran off to join a travelin' show and he won't be back for YEARS!"

Grace told Lucinda all about the Wild West show and their encounter with Buffalo Bill.

"And now your heart is breaking, isn't it, *Mitakŏja ke,* my precious granddaughter?"

"Who knows how long he is going to be gone, Granny? What if he dies and I never find out about it? What if I have to wait fifty years and he comes back and I'll be too old to have any children?"

"Gracie, a man's mind works differently from a woman's. You have to put your faith in *Wakaŋ Taŋka,* the Great Spirit. Trust this old woman when I say I see him coming back very soon."

Grace stopped crying with a new hope creeping into her heart. "Really, Granny? Do you really think so?"

"Yes. I have been seeing visions during the night when I close my eyes to sleep. You have been weighing upon my mind, *o iyokîpî,* my lovely. I see your *teĥila* returning to your side. I do not know when because my age sometimes blocks what I want to see the most."

Grace turned red at her grandmother's use of *'teĥila'.* She had sat at her grandmother's knee too often to not know its meaning as 'lover'. But her heart soared at hearing the reassuring words. She had never known her *ŋikusïki* to be wrong in her visions.

Lucinda placed her gnarled hands over those of Grace. "I have something for you. There on the shelf, next to my flour tin, fetch me the small bag."

Grace retrieved the bag and handed it to her grandmother. Lucinda took a dull knife, cut off a lock of her stringy hair and placed it in the bag.

"I will not always be with you, little one. One day, you may find you have need of my counsel. This bag now contains a lock of my hair but what else is in there is of far more importance. It has some special herbs that I have grown in my garden. When you feel you need to talk to me but I have gone to the Other Side,

I want you to take out the bag, put my hair into a small bowl and burn it. Do not use a Sulphur match but use the embers from a fire built with sticks from the oak tree. Add the herbs and a cup of water from the stream. Mash it all together and then simmer it over the fire, letting the smoke pour over the cup. Bring it to a boil and then let it cool for about two minutes. I want you to then drink this mixture. I will come to you in your dream and we can talk."

"Grandmother, I cannot bear the thought of you not being here. You are always near when I need you."

"These bones are growing brittle, *Mitakŏja ke*. I will be joining Isaac before too long, I think." She reached out and wiped away Grace's tears from the corners of her eyes.

Grace took the precious bag and tied it with a string around her neck. She kissed her grandmother on the cheek and returned home in sorrow.

10
Hannah, 1884

Mary Jane hurriedly packed what she could after her fight with her husband. She managed to find enough money in the house to rent a wagon and a horse, loaded up her children and fled to live with her brother Asel in Colonna, south of Moline. Asel had six children of his own and when Mary Jane appeared on his door step with Hannah and Frank, he did not hesitate to take them in and care for them. The three room house he had built for his family was now bursting at the mud caked joints with eleven people.

Mary Jane's affliction proved doubly hard not only for her but for the rest of the Day family as well. Hannah's resolve to tend to her mother was the only way the Day clan could cope with all it was doing. Asel was able to put food on the table for everyone and nobody ever went hungry. He had a very large garden that the entire family, except for Mary Jane, tended to, weeding, pruning, and harvesting its crops. Their herd of 25 goats provided milk, cheese, meat, and a steady birth of kids.

Hannah's thirst for education did not stop merely because she had to drop out of school to take care of her mother and brother.

Whenever she had the opportunity to get a book, she would read it from end to end several times by the lantern light or fireplace fire. It was from this self-taught schooling that Hannah found useful in helping provide. She found a job with a local bank. Her ability to use numbers and to understand them so impressed the bank's president that he promoted her from sweeping floors and taking out the trash to teller within a month after he hired her. The girl was just fifteen years old but carried herself with the grace of a woman much older.

It was an extraordinary thing to find a woman, and a young woman at that, standing behind the counter in a position where you would always find a man. Men entering the bank would sometimes stand in a long line of the other teller, who was a male, while Hannah's window stood empty. Most often her customers were women and even some of them were mistrustful of a woman taking a man's job.

Mr. John J. O'Dea, the bank's president, ignored the snubs Hannah was getting and when she stood at her window with no customers, would make her do the books. Her proficiency with numbers helped her earn two dollars a week. She promptly turned the money every Friday over to her uncle Asel. Once in a while, Asel noticed her dress was wearing thin and allowed her to keep enough to either mend it with new material or buy a new one from a catalog. Hannah never asked to keep some of her money from him, knowing it was needed to help pay for her family's lodging and food.

One day, as Hannah was standing at her post, she dropped several bills on the floor and stooped to pick them up.

She heard the door to the bank open and decided it was probably just another man who would refuse to come to her window.

She heard a drunken voice that turned her blood to ice. *"Need some service here! Where the hell is the teller at this window?"*

Hannah stood up and said, "Sorry, sir, may I hel …?" She cut off in mid-sentence as she looked right into the red-rimmed eyes of her drunken father. It had been six years since she'd last laid eyes on him. She could tell he had lost a considerable amount of weight as his ragged clothes hung very loosely on him. The stench of sweat, dirt, and unwashed clothing permeated the air within ten feet of him and other bank customers steered around him.

A brief puzzled look came upon Walter's face as he thought he might know this girl from somewhere. Hannah had grown into a young woman and the dress she wore certainly had more curves than it did when he had last seen her.

"Hey, don' I know you?" He slammed his hand down on the counter. Hannah could see it was missing its forefinger. She tried to get words out but they seemed kind of jumbled, even to her own ears.

"I … I don't think so, sir. Would you like to make a deposit today?" Hannah's heart was beating wildly in her chest, praying the man wouldn't recognize her.

"Hannah?" Walter's eyes flickered in recognition. His slurred word came out as raspy.

"Hannah! You little bitch! I knowed it was you'n." He reached through the window and grabbed her by the throat.

"Where's that worthless slut you call a Mother?" he screamed at her.

Hannah's eyes started to bulge as she gasped for breath. Fear drove daggers through her heart as she felt certain she was about to die.

Walter suddenly let go of her as someone knocked him to the ground with a powerful slam to the back of his head. A young man stood there, towering over the fallen figure. "Someone go get the sheriff!" he yelled at one of the men standing nearby. As the man ran out of the bank, Mr. O'Dea ran out from his office to see what the commotion was all about.

He saw his young teller gasping for breath as she held her throat and a young man standing on the other side of the window. He pulled a gun out from under his waist coat and aimed at him with every intention of shooting him if he so much as moved an eye lid.

"No! No!" several people yelled at once. An older woman spoke up, "John, it wasn't him. It was that man on the floor."

The bank's president walked around from behind the counter and leveled his gun at the moaning man curled up on the floor. "Sorry, young fella," he said the young man, "I almost shot you, thinking you were trying to kill my clerk."

"No, sir," he answered. "I could see she needed help and I did the first thing I could think of and whaled him from behind." He turned to Hannah. "You Okay, miss?"

Hannah finally found her breath and was rubbing her throat where her father had held a death grip just a few moments before.

"Hannah, are you all right? Who is this man? Do you know him?"

"Yes, yes, sir," she said in a hoarse whisper. "He's my father." Her throat ached from where he had squeezed it and she could barely talk.

"Your *father*? Why was he trying to kill you?"

"I haven't seen him for several years, Mr. O'Dea," she squeaked. She jumped back behind Mr. O'Dea in fear as Walter groaned on the floor and tried to sit up just as Sheriff Thomas C. Williams came through the door. The powerfully built lawman filled the doorway as his huge mustache twitched and he took in the scene.

"What's going on here, John?" The sheriff moved over to where Walter was still struggling to get to his feet. "You stay right there, fella, 'til I figger out what's what." He pushed down on Walter's head bringing a stab of pain to the spot where he'd been hit behind.

"Tom, this gent came in and tried to strangle Hannah. She says he's her father."

The Sheriff turned to Hannah, looking over his large bulbous nose. He didn't say a word but let his gray eyes ask the question.

Hannah had finally caught her breath and told Sheriff Williams that the man on the floor was, indeed, her pappy, how he'd beaten her mother, and how they fled over six years ago.

"Sheriff, I want him locked up or he'll come and kill us for sure," she said.

The two-hundred-fifty pound lawman picked up Walter by the back of his shirt as if he was no more than a sack of flour and dragged him back out the door. "Don't you worry yourself about that, Miss," he growled back over his shoulder. "I have the feeling he's going to leave town real soon."

Hannah was still shaking when she turned to Mr. O'Dea. "I'm sorry, sir, for the stir. I'll understand if you want to end my employment."

The bank's president turned to Hannah and laid his hand on her shoulder. "What? And lose the best clerk I've ever had? I don't think so." He turned to the young man who had hit Walter from behind. He had gotten back into line to finish his bank business. "Come over here, fella," he motioned to him.

"Tell me . . . what's your name?"

"Reynolds, sir, my name is Aaron Reynolds."

11
Charlie, 1902

T he days and the river went swiftly by as the seven steamers wended their way down the Mississippi. The Wild West show had played Memphis and St. Louis drawing crowds of thousands to see the extravaganza.

Charlie had been working on putting together a fairly good orchestra of musicians as Buffalo Bill had given him a blank check to hire fiddlers, guitarists, and a banjo player. He added a brass section of two buglers, trombonist, tubist, and a trumpeter. He rounded out the group of music makers with a drummer and pianist. They had no more shows until they reached New Orleans and met the ship that would carry them to London so the troupe spent hours rehearsing as they drifted down the river.

People in river towns heard a mismatch of sounds as Charlie struggled to lead the ensemble into a cohesive group of musicians. The towns closer to New Orleans heard a better rendition of Souza's *King Cotton March* than those just south of St. Louis. Bill sometimes paused on his walks around the steamer to listen to them as Charlie tried to keep order amongst those that played well arguing with those who probably never should have been hired on. Was he wrong in putting such a burden on a fifteen-year-old boy who had never been more than a hundred miles from his home in his whole life? He winced as some of the discordant noises coming from the brass section but he had confidence in the young Charlie and knew they would be making better music by the time they reached London.

The string of steamers finally made port in New Orleans in December, 1902. Bill got hardly any sleep as he directed his entourage in the massive job of transferring people, horses, buffalo, cattle, equipment, and rigging onto the ship destined to depart one week hence. The levee at Canal Street had a dock nearly half a block wide and block long, holding goods in sacks and barrels, bales of cotton, and stacks of lumber. Amidst all of that were dozens of stevedores helping unload the steamers onto the dock and keeping them separate from other ships as the Wild West show was to be re-loaded on the *Eastern Star,* a giant ocean liner that had made dozens of trips back and forth to England.

Bill sought out Charlie whom he found to be throwing a rock at a large, brown rat that was trying to get into a sack of oats. Charlie's well-placed aim hit the rodent on the head, killing it.

"Good aim, boy," said Bill.

"Yes, sir. Thank you, sir."

"You've been doing a great job with the orchestra, Charlie. I'm thinking you need a little time to rest before we disembark tomorrow night. Why don't you go into N'awlins and have some fun? Get drunk, find a girl, but you have to be back on this ship by no later than noon tomorrow to get things in order."

"Yes, sir. Thank you, sir, but I'm gonna skip the part about the girl. My Gracie is waiting for me back home and I'll be sending most of my wages back to her to save for us to get married."

"Well, suit yourself, but you get off into town for a while and relax." He turned to go, stopped, turned back to Charlie and pointed his finger at him. "Now don't forget . . . noon tomorrow. We aren't holding up for anybody."

"Yes, sir. Thank you, sir." Charlie turned back to a team of horses he was leading before he had been distracted by the rat. "Come on, Joe. Giddyup, Mac. I'm gonna go see me somethin' I ain't never seed before . . . New Orleans."

12

Buffalo Bill

Bill Cody was always an early riser and this morning was no different. He had gotten little sleep and was ticking off in his mind all the details he had to think about in moving his entourage on their trip down the Gulf, rounding the state of Florida, and then across the mighty Atlantic. Weather reports were sketchy at best and being in these waters during the hurricane season was a risk he had to gamble. This was to be his fourth and final tour of his Wild West show in Europe.

He stepped out on the deck of his steamer cabin and the more pleasant humidity of an October day in the port city of New Orleans was a welcome change from the heat of the summer and his trek down the Mississippi. He looked across the harbor and the early stirrings of hundreds of longshoremen as they loaded the *Nebraska* for his trip confirming they were lading the last of the equipment he would need.

He bit off a piece of jerky for his breakfast and downed it with a cup of the strong chicory coffee that was the drink of choice in this southern city. He returned to his cabin, pulled on his fringed leather vest and grabbed his valise to carry over to the ship.

As he strode up the gang plank of the *Nebraska* he found his show manager, Nate Salsbury, standing at the rail with his packet of papers, checking off each crate as it was loaded.

"Morning, Bill!" he shouted over the racket of cursing longshoremen. "Just a few more animals to be on-loaded and we'll be good to go!"

"Good work, Nate! Still having trouble with those Injuns that don't trust something this big that sits on water?"

"No. I got 'em good and drunk last night like you suggested and all of them are sleeping it off below decks."

"Good! Good!" Bill pulled out a cigar and lit the tip of it, flipping the match into the water below. "Everybody else accounted for?"

"Almost," he answered, checking another of the pages listing the passengers. "A couple of the ramrods haven't reported yet. Let's see . . . a cook, Yun Chin. Concession Manager James Brock. Your musician guy . . . Charlie Fisher and one of the riggers, Patrick O'Connor still haven't checked in."

Cody's brow furrowed as he contemplated the list but was most concerned about his newest protégé, Charlie.

"Well, they have a couple more hours before we pull up the gangplank, so no worries."

"Ah, there comes Yun Chin now and looks like Brock is right behind him."

"The others will be along soon," he replied. "I'm going to go check on the animals."

"Yes, sir," Salsbury said to the back of Cody who was already making his way over the deck, before disappearing through a portal to the lower decks.

With all the animals under his charge, he cared as much for their welfare as any of the people in the entourage. His menagerie of animals provided the backbone of his extravaganza and he needed them to stay healthy.

It was nearing the time to put to sea, and Bill nervously chewed the end of his no longer lit cigar. Maybe he shouldn't have given Charlie free rein to go into the center of this rough city. The French Quarter was full of drunks, prostitutes, and every kind of lowlife possible in a cesspool of humanity. He knew of men who went into some of the hovels along Bourbon Street and were never seen again. He should have warned Charlie to stay away from the Quarter but wanted to put some aging on a kid that was still fairly green.

As he paced the deck, Nate Salsbury approached him. "Time to pull the plank, Bill. The Captain wants to ride out on the ebb tide and is anxious to get started."

"'Nother minute, Nate. You sure Charlie Fisher isn't on board."

"Yes, sir. Everybody but him and Patrick O'Connor has checked in."

"Damn it," he muttered under his breath. Why had he suggested Charlie go ashore? The young man could take care of himself but it was all of those whom he might meet that worried him.

His thoughts were interrupted by a long, shrill blast of the ship's horn.

"That's the Captain, Bill. He's telling them to pull the gangway."

"Alright. We've got a schedule to keep. I hope to God the lad is Okay. I'm not sure what's going to happen without his leadership of that orchestra."

"Well, you know, sir. I can read music and I play the guitar pretty well so maybe I can add that to my chores."

"Pull the gangway, Nate. Let's be on our way."

"Yes, sir," he said as he turned to give the order.

Bill put his hands on the railing and scanned the waterfront, hoping to see Charlie running to board but there were only well-wishers waving their good-byes, longshoremen turning to the next ship to load and a scattering of pickpockets making their way through the crowds.

"Where are you, Charlie? Where are you?"

13

Charlie

Charlie had never seen such blackness or felt such pain. It was a dark tinged with a great hurt that started somewhere in the deepest recesses of his fogged brain. It was like a nightmare from which he couldn't awaken and wondered if this was death. He couldn't remember what happened and he wasn't even sure who he was at this time, at this moment.

He tried opening his eyes but something was keeping him unconscious. He tried to lift his arm to feel his head but it was like trying to lift a hundred-pound crowbar. The signals he was sending to his arm somehow were not reaching it. He became aware of a stench that he tried to identify but wasn't sure of its source. Something rotten with horse manure, he thought.

And, why was the side of his face all wet? Was it blood? *His* blood?

He knew he had to get up but his legs could only tremble under him, twitching uncontrollably. Finally, the rotting smell forced him to get himself propped up on his elbows before he lost whatever might be left in his stomach.

The darkness was pierced with a blurred ray of light that was a pinpoint off in the distance . . . a mile away? Ten feet? Or was it the Lord calling him home?

With a tremendous effort, he painfully sat himself up with his legs flayed out in front of him. He pulled his arm up to feel his head, pulling it away to see if he was bleeding but his eyes still couldn't focus as the ray of light started to take shape across the street from where he lay. He became aware of a cacophony of sound. A throbbing pain pulsed through his brain with each beat of his heart, sounding like someone was beating a drum inside his head. He heard voices, laughing drunkenly and the light came into sharper focus as he saw a bar across the street full of drinking sailors, painted women plying their particular brand of trade, and a horrible music coming from a piano that obviously was out of tune and pounded on by someone who didn't know a chord from an anchor.

He tried to remember why he was sitting here in the offal of a town that had no waste system other than the gutters into which they threw their buckets of foul refuse. In a city of horses, their daily tons of waste and gallons of urine kept New Orleans streets a quagmire of manure and ammonia.

Bill! Buffalo Bill! A repetitive phrase kept going through Charlie's mind as he tried to make sense of what it meant. He crawled to a gas lamp pole and pulled himself up, hand over hand, using every bit of strength he could muster. Every muscle in his body screamed out in protest and he groaned out through clenched teeth.

Across the street, a voice pierced through his blackness. "You, slimey, get back here and pay your bar bill. You owe me ten dollah!"

A high laugh was thrown back. "Try ta collect yer bill, swine. Yer beer was warm and tasted like piss."

Charlie heard more arguing but the pain inside his head was beating out what the words were meaning. Bill? Bill! What did it mean?

As the clouds began to lift from his head he realized it was turning dusk. He held on to the lamp post to keep from collapsing back into the gutter and its retched refuse. A group of laughing longshoremen came along the sidewalk and one of them kicked Charlie back into the street, and he landed painfully on his hands and knees.

"Outta way, you blimey sod," laughed the man. He turned back to his friends. "You'd a thunk the city would do sumptin 'bout the likes of him, stinking up the street." They all laughed and moved on.

Again, Charlie crawled to the lamp post and hoisted himself to his feet.

"Bill! Noon!" he yelled to himself. "Noon! Bill! Buffalo Bill!" He knew he was supposed to be someplace at Noon with Buffalo Bill. But what?

He tried to locate the sun. If it was overhead, it would be about noon, but the shadows cast on the building across the street told him it was much later than that.

The ship! He was supposed to be back at the ship before noon. A horrible realization came over him as he realized he had missed his opportunity to see the world with his hero, Buffalo

Bill Cody. Bill had told him that he would be putting to sea at noon and had to be on the ship before that. He told him he wasn't holding up for anybody!

He stumbled down the street in the direction of the port, hoping against hope that somehow the ship had been delayed and he still had a chance.

The ladies of the evening were starting to come out onto Bourbon Street and he picked out the closest one and asked her if she had the time.

The woman had hoped for a potential customer but when Charlie had gotten ten feet from her, she backed up holding a soiled hanky to her nose as the manure-coated boy approached her. "Whoa, back up there, mate! I don' do anybody that can't keep hisself clean."

"I just want to know what time it is, ma'am. That's all."

"Do I look like a bloody clock, mate? Be off with ya now and go get a bath, fer God's sake."

She turned back to the group of women she was standing with who were watching with disinterest. "Geezus," she said to no one particular. "I got's my pride, don' I?"

Charlie's urgency forced him into a painful jog as he tried to clear his mind on how he got into this predicament.

When he left Bill, he had tied off his team of horses to the gangplank and made his way into the city. He passed shanties of black people. This was the first time he'd ever seen any up close like this, except those that happened to serving on some of the riverboats that passed through Port Byron. He had never talked to any of them because he wasn't even sure they spoke English.

All he could make out from their banter was language that could only form, in his opinion, a crass and guttural sound.

The blank stares of women sitting in their doorways, naked children running about, men who seemed to have no occupation other than sitting in groups of three or four others, drinking who knew what from stained brown bottles.

Charlie had come from a poor family but he was unprepared for the images of a people he barely knew existed. He began to consider himself rich compared to what he was seeing as he passed them by.

It wasn't that long since the War Between the States and, in his mind, he thought black people were still bound to a master so he stared in wonderment at these people freely walking about. He started to realize just how little he knew about life other than just what happened around him.

He remembered some stories from the boats that docked in Port Byron and the adventures they'd experienced in a town called New Orleans. They told of nights spent drinking and the brawls they would get into every bar they entered.

He recalled the stories from Ratface who had a reputation for a quick, mean temper and for fists that were even quicker. Charlie never knew the real name of Ratface, so called because of his long slender nose and the hairs growing out of his nostrils. His pocked face told of a bout the man had with the smallpox when he was a child. He boasted that if he could survive that deadly disease then he could whip anything, anyone, anywhere that he might take a disliking to.

Ratface had taken a shine to Charlie because the kid was wiry and obviously used to hard work judging from his muscular upper arms. He had kicked Charlie in the rump when they were on the Port Byron dock just for fun and for a chance at some bare knuckle fighting.

Charlie landed face first on a bag of oats, but came back up snarling at such an indignity and managed to land a blow on his attacker's jaw before another kick put the kid back on his backside.

Ratface laughed and jumped out of the way when Charlie made a second charge. Side-stepping the boy, Ratface held up his hands in mock defeat.

"Hold on there, young fella. You're awright. You don't take no shit from nobody. I like that." He extended his hand for a handshake which Charlie warily eyed with suspicion.

"C'mon, kid. I like you. How old are you?"

"Twelve," Charlie replied, "and you ever kick me like that agin, I'll give you sumptin you ain't nevah gonna forget."

Ratface laughed again. "C'mon, shake my hand. I was jus' funnin' ya."

Charlie knew he would have come up on the short end if he had tried to get his revenge so he held out his hand and took his attacker's gnarled hand and shook it firmly.

"Hey, ya gotta good grip, kid. My name's Ratface."

Charlie gave him a contemptuous stare and then smiled when he realized that the man did indeed have the face of a rat. In a bit of irony, a wharf rat scampered right through Charlie's legs and past the river man.

Every time Ratface passed through on the Mississippi and made port in Port Byron he sought out Charlie and regaled him with stories on the river and the many towns he visited along the way. Charlie loved the tales but mostly those about Ratface's adventures in N'awlins.

The river man told of his encounters in the French Quarter and the best places for entertainment. It was those haunts that Charlie most wanted to see when Bill Cody told him to take the night off.

As Charlie walked deep into the French Quarter he was amazed at the boisterous din seemingly coming from every bar, building and alley way. He heard music that was advertised on a hand written sign posted on the doorway of a saloon read *"The best Jazz of New Orlans is heerd right here ever night sundown to sunup."*

An old black man was sitting on a stool held up by three spindly wooden pegs that looked dangerously close to collapsing. He was playing on a dulled-brass saxophone that had seen many, many years of use. The man's music he made on the beat-up instrument belied its age. A rich melody came from the horn that seemed to beg from a mournful soul. Charlie had never heard music quite like that and wondered if he would be able to use some of those tunes when he got back to the Wild West show. He didn't have a saxophone in his makeshift band and wasn't sure how to get one. He wondered if the man would consider following him back to the ship with the promise of a steady job but thought better of it, not knowing how Cody would feel about it.

The cursing, laughter, and ravings of drunken sailors was heard everywhere.

He smelled a mixture of odors completely foreign to his nose . . . boiling crawfish from vendors in the side streets, tobacco juice that had been spit and dried on every square foot of the wooden sidewalks, the horse dung that lay in the ruts of many wagons that had passed through the city.

Charlie stood at the corner of Bourbon and Toulouse Streets watching in wonderment at the wave of humanity passing him by . . . drunken sailors, prostitutes of every size and shape imaginable, Cajun Indians hawking grotesque dolls that resembled a dead, shrunken head, black children working the crowds and picking pockets as they found easy marks, and people dressing themselves up as statues looking for contributions to their tin buckets in front of them.

"C'mere, sonny," Charlie heard from a voice behind him. He turned to face maybe the ugliest woman he had ever seen, or at least he assumed it was a woman from her high pitched voice. Her face was a cross between a dark piece of chocolate and a pecan. The furrows creasing her dark face rippled with every movement she made. Black, scraggly hair poked out from under a dirty scarf wrapped around her head. She was dressed in a filthy smock that was probably a beautiful piece of cloth decades ago but now showed the non-washed wear of years on the street.

"C'mere, sonny," she repeated and thrust one of the foul dolls into his face. Her voice had a slight cackle to it and he was sure this is what they called a witch. "Ya nee theese fer your worse enmy! Garteed to make him die by morn. Steek a pin into his head tanite at meednite, full moon! He die mebbe three, fo' our. You r'venge be compleet."

Charlie backed away from the crone, hoping he wouldn't trip into the muck of the street. "No! No, thank you!"

"Yo' be sorry! I now sell to yo' en'my and YOU be one ta die! Mebbe I do it me sef!"

She pulled a long black pin from her scarf and pricked the head of the doll as she mumbled some sort of harsh language that Charlie had never heard before and hoped he would never hear again. Its' shrillness seemed to make his teeth ache.

He felt a sharp pain in his right temple that responded in the same place the old woman had poked the doll. He grabbed his head with a cry and raced to the other side of the street. The pain almost made him pass out as he tumbled into a saloon door, hearing the hag's cackle following him.

The bar he fell into was full of laughing men, loud music and somebody singing an off-key song. He stumbled and fell at the feet of a man standing at the bar. The pain in his head started to ease up and he stared at the scuffed black boots of whoever it was he had sprawled into. One boot was on the dirt floor and the other perched on a filthy spittoon.

"Wha' the hell?" said the man as he reached down and pulled Charlie up by the back of his shirt. "I'll teach you not to interrupt a drinking man." He pulled back his fist and was about to slam it into Charlie's face when he stopped in mid-air. "Well, I'll be a sumbitch. It's Charlie Fisher."

Charlie looked into the red face of Patrick O'Connor, one of the hired hands from Bill Cody's ship. "Wha' the hell ya doin', Charlie? I neered put you inta the middle of next Thursday."

Charlie recognized O'Connor as one of the riggers Cody had hired to help put up the tents for the show. The big, ox-shouldered Irishman often stopped what he was doing to listen to Charlie rehearsing on his fiddle.

"I don't rightly know, Pat. I was standing on the street when some old woman stuck a doll into my face and now I got a fearsome headache. I barely made it into here. Thought I was 'bout to die from the pain."

"Ay, mate, ya musta run into Voodoo Violet. She hawks them ugly things and gets all riled up when no one buys from her."

"Voodoo? What's voodoo?"

"Son, you truly are green offen the farm, ain't ya?"

Charlie shifted his feet, embarrassed he had little knowledge of the world outside of Iowa and Illinois.

"Voodoo is a ancient magic practiced by the Cajuns down here. They made up those images of people in the form of a doll, don't you know, and stick pins in 'em. Somes claim that voodoo in the hands of a ace is the sure path to a horrible death." O'Connor slapped a coin on the bar. "Hey, Johnny, a beer for my fren."

The bartender grabbed a mug and used his filthy apron to wipe it out. These places couldn't be bothered with washing out the dishware after every use. That cost too much money. He pulled out a bottle from underneath and filled it to the top, splashing the beer over the counter.

O'Connor raised his own mug in a toast. "Here's ta the best damn fiddle player that strummed the Mississip." He pounded Charlie on the back and downed his drink in one long swallow, belching out the worst breath the boy had ever smelled and that included the passing of gas from his milk cow back home.

Charlie knew it would be an insult not to consume the foul smelling brew so he raised his mug and tried to imitate O'Connor by consuming the drink in one swallow. He realized half way through that he would never make it and choked, spewing some of the drink back onto the bar.

O'Connor roared in laughter with the bartender who used the same apron to wipe up the mess Charlie made.

"You alright, Fisher, you alright. Johnny, pour him another."

Charlie was squeezed in between his new rigger friend and a surly, drunken German who just kept staring into his own glass and muttering something about a Kaiser. Charlie had no idea what a Kaiser might be and deemed it prudent not to ask.

O'Connor kept insisting that Charlie just have another and then another. By his third beer, the room seemed to be spinning. Charlie held on to the bar with both hands to keep from falling to the floor.

His rigger friend was absorbing the drinks like a fish in a pond but the more he drank, the more belligerent he became and soon found himself challenging anyone in the bar to a knockdown.

"Can whup anyone here," he was yelling to no one particular. "Who here thinks he can take on an Irishman? I can take on two you'ns if you a mind ta. I could lay out John L if he wuz standing here."

The barkeep leaned over the bar and grabbed O'Connor's shirt. "None of that stuff in here, Paddy. Mind you self!"

O'Connor took that as a challenge and swung a haymaker at Johnny, clipping him on the chin. The tavern owner, who outweighed the drunk by a good thirty pounds, was over the bar in in less time than it took to say it and hauled him through the saloon doors and hurled him into the street.

Charlie's brain was in a haze but saw someone attacking his co-worker and jumped up on Johnny's back and tried to put him into a headlock. It was like hitting the side of a barge, stunning Charlie. Johnny reached up over his shoulders and flung Charlie through the same swinging doors, right onto the prone O'Connor who was trying to stand up.

Both men tumbled over each other, with Charlie's arm caught at an impossible angle under the Irishman. It felt like the limb was being ripped from his shoulder socket. Their heads collided and Charlie was knocked unconscious.

It was several hours before he woke up to an unimaginable pain without any idea where he was or if he was even still alive.

As Charlie painfully jogged through the streets back to the docks, he prayed that somehow the ship had been delayed or that Cody held up their departure to wait for him. Toulouse Street ended at the water's edge and the berth where Cody's ship was anchored, was empty. He looked up and down the wharf hoping that maybe the ship had been moored to a different spot, or maybe he was in the wrong place. The only thing he saw were other ships with a new one moving into the spot vacated by the *Nebraska*.

Charlie's heart rose up to his throat as he realized he would never see Europe or his friend William Cody ever again. He sank to his knees in despair. All his belongings, whatever money he had saved, his fiddle . . . was all on the ship headed to Europe. His head still hurt from where he had collided with O'Connor and the same spot where the old hag had stuck a pin into a doll. He fell over onto his hands and threw up into a fresh pile of horse dung, flushing some of the alcohol from his belly.

He had no idea what he should do next.

14
John L.

A heavy, right cross brought Jim McCormick to his knees. He
stared blankly at the huge man standing over him and then
pitched forward on his face. The crowd around the ring pushed
forward and counted to ten with the referee. A roar come out of
the mass of men as they all shouted, *"Ten!"*

The referee turned to the victor and raised the hand of John
L. Sullivan, former Heavyweight Champion of the World. It was
an exhibition fight and it was his last time to ever step into the
ring. He ended his career as he had begun it in 1878 . . . with
a knockout.

Sullivan stepped over the prostrate body of his fallen opponent
and circled the square ring with his arms raised high, soaking in
the melee outside the ropes that his performance had inspired.
It took just two rounds to bring down McCormick. As his aides
rushed to his side, Sullivan stood and watched as they put the
man on a stretcher and carried him to a nearby horse drawn
ambulance. It would be two days before McCormick woke up, his
face still puffed up from the pounding he had taken.

John L. Sullivan had lost only one fight in his life and that was to "Gentleman Jim" Corbett back in '92, costing him the title of Heavyweight Champion of the World. The match lasted 21 rounds and Corbett landed a left hook that was heard from ringside up to the last row even over the roar of 10,000 screaming boxing enthusiasts in the New Orleans' arena. Three of his fights had been bare-knuckled, and he was the last bare-knuckled fighter to ever do so professionally.

Sullivan climbed out of the ring and made his way back to the dressing room. Men all along the exit reached out to touch the most famous man in sports in the world. Anybody who even made eye contact would tell friends how they knew John L. Sullivan personally.

John finally made it through the throng of well-wishers and pushed into his locker room, only to collapse on a stool. The pains and aches of hundreds of fights made him weary. "Bill, I think I've just had my last fight. I'm getting too old and too tired to carry on."

"I've been telling you that for the last five years, Champ. I can patch you back up only so many times."

"I know, I know. Maybe I should have taken better care of myself and stop going to a bar every time I won a match." Even his own mention of a drink made him thirsty.

"Champ, you're gonna miss the ring, I know, but it's time to slow down, do some traveling to a town where you're not expected to step through the ropes. Find yourself a good woman and enjoy life."

Bill McGee continued to massage Sullivan's muscles. He took a swab of cotton and applied it to the gash above the fighter's left eye.

Long known as "The Boston Strong Boy", John L. Sullivan had lived a life that included drinking, carousing in the bars of every town he ever fought, and using his fists as much and more on the outside of the ring as he did within it.

Born to Irish immigrants Michael Sullivan and Catherine Kelly in 1858, John had grown up on the streets of the South End and its adjoining neighborhood of the Highlands. He never cared much for school, preferring to get his education using his fists. He dropped out of school when he was 13 and didn't get into too many fights at his early age because most of the boys he tumbled with knew they would be in for a thrashing if they dared challenge him.

"What do you think you're going to do, Champ?" asked Bill.

"I dunno. What town are we in again?"

"Grand Rapids, Michigan. You heading back to Boston?"

"Maybe. I dunno. I got some kin folk down in Illinois on the Mississippi I haven't seen in several years. Maybe I'll grab a steamer and head down that way. Then stop off in St. Louis. What are you gonna do, Bill, without me being around to patch up?"

"Don't worry about me. I can always find something." He put a bandage over the cut on John's eye. 'That ought to keep you a while. Don't take that off for at least a day."

"Yeah. I need a drink."

"Champ! No drinking. Try to start healing your body."

"Yeah. Okay. Guess I'll go catch a boat."

"Well, whatever you do, stay in touch."

"Sure, Bill. Thanks. I'll wire what I owe you when I get paid."

The men shook hands and it was the last communication they ever had with each other.

Sullivan went out a back door and headed for a bar.

The paddleboat *Julie Belle* stopped in Port Byron to drop off a single passenger. As the broad shouldered man with the thick mustache stepped on to the gangplank, he carried with him the scars of over 450 fights.

John L. Sullivan, worldwide renown, was weary but confident in his decision to leave the ring for good.

He had wired his niece Hannah Reynolds he was going to arrive. He was twelve years her senior and had met her a couple of times over the years. Hannah knew her uncle was some kind of fighter, but didn't give it much thought. She read the wire to Aaron who became quite excited.

"Becky, you never told me you was kin to a great man. How come you never mentioned it?"

"Why would I?" she answered. "What's so great about him anyways?"

Aaron was incredulous. "Are you serious? You don't know that John L. Sullivan is the world champion bare knuckle fighter and one of the most popular men in the world? I can't believe this . . . John L. Sullivan right here in this house."

"You're carrying on like he was married to your queen of England. I never heard such nonsense. I don't give much truck to people brawlin' in the streets."

"Becky, he is a lot bigger than Queen Victoria. He's . . . he's John L. Sullivan!"

"Well, I'm not sure where he's going to sleep. We've no room in this house for him."

"I'll go down to the Port Hotel and reserve him a room. John L. Sullivan . . . sittin' at my table. Lord o' mercy!"

It was the kind of news that Aaron couldn't keep quiet. The word soon spread that the Champ was coming to little Port Byron and when the John L. stepped off the boat, nearly every man, woman and child that lived within ten miles was there to greet him. The mayor had arranged for a small ensemble to play a fanfare and when the crowd saw him step onto the plank coming off the boat, there was a cheer that could be heard across the river.

Hannah thought it was a lot of foolishness and said as much but she was still in the throng of people who greeted him.

"Hello, Hannah," he said in his booming voice and she was suddenly the most widely held-in-awe woman in all of Rock Island County.

"Good morning, John. Sorry about all the ruckus and carry-ings on. It's not my idea."

John laughed heartily. "Hannah, I get this wherever I go, so I'm used to it."

Hannah introduced him to her husband, who still couldn't find the words he had practiced for a week. Aaron pumped John's hand. "It's your honor, sir, to meet me. Uh, I mean . . . uh."

John's smile widened under his great mustache. "Aaron, you married a fine little gal here. Hope you're taking good care of her."

"Oh, yes, sir. I'm a big favorite of hers. I mean . . . oh, damn, you know what I mean."

"Indeed, I do, Aaron, indeed I do. Now who are these sweet little girls peeking around from behind you?"

Hannah rescued her husband and pulled Hattie's hand forward. This is my oldest . . . Henrietta.

Hattie gave a curtsy that she had been practicing. "How do you do, Mr. Sullivan, sir."

"Now, none of that 'mister' and 'sir' stuff, Henrietta. You call me Uncle John."

"Yes, sir."

"And just who is that little wisp of a redhead standing behind you, Aaron?"

"This is my daughter Grace, champ."

Grace came forward but she wasn't about to curtsy to him or anyone. She thrust her hand forward and gripped John's hand as tightly as she could, pumping it like a well handle.

"I'm Grace, Uncle John, and I've got a boyfriend Charlie."

"I do believe that is about the strongest handshake I've ever gotten from anyone. How do you do, Grace? Where is your boyfriend Charlie?"

"He went off to Buffalo Bill's rodeo show and is somewhere in England right now, I 'spect."

"Buffalo Bill, huh? Did you know I did a show with Bill Cody a few years back? Well, your Charlie sure has a good eye for pretty girls."

"Thank you, Uncle John."

Aaron put his hand behind John's waist to guide him through the crowd. The fighter flinched and pulled the hand away. "Sorry, Aaron, but no man ever touches me lest I want to be touched. I've broken a few arms because of that."

"Oh, uh, sorry," an embarrassed Aaron said.

"Now you know."

"Yes, sir. I was just going to steer you towards the hotel. We ain't got much room up to the house and thought you would be more comfortable with clean sheets every day and maid service."

"That's fine. I'm sure it will be most satisfactory. What say I go freshen up a bit and then I come to the house for some of Hannah's fine cooking?" He turned to his niece. "You are a fine cook, ain't you, Hannah?"

Grace grabbed John's hand giving no thought to the admonition given her father. "Uncle John, she's about the best damn cook in town!"

Aaron and Henrietta swung around in disbelief. Aaron had never heard his daughter use that kind of language, and Hattie smiled inwardly knowing her sister was going to get a thrashing from their mother.

Hannah froze when she heard Grace and bored her steel gray eyes right through to the back of Grace's head. "Grace May, when we get home, make me a switch!"

John threw back his head and roared with laughter. "Grace, you and I are going to get along just fine. Hannah, it's Okay. She meant nothing by it. 'Sides, I believe her. I just bet you are the best damn cook in town."

Hannah turned her fury to her uncle. "This is a family matter, Uncle John. I will not have that kind of language used by my daughters. So kindly keep your nose out of it."

John, who had been in a thousand bar fights with men who oft times were bigger than his 225-pound frame, now stood meekly before the Reynolds family. He had just been verbally whupped by a no-nonsense, one-hundred-and-thirty pound woman. "Yes, ma'am. Sorry. Grace, you best learn from this woman because I got a feeling she will not be crossed."

Hannah was pacified, but her tone still carried some ice with it. "Thank you. Dinner is at seven o'clock. Be on time." With that she turned towards home, holding Grace by the elbow, leaving Aaron standing by John.

"Damn, Aaron. You married a wildcat."

After a short nap in the hotel, John put on his best clothes for dinner. Looking into the mirror hanging over the ewer on the bedside table, the face looking back at him carried the scars and damage from the poundings of many a fight, both inside the ring and out. His nose had been broken so many times that he'd lost count after twenty-five or so. Still, the face was a handsome one with short cropped hair and a great bushy moustache that spanned the width of his head. His deep steel-blue eyes belied a softness he had for women and whiskey. He straightened the wide ascot wrapped around his neck, picked up his gold-knob cane and stepped out into the hallway. He didn't really need the cane but used it as a prop for a finely dressed gentleman. He was determined to leave his fighting career behind and find a new way to occupy his time. He felt into his pocket for the silver dollar he placed there for a quick drink at the hotel bar before Aaron was due to pick him up for dinner.

As John rounded the corner and came to the top of the stairs, he looked down on a crowd of men and a few curious women who wanted to see the great man in person. A voice in the throng yelled, "Hey . . . there he is!"

Questions started assailing him before he even descended one step.

"Hey, John L.! When's your next fight?"

"Who you going to face next?"

"You gonna face Corbett again and take back your title?"

He stopped on the first landing and held out his hand to quell the noise from the crowd.

"Thank you, gentlemen, for your kind words." He tipped his hat towards a rather pretty young woman in the front of the pack. "Madam. How do you do?"

The blonde blushed and gave him a demure smile.

"Now, as to your questions, perhaps you hadn't heard of my retirement from the ring."

A chorus of "Oh, no" filled the hotel lobby.

"Oh, say it ain't true, Mr. Sullivan."

"You're too young to quit now."

"Not before you get your revenge on Corbett."

John held up his hand a second time. "I know how you feel, but I've come to the end of a great career, and this body can't keep up with the travelling, the bad hotel food, and the aches and pains of so many fights. Now, if you'll excuse me, I believe I'll have a drink before dinner."

He made his way to the bottom of the stairs and tried to shake the hands of those who offered them, stopping to sign a few autographs.

As he made his way through the crowd he noticed a young man hanging back by the door. His biceps stretched the limits of the shirt he was wearing as he chewed the end of an unlit cigar. He had a sneer of contempt on his face as he kept clenching his fists. One eye sagged a bit to the right side of his face and he kept making sniffing sounds, obviously from a broken nose that had never properly healed.

John brushed past him with a nod and stepped into the street headed for the bar across the way. The crowd hustled into the street, some still hoping to shake the hand of the great Boston Strong Boy.

A voice boomed out over the mass of people, stopping John in his tracks.

"Hey, mister tough guy! You don't look so hard hittin' to me. That bunch of pansies you faced in the ring can't even come close to what I can do to ya!"

The crowd immediately hushed into a silence as the man at the door stepped out into the street.

John turned around to see someone who outweighed him by twenty pounds and was a half-foot taller. Young man, maybe no more than eighteen, he thought. He sized up the challenger. Farm boy, he thought, and full of himself. No, he decided he didn't want to get into a fight with him.

"Sonny, I believe I made meself quite clear that I'm done with the ring and fighting. Now you look like a good, stout fellow who can take care of himself. I've no doubt you've been in a few go-rounds yourself. I merely want a drink before dinner and enjoy a pleasant evening with my kin. As a matter of fact, why don't you join me? The drink is on me."

"Don't want no stinkin' drink with a stinkin' bleedin' mick. I betcha do your own mother, don't you, mick?"

John's jaw tightened as he clenched his teeth. "What did you just say, sir?"

"I said your mama's a whore and your daddy is an arse biter." The man stepped into John's space with a grin, letting loose with a wad of tobacco juice on the champ's freshly shined boots.

The man made a sudden move with a fist that caught nothing but air as John feinted to the left.

The man never saw the famed right hand of the former World Champion smash into his face. Two spurts of blood shot out from both nostrils of a re-broken nose. The larger man was lifted off his feet and staggered backwards, falling into a fresh pile of horse dung right at the feet of Grace who stood unbelieving at what she had just witnessed.

The silenced crowd suddenly erupted into cheers as they were fortunate enough to see John L. Sullivan lay out the Port Byron bully.

Grace allowed a thin smile and then putting one foot upon the man's chest, stepped over him, and walked up to John as he straightened his ascot. "Uncle John, Mama sent me down to fetch you up to the house for dinner."

"Well, thank you, Grace." He offered his arm to the girl. "Excuse me, folks." The awed crowd parted down the middle as the two headed to the house.

As they walked back to the Reynolds home, John felt a sudden surge of warmth for his grand-niece.

"Gracie, I hope you weren't offended by what you just witnessed," he asked in his thick Boston accent.

"Uncle John, that man's name is Duggie Hayes and has bin pestering folks around here going back five year. I've had a run-in

with him myself. It done us all a world of good to see him sittin'
in a pile of horse shit."

John chuckled at the brazen language of the red-headed
girl. Yeah, he thought, that girl has got some Sullivan blood in
her, no doubt.

"Well, I'm glad I could oblige the good folks of Port Byron. I
wants me and you to sit down after dinner and have a little chat."

"That'd be fun!"

During dinner, John kept up a steady chatter of things he
had seen, people he'd met and places he had been. He related
his fight with Gentleman Jim Corbett when he lost his World
Champion title.

"I liked Jim. He had a punch that would knock down a mule,
but outside the ring he was a true gent and all the ladies especially liked him."

"What about your own ladies, John?" asked Hannah. She was
well aware of his first two wives and how his carousing had left
them heartbroken.

"I'll admit I've had some afterthoughts about how I treated
them. It's important for a man to have a good woman's love, and
I lost sight of that in all my travels. As a matter of fact I've been
thinking of how women have been treated and this suffrage
movement that's all the rage right now. I truly believe, and the
time is coming, that women should have the same rights to vote
as a man."

Hannah raised an eyebrow. Because of the abuse suffered by
her own mother, Mary Jane, she had been forced to make her
own way in the world. Had she not met Aaron on the day her

father accosted her in the bank, she would most likely have been a vice president by now, a position that very few women held.

John pushed his chair back from the table. "Hannah, that is just about the finest meal I've had in a long, long time. Mind you, I've had my feet under the table of some folks who employed first class chefs." He absent-mindedly stroked his moustache. "I tell you nothing can hold up to what you can do with fried chicken and greens."

Hannah blushed at the praise, got up and started clearing the table. "Nice of you to say so, Uncle John."

"Gracie, let's you and me go sit on the porch a spell. That is, Hannah, if we may be excused."

"That's fine. There's a nice breeze this time of the evening."

As John and Grace settled into their rockers, he pulled out a cigar and put a lit match to the end of it. "Now, Gracie, tell me more about this young man of yours."

Grace told him all about Charlie, his music, and the story of how Duggie Hayes had cut off one of her pigtails.

"Now if I'd have known that when that gent stirred up a fight, I would have hit him harder." John blew out a puff of smoke. "But he shouldn't have said that about my mother. He had no cause for that. Gracie, always honor your mother. And your father, too. Those are two fine people."

"Yes, sir."

Aaron and Hattie came out onto the porch and sat down on the steps, looking up at John.

"Now you say he went off with Buffalo Bill?" John asked. "I went to England one time and did an exhibition match for his show. Then we rode in a parade with Queen Victoria herself."

Aaron jumped up off the step. "What? You tellin' us that you knew Queen Victoria?" Aaron's admiration for his new-found-uncle-by-marriage increased a hundredfold. "Lawd Amighty!"

Hannah's voice came through the window. "*Aaron!* You know I don't hold with profanity in this house!" Sheepishly, Aaron sat back down on the step.

John chuckled at Aaron's discomfort. "Yep, met her back in '87 during what she called a 'Golden Jubilee'. Fifty years a queen. There were kings and queens from other countries, princes, and a whole bunch of other royalty I can't rightly recall now."

John talked into the night of his exploits both in the ring and out. Finally, Hannah came out on the porch, wiping her hands on her apron. "Been listening through the window at all of your stories, Uncle John. If even half of them were true, I'd say you are a well-travelled man. Right now, tho', I have to get my two young 'uns to bed. Girls, you have a lot of chores tomorrow, so off to the loft with you."

Knowing better than to argue, Hattie and Grace stood up and said their good nights.

"Hope to hear some more stories tomorrow, Uncle John."

"Sorry, Gracie, but I'm booked on the steamer out tomorrow morning early."

Both Grace's and Aaron's face showed their disappointment at the same time.

"Ah, that ain't fair," moaned Grace.

John leaned over and cradled her face in his giant hands. "Let me tell you what my mama always told me, Gracie. 'Only three things in life are fair; ... fair skies, a fair complexion, and a place where you take your prized pig.' Now off to bed with ye!"

When Grace got up the next morning, John was already on the steamer, heading south to St. Louis. At his side holding on to his arm was a pretty young blonde.

Grace never saw him again.

15
Charlie

Y oung fellow, you look like you don't have a friend in the world."

Charlie looked at a pair of white polished boots from his seat on the curb and turned his gaze from there to the neatly pressed white pants, past a smartly tailored white suit coat and finally to the lips of a man who had a broad smile. A great unruly graying moustache framed a face that had penetrating steel blue eyes that had several crinkles marking a path back into his white hair that looked as if it had never seen a brush.

"Do you have any friends, my dear sir?"

Charlie was taken aback. "What?"

"I asked if you have any friends. Surely a friend would not leave you in such a deplorable condition."

"I had a friend, Buffalo Bill, but I don't think I'll ever see him again. I was supposed to be on his boat to Europe and I missed it."

"Ah, yes. I saw Mr. Cody's show some years back and I was quite impressed. His spectacles in the arena greatly matched some of my own experiences when I roamed throughout what they call the Wild West."

"I was supposed to be his musician but I went into the French Quarter and got into a tussle. Now I'm sitting here with no money, no friends, and no idea what I'm gonna do."

The man tapped his white cane on the curb three times. "Well, come, come. Let's see what we can do about your predicament. Maybe get you cleaned up, share a bowl of soup, and go from there."

"I'm sorry. Why would you do that for me?"

"I guess because I see something of myself many, many years ago. What's your name, young man?"

"Fisher. Charlie Fisher."

"Well, Charlie Fisher, let's go back to my hotel and get your life turned around."

"What's your name, mister?"

"You can call me Samuel." With that he turned on his heel and walk away.

Charlie jumped up and followed.

The Hotel Monteleone in the French Quarter was known for its hospitality and famous guests who had stayed there. But when one of those famous guests showed up in tow of a young man dressed in clothes that reeks of the offal of New Orleans streets, the concierge moved to block the path of the two.

"Monsieur Twain, why you bring this into our hotel? We cannot allow this person to offend our guests."

"Well, my dear Abelard, I anticipated your objections and just want you to know that if we cannot pass through your lobby and to my room, there will be repercussions such that you most likely will lose your position."

Abelard blanched with the threat. "But, Monsieur . . ."

Twain waved him aside and crossed the lobby with Charlie. "Abelard, I want a hot bath drawn for my young friend and please bring him a fresh change of clothes."

"Oui, Monsieur."

Two hours later, Charlie was sitting at the dining table with his new friend, enjoying a meal like he had never seen.

"What's this stuff called, Samuel?"

"That's Oysters Rockefeller, Charlie? You like it?"

"I ain't never tasted anything like it."

Mark Twain was taking a new look at his dinner companion because he reminded him so much of Huckleberry Finn. An idea was forming in his mind.

"Charlie, do you know who I am?"

"No, sir."

"My real name is Samuel Clemens, and I write books under the pseudonym of Mark Twain."

"Oh, you're that Huck Finn guy. My daddy had a book of him and I read it a couple of times. I think he's the reason I wanted to get out and see the world. What's a pseudonym?"

Twain chuckled. "You know something, Charlie? I like you more and more with each passing minute."

"Yes, sir."

"Charlie, I'm about to board a steamer going around The Keys and up the east coast. I can use someone like you to carry my things for me."

"Well, I reckon that would be alright. What's the job pay?"

Twain chuckled. "Well, you do get right to it, don't you? Well, I pay room and board and can give you two dollars a week, but you will be working every day with no time off. Is that satisfactory with you?"

"Yes, sir, it surely is. I can send some of that back to my Gracie."

"Ah, a lady in your life. Tell me more about Gracie."

Charlie spent the next two hours telling of his family, how he came to meet Grace and his misadventure with Buffalo Bill.

The next day they boarded the *SS Carolina*, a steamer bound for New York.

16

Charlie

Charlie awoke on New Year's Day, 1903, to the steady whish-whish-whish of the schooner as it swept up past the coast of Georgia.

He dressed and left his cabin to the brisk salt air spraying over the deck. He leaned against the railing and marveled at the vast expanse of water, never imagining he would ever have had the opportunity of seeing an ocean. He mused about where his life was taking him. He didn't feel quite right with the new clothes he was wearing because it was the first time he ever had any. The hand-me-downs from his father seldom came to him without a hole, a patch, or sweat stained from years of grime. He never even heard of the term "knickerbockers" until Mr. Clemens had insisted he wear them. The pants came down only to his knees and were quite loose around his legs, making them look twice their size. He was also told to wear long stockings with new leather shoes. They creaked whenever he took a step and were maybe a half size too small, making his feet ache after wearing them for only an hour.

Still, Mr. Clemens seemed to approve of his attire so he just kept a smile on his face whenever the two of them were together.

His position was certainly different from anything he had ever experienced in his sixteen years. Everything from pitching hay to castrating pigs, pulling tow lines to shoeing horses, keeping furrows straight behind a horse-drawn plough to knocking out tunes for two hours at barn dances, now seemed a long time ago.

Mr. Clemens had him laying out clothes, toting several pieces of baggage, drawing his bath and a minion of countless errands. He thought he could really get used to this kind of life. Putting his hand and arm deep into a cow whose calf had gotten twisted around before birth certainly made him hope he never had to go back to that kind of life.

"Charlie!"

His thoughts were interrupted by Mr. Clemens who had forgotten where he had stashed his imported boxed-collection of Cuban cigars. He found a couple of them and cupped a match in his hand as he drew in a lung-full of blue smoke, blowing it out, watching as the wind caught it, disappearing into the sea mist.

"Nothing beats an early morning smoke after a cup of chicory, Charlie. A nasty habit, it is, but I'm too old to change. Why don't you join me?"

"No thanks, Mr. Clemens. The last time I tried those was with Mr. Cody and I swore that it would be a pipe from now on for me."

Mark chuckled and took another draw. "Why I do believe that is Savannah we're passing. Ever been there, Charlie?"

"No, sir. Can't say that I have."

"Savannah is a great little city. Has some of the oldest churches in the country. What's your religion, Charlie?"

"Baptist, sir. Daddy was always pretty strict when it came to the Lord."

"Presbyterian myself, but I don't put too much stock in any organized religion. I'm pretty sure there is an afterlife. Seems to me there has been nary any evidence of a molecule of life everlasting. Still, I most certainly expect to have one."

Charlie nodded as if to say he understood, but truth be told, he did not.

"Where did you say we were going on this trip, sir?" He was anxious to turn the conversation to something he could understand.

"Washington, D.C., Charlie. I'm scheduled to give a series of lectures at the Smithsonian in a couple of weeks. From what you've told me, I know you've never been there. A lion's den of politicians, it is, each one all-fire sure that what they believe is right and the only way to save the nation. Only the fools in Congress would appropriate ten-thousand dollars in an agriculture fair to display forty dollars' worth of pumpkins."

"Now that is a place I would like to see."

"You'll get your chance, Charlie Boy, but don't expect too much. My doctor told me that if I wanted to live three score and ten, I must go to bed early, avoid social excitements, and behave myself. I can't do that in Washington. Don't know of anybody that can. Soon as I get there, I'll be counting the hours . . . no, the minutes . . . when I can leave again."

Charlie, at the age of almost 16, was tall enough to look Mark Twain in the eye. He turned to him and said, "Sir, you sure do talk pretty!"

Twain chuckled, "Then I believe I have hoodwinked you as much as I have most of the men I've met." He turned and headed for the port door. "Let's get some breakfast, Charlie."

17

Grace

At the same time Charlie was breaking bread with Mark Twain, Grace was bundling herself up to step out to the hen house and gather eggs. Six inches of an early fall snow overnight had her father busy trying to shovel a path to the barn. She fell in behind Aaron and patiently waited until she was close enough to make a detour to the chickens.

He stopped after lifting yet another shovelful and turned to his daughter. "Good morning, Gracie."

"Good morning, Poppa. Ma wants some scrambled eggs for breakfast this mornin."

"Well, you tell her I'll be in shortly."

"Yes, sir," she said as she plunged into a drift that came up to her knees. As she broke the layer of ice on the hens' water dish, she wondered what Charlie was doing right at that minute and if he was staying warm. Her heart was heavy with loneliness and worry at his health.

She trudged back to the house and put the basket of eggs on the table as Hannah pulled a pan of biscuits from the wood-fired oven.

"Set the table for breakfast, Gracie. Henrietta, yell out the back door for your pa. Eggs and bacon will be ready in about ten minutes."

"Yes, ma'am," they both responded in tandem.

As soon as Aaron came in and took off his coat, the family sat down to their morning meal. "Grace," said Hannah, "your turn for the blessing."

They all joined hands and bowed their heads. "Dear God, we give thee thanks for all your blessings and for this meal and the hands that prepared it. Be with those we love and keep 'em safe. I pray specially for my Charlie. Don't rightly know where he be right now, but I want You to watch o'er him till he comes back. In Christ's name, amen."

A round of "amens" went around the table as Aaron reached for the plate of biscuits. "I reckon Charlie can take of himself, Gracie. Why don't you trek over to your grandma's house after breakfast? She always seems to make you feel better."

"Take Granny some of the sorghum syrup I made last week," said Hannah. "She claims it always makes her rheumatiz feel better."

"Okay, Ma."

After breakfast, Grace bundled up to stay warm, grabbed the sorghum and waded through the snow to Granny Cindy's ramshackle hut two miles north in Coe. She refused to move in with

Aaron and Hannah saying she was going to die in her own bed
in her own time. Nothing said by her son and daughter-in-law
could change her mind.

Grace walked in and found it to be fairly warm as her grandmother sat by a small pot-bellied stove. Lucinda had a fire poker
in her hand and was stirring up some glowing embers to ignite
a dry log.

"Well, gracious, child," she said. "Look who's comma callin'!
Come warm up by the fire. Is that a jar of your mama's syrup?"

"Yes, ma'am. How are you feeling?"

"Lordy, 'nother year past. Been ten year since your
Tuŋkaŋsidaŋ passed. Don't mind if I could join him soon."

"NO!" exclaimed Grace. "I don' know what I'd do iffen you was
to go and die."

"Gotta happen sometime, child. Every winter seems like it's
colder than the last and it's making me too tired to even walk
out to the wood pile." Lucinda noticed Grace's depression and
immediately guessed as its source. "What's going on with your
Tu'wewašhada, sweetheart, Gracie?"

"Ain't got but one letter since he's been gone. I don't rightly
know where he might be."

"Gracious, child, you gotta burden. Fetch me 'nother log and
sit yourself down for a story."

Grace complied and sat down at Lucinda's feet, wrapping her
arms around her knees. The old woman poked at the fire and
then wrapped her shawl around her as she looked at her granddaughter with love. She began her story.

A long time ago, a Lakota mother was becoming concerned because her young daughter was getting to the age when she should be getting married. A man in the house could then care for them both. She told the girl that the man should be a wotihŋisa, *a great hunter, so they could live out their days with plenty of food and provide a warm place to keep the winter's bitter wind begging at their doorstep.*

The girl said she knew of no young man like that and she feared it would mean a lifetime of loneliness, hunger, and no shelter. It continued like that for more than a year as the mother fretted more and more that she would not be taken care of in her old age.

One day as the child was out gathering strawberries, a young man appeared at the edge of the forest and spotted her in the meadow. 'Oh,' he said to himself, 'what a nice looking girl that is. I think I shall marry her, and she can keep my bed warm at night, fill my belly with cooking from the fire, and give me many children.'

He approached her, startling her as she picked a ripe strawberry from a vine. When he told her he would like to marry her, she said that it would be possible only if he could prove himself a good hunter. He assured her that he was, indeed, a great hunter, but the girl said that her mother would demand proof of his skills before he could marry her.

The young brave said he would prove it and left for about an hour. He returned, carrying a freshly killed maštíŋča . . . *a rabbit. 'See,' he said, 'this proves I am a great hunter.'*

The girl took the rabbit to her mother and told her of the young man and his desire to marry her. The mother was suspicious, at once. 'Child, I can kill a rabbit. This young man must provide more proof if he is to become my takosku . . . *son-in-law.'*

The girl returned to the young man and told her what her mother had said.

The brave grew perplexed. 'I shall prove it to your mother. I will be back with a great bounty and then take you for my bride.'

So the man left. He went to the mato, bear, *and told him, 'I need to kill you so I can take your tanned hide back to my intended bride so she can see I am a great hunter.'*

The bear replied, 'I am sorry but I have a cub I must care for so I cannot let you kill me.'

The hunter said he understood and went to the hehaka, elk. *'I must have your meat so I can provide food to my intended bride and she can see I am a great hunter.'*

The elk thought on this and said, 'I can see your problem, but I am the leader of an entire herd and they rely on me to find the best grass to eat.'

Again, the hunter said he understood and went to the ca'pa, *beaver. 'I need your pelt so I can show my intended bride that I am a great* watihŋisa.'

The beaver pondered this and tried to come up with a solution. 'I think I can honor your request but you must do something for me in return. I am getting old and my teeth are no longer good for gnawing at trees to make a good hut for the coming winter. If you will bring me plenty of long branches, I can build a shelter for my family.'

The hunter agreed and went into the forest. For several months he cut down trees and moved a great supply of branches back to the beaver. 'Now you must keep your part of the bargain, Beaver. I need your pelt to prove I am a great hunter.'

The beaver, however, is a very clever fellow and told the man, 'You must allow me time to build my shelter. While I am doing that, I need you to gather many roots and edible tubers for my family to survive after you kill me.'

The young man saw that as a very reasonable request and spent another two months gathering roots and tubers. He returned and saw that the beaver had built a great lodge for himself and his family. 'I have done as you requested, Beaver,' he said. 'Now I need your pelt so I can take it back to my intended bride.'

The Beaver knew he was running out of options, so he had one more request. 'I am ready to give myself to you if you would do one small favor for me.'

The brave was growing impatient. 'I will grant one last request, Beaver. What is your need?'

'I need the moss from the ground on the far side of the mountain for lining my shelter to keep it warm. This moss is the only thing acceptable. When you return, you can have me.'

The young man agreed and spent more than two months gathering the moss. When he returned, he called out. 'Where are you, Beaver? I have gathered the moss you need to keep your shelter warm.'

He searched several days for the beaver and came to realize he had been tricked. He was sad as he realized he would not be able to marry the young girl. He had failed as a great hunter. On his way back to her and the mother, he came to realize that all the time he had been gone, his adventures had given him considerable skills in his quests to supply the Beaver with his needs. Surely he could use these same skills to provide for the girl and mother.

When he returned home he made no contact with the girl. No, instead he set about to cut down trees and made a good solid cabin in which the three of them could live together. His new knowledge of roots and tubers helped him to grow a great garden of corn, peas, potatoes, and cabbage. He found moss to plug up the cracks of the cabin, keeping it warm in the winter and cool in the summer.

Two years had passed, and the young girl grew anxious in her despair, thinking she would never see the handsome, young brave again. Her mother had died the previous summer and her loneliness preyed upon her mind. As she gathered strawberries in the same field where the young man had appeared, she looked up and her heart beat wildly within her breast, for standing there was the young brave, looking more muscular than she recalled.

Taking her to the lodge he built for her, he proved he could, indeed, provide for her and she could give him many children.

Lucinda reached down and placed her hand on Grace's head. She closed her eyes and mumbled something in the Lakota language. Grace did not understand the words but waited patiently for her grandmother to explain to her.

Finally, Lucinda broke out of her trance and smiled at her. "Grace, I see your future and, like the young brave in my story, your Charlie will return to you in three, maybe four years. You will not recognize him at first because of his wanderings and what he has seen and done. I see you getting married and having children . . . three fine sons and a daughter.

Lucinda leaned back in her rocker and, again, closed her eyes as she drifted off to sleep. Grace quietly got up, dressed and made her way out the door, silently closing it behind her.

Charlie . . . marriage . . . three sons and a daughter. She had never known her grandmother to be wrong in anything. Wrapping her scarf tightly around her face, she stepped back into the snow and made her way home.

18
Charlie

Mark Twain was biting off the end of a Cuban when Charlie joined him on the bow of the ship as it sailed toward its destination. "Some mean looking clouds coming in from the northwest, Charlie. I think we're going to have a blow."

Charlie looked into the sky but could see only a few wispy clouds. "No, sir. I think it looks like a nice, warm day. "Sides, don't you think mebbe the climate is wrong for a blow this time of year?"

"Well, son, I've been standing here for the past hour and the wind has shifted almost to a right angle. The temperature has dropped at least ten degrees in that time. Climate is what we expect. Weather is what we get."

"Yes, sir."

"See to the things in my cabin, Charlie. Need to batten down. Anything that might fall to the floor should be secured."

Charlie looked at the sky again and shook his head, but Mr. Twain was paying his way so he went to do as the man asked.

Half an hour later, Charlie went back out on the deck. The temperature had dropped another ten degrees and massive clouds were building up over the western shoreline. He found Twain in a spirited conversation with the captain of the steamer.

"I'm certain that we are heading right into a big blow," said the captain. "By the morrow, we'll be right in the middle of it."

"I concur, sir", replied the author. "What's the plan for putting ashore?"

The Captain pulled his coat collar as a gust of wind buffeted his ship. "We're about seventy-five miles from the Oregon Inlet of the Outer Banks. We can squeeze through there and make for port in Manteo in the Shallowbag Bay. We can weather the storm from there and when it passes, move back out to continue the trip. My advice, Mr. Twain, is to stay inside."

"A most welcome suggestion, sir. I take my leave."

As he turned he saw Charlie standing near the cabin door. "Best come with me, my boy. We're in for quite a ride."

"Yes, sir," he replied. They both hustled off to their respective cabins . . . Twain to his rather spacious cabin and Charlie went below to the crew's quarters in the steerage.

When he got there he found no one there as the crew was already preparing the ship for a winter storm on deck. He thought this would be a good time to write Grace a note and let her know where he was and what he was doing. He found a stub of a pencil and piece of paper.

Dear Little Bit,

Sorry I haven't bin able to write much. I tole you I was sad to miss going with Bufalo Bill as I got waylaid in Nu Orlins and mist the ship. I bin busy doing the work of the man I work for. You mighta heerd of him. Mark Twain the book writin' fella that done the Huck Fen stories. Ima takin care of his belongins on a ship and wes hedded tup Washentin DC way. I think of you everey day and the carrot hared girll that I can call in my dreams anytime I want. I even writ a song 'bout you and can't wait to sing it to you. I'm determined to make nuff money that me and you can settle down in our own place and raise sum children. I emclosein' a five dollar coin that you can lay aside for futur use.

Yore Charlie who loves you.

Charlie was about to erase the part that said "loves you" when he changed his mind and left it as he had written. He wasn't much given to expressing his feelings but thought she might like to hear it anyway. He folded up the paper and stuck it in his coat pocket. He would give it to Mr. Twain to post when they got to wherever they were going.

He decided that since there wasn't much left to do, he might as well lay down for a nap before dinner. The wind must have been picking up because the steamer was groaning with a din of creaks as it tried to make its way through the swelling waves. He drifted off into a troubled slumber in which he did, indeed, dream of a carrot-haired girl swinging on a gate.

GRACIE AT THE GATE

by Charlie Fisher

The heart knows what it is feeling

It's heavy with regret

I find it hard dealing

With knowing you're so upset.

The last image of you stayed in my mind

As I rode away to my fate

The red-haired girl I left behind,

My Gracie at the gate.

Many adventures I have seen

In a world on land and sea

The people I've met, the places I've been

That thought keeps coming back to me.

The last image of you stayed in my mind

As I rode away to my fate

The red-haired girl I left behind,

My Gracie at the gate.

My wandering lust is still not fed

Our dreams will soon come true

The roads behind will be the roads ahead

I'll come home to you.

Your image carries me through

Soon you will no longer wait,

You are my red-haired girl feeling blue,

My Gracie at the gate.

19
Charlie

Charlie woke with a jerk as he was violently thrown from his cot. He forgot where he was for a few seconds. He sobered up quickly as the ship rocked back to the left, striking his head against the iron post of the bed. He scrambled to his feet and tried to make his way to the door. He heard men yelling above as they struggled to maintain their own balance.

He finally made his way to the ladder leading to the hatch on the next level. As he grabbed the handle, the ship pitched to the right and he was left swinging by one hand. The steamer rolled again the other way and his body slammed into the ladder, each rung painfully digging into his torso and legs. He was able to hang on and pushed the hatch open.

He climbed into a dark passage way and started making his way to the stairs up to the main deck. The ship rolled again knocking him against the opposite wall. Reaching the stairs, a shower of cold rain, mixed with hail stones swept over him. He made his way to the upper deck, wiping the water from his eyes, and stepped out into a storm of immense power. The hailstone pellets pummeled his body, each one hitting with the force of the

Devil behind it. He grabbed the rail attached to the bulwark and pulled himself along trying to reach Mark Twain's cabin.

The din of the howling storm nearly drowned out the occasional shouts he heard from the ship's crew as they barked orders at each other to batten down as much of the loose equipment as they could. Charlie, in the darkness, did not see another passenger making his way in the opposite direction, colliding into the man, almost losing his grip on the rail.

"Is the ship breaking apart?" screamed the frightened traveler. *"I can't see anything! We're going to die!"*

Charlie felt a door knob with his free hand, opened it and grabbed the man's arm shoving him through to safety. He continued his own trek in trying to reach his employer's cabin.

The *Carolina* pitched to port causing Charlie to lose his grip, smashing him against the outer rail. A flash of lightning exposed a life preserver tied to a cleat and flopping against the rail. In a desperate attempt to keep from going over the side, he grabbed at the preserver. It had not been tied securely and came loose in his hand.

Charlie's forward momentum carried him over the railing and he fell into the sea, still clutching the preserver. The sudden shock of cold water nearly knocked him unconscious. He tried to grab a breath only to take in a mouthful of salty sea water. He also knew that the powerful pull of the paddle wheel at the aft of the steamer would mean sure death if he were swept into its path.

Desperate to get away from the ship, he knew it would be the end if he lost his grip of the life preserver. Years of work on the farm paid in dividends now as he furiously pumped his legs in the freezing water. He looked towards the ship and made out

its dim lights through the howling storm. As it passed him by
he could see the ship's bridge and barely made out the form of
a man. He had a broad, white moustache and he was peering
through the darkness trying to see. Mark Twain had seen Charlie
go over the side of the ship in a flash of lightning and now stood
helpless behind the glass. He was certain his young friend would
be swallowed by the deep, never to see his Grace again.

Charlie was becoming numb to the cold, his fingers wrapped
tightly around the rope of the life preserver were so cramped
he didn't think he would ever be able to straighten them out.
The darkness only added to his misery, encompassing him in a
shroud of impending doom.

Thoughts of Grace shot like arrows through his semi-con-
sciousness. He was becoming more certain that within the
next few minutes he would surrender to the depths of the
Atlantic Ocean.

"I'm sorry, Little Bit," he whispered to the cold rain driven
night. "I never thought it would end this way." He tried to wipe
the water from his eyes, giving hope the ship would turn around
and come back for him, but the darkness held no light . . . no
Carolina, no shore, no moon, no stars.

It must be true, he thought, that your life really does pass
before your eyes at the point of death. In his gloom he saw Grace
losing her moccasin in the river, then holding her hand on the
ferry going to see Buffalo Bill's show. He gave a thin smile at the
satisfying blows he planted on Duggie Hayes' face. The recurring
image of Grace at the gate flashed through his mind. The brawl

in New Orleans. Sitting in the gutter only to be taken in by the kindly Mark Twain.

Charlie felt his legs giving out as he drifted towards his certain oblivion. He was tired beyond anything he'd ever felt before and his exhaustion led to hallucinations.

He saw Grace as a little girl, giving her a rude carving of a horse for Christmas. As she clutched it to her heart, her red hair started coming loose from her head as she floated away into the invisible night. Charlie reached out to her, trying to grab her hand and pull her back but only heard her cries, "Charlie, help me!"

The hallucinations kept getting interrupted by images of Grace standing at the gate, water from some unknown source swelling over her and sweeping her off into the night.

Charlie was about to give himself up to the unrelenting pull into the deep when his nearly deadened legs struck sand. He could barely feel anything below his chest but he had definitely hit something solid. He took a step and even with the waves crashing around him he knew he had landed in some shallow waters. Struggling against the rip tide and not knowing which direction the shore might be, he took hesitant steps until he could feel the water level going down.

When he finally reached the sandy beach he took five more steps and collapsed in utter exhaustion. He thanked God he was alive and fell into a deep sleep, unmindful of the rain and the cold wind still thrashing his body.

20

Grace

The same storm system that swept Charlie off the steamer had also dumped up to a foot of rain across parts of Minnesota, Wisconsin, and into northern Illinois. Tiny streams became creeks which would dump into lesser rivers before joining the Mississippi. Roads washed out, trails between towns transformed into quagmires, and the onslaught of water saturated the ground. Without the ability to soak into the soil, the water that was so necessary to life became the harbinger of death.

Tributaries were pouring millions of gallons of water a minute into the Mississippi and had no place to go but downstream. Towns and cities on the banks of the mighty river were helpless against the onslaught of water. It was now headed towards a tiny village in Illinois and then beyond . . . Port Byron.

Grace was gathering eggs when she noticed the first few drops of the approaching storm. She hurried to collect the rest before it came down harder. She looked to the sky and saw the roiling black clouds and decided to abandon the chicken coop while she still could. The sudden onrush of wind carrying the rain ceased to dropping vertical and now whipped into undulating sheets of water. She felt a sting on her forehead as hail stones began pelleting the ground. She stepped back into the coop as the hens flapped around her in their own frenzy to get into the shelter.

The hail pounded the tin roof of the coop making a racket so deafening she couldn't even hear the cries of the fear driven chickens. Water ran in rivulets through the wire gate and over her feet into the straw on the coop's floor. Hail stones as large as her fist followed the rain and she backed into the shed even further in an effort to stay away from them. Loud cracks of thunder followed dizzying flashes of lightning further adding to the cacophony.

The sky suddenly grew very dark and as she looked across the yard towards the barn, a lightning bolt split the air with a huge boom, and she could see her father motioning from the doorway to stay right where she was. "Oh, right," she thought to herself, "like I'm going to step out into this."

Her fear of the storm suddenly gave way to a new thought that a tornado could be coming through. The chicken coop is the last place she wanted to be if that happened. Defying her father, she picked up the basket of eggs and dumped them on the ground, not caring if they cracked or not. Putting it over her head, she leaped through the gate and headed for the barn to be with Aaron. He always protected her and he would do so now.

The hard packed dirt of the yard was now a mass of mud. Halfway to the barn, she slipped and came down hard face first into the ooze. She lost grip of the basket and the hail stones kept coming hard. A chunk of ice caught her on the side of the head and she lost consciousness, mindless of the mud clogging her mouth and nose.

The first thing Grace noticed was the flame from a lantern flickering in her eyes. A horrible pain was shooting through her head, and she lifted her hand to feel a huge bump just over her right ear. As she tried to focus her eyes, she heard the comforting words of her father.

"I think you're going to be all right, Gracie, but why, in God's name, didn't you stay where I told you? I had to run out there and gather you up before those hail stones killed you. Took a couple of knots myself."

"I'm sorry, Papa," she whimpered as she tried to sit up. "I was skeered and wanted to be with you, not those fool chickens."

"Well, we've got bigger worries right now. The rain ain't letting up and I'm afraid of what's going to happen if it keeps coming down the way it is. Port Byron's got a system that if we get a frog strangler like this'n, all men are to meet down by the river in case of flooding. You gonna be all right?"

"Don't leave me, papa."

"I'm gonna carry you up to the house and let your ma tend to that bump on your head. Then I gotta head to the river."

"Okay, Papa."

As the rain continued to fall, Aaron walked the half mile from his farm to Port Byron. At least the hail had stopped and when he got there several other men had also gathered. The river had already risen to the level of the dock. When it became obvious there was no one in charge, Aaron spoke up trying to yell over the din of the storm.

"Miller, Beery, Schmidt. Go round up as many bags as you can. I know the feed mill has a whole stack of them."

Glad to have someone who seemed to know what to do, the three men scurried off.

"Cox, Crawford, Bosley. Get your buckboards and go to the quarry. Take your sons with you. Load up as much of the sand as your wagons will allow. Get back here pronto!" The trio ran to get their teams hitched up to their wagons

"The rest of you men go grab shovels and picks."

Aaron knew they would never be able to hold back the river but if they could fill enough sand bags to keep the water out of the stores and homes along the banks, they could at least try and keep Port Byron from washing away.

As Aaron and the men labored through the night building their levees around the town's structures, Hannah, Hattie, and Grace did what they could to shutter up the house, coop, and barn from the strong winds. Water was leaking into the kitchen and bedrooms so they hustled to put as many pots and pans under the drips as they could find.

With the hail storm having passed, Grace ran to the chicken coop to fasten the gate and door, keeping the birds safe and dry as well as she could. Then all three of the Reynolds women worked in the barn. The horses were still jittery from the thunder, and Hannah found it difficult to quiet them down in their stalls. Hattie dragged bales of straw up against the doors to keep them from whipping off their hinges while Grace tended to the milking of their three cows. The knot on her head was still throbbing and she felt as if she might faint from the pain.

Once those chores were done, they leaned into the wind and finally got back to the house where they sat down exhausted. Grace fell onto the wet sheets of her bed and tried to sleep but the thunder and her worry about her father kept sleep at bay. She just had to know if he was okay.

Knowing her mother would forbid her from going out into the rainy night, Grace slipped on her parka and snuck out the back door. She went to the barn, found a lantern and then started making her way to the river. If her father had gotten hurt, she wanted to take care of him just as he had done for her.

It was difficult to see through the darkness with a lantern that kept flickering and threatening to extinguish itself from the water that kept pounding at the glass chimney. Reaching the town, she made her way down to where she thought the dock might be only to find no one there. Where could her father be?

She turned to step onto the railroad tracks that ran parallel to the river but stepped into water that came up to her knees. The swirling current pulled at her legs and, losing her balance, she dropped the lantern and fell into a mass of water, mud, tree branches, and other debris. As she struggled to get to her feet, the muddy water got into her mouth as she tried to gasp for breath. She could not stand up and was desperately struggling to keep her head above the water. She knew she was in trouble as she tumbled over the rail and painfully banged her knee.

"Oh, God, please help me," she cried as a massive wave swept over her dragging her under.

Suddenly she felt a hand grab at her arm and pull her back to the surface. She couldn't see who her savior was but his voice was certainly one she recognized.

"Well, I ain't no God, but I bet I can get that kiss now."

Pulling her up to his face, Duggie Hayes kissed Grace full on the lips. Lifting her up, he put her over his shoulder and worked back up the bank, slipping in the mud several times before he reached the road.

Grace was in full conflict of her senses. She cringed from the rough buss her sworn enemy had given her but felt genuine gratitude he was there to pull her from certain death. She sat in the mud gasping for breath as the rain continued to come down, mixing with her tears.

"Duggie," she cried over the thunder, "I'm mighty grateful fer you and whut you done but don't you ever do that again!"

She got to her feet and started back home. She managed to cleanse herself of mud from the rain, slipped back into the house unnoticed, and crawled back onto her bed. She kept trying to wipe the kiss from her lips as she fell into an exhausted sleep.

She never told her father, mother or Hattie of what had happened that night. Neither could she come up with a reasonable explanation of what happened to the lantern.

21
Charlie

Contending with his own brush with death, Charlie felt the gentle caresses of waves on his face as he slowly regained consciousness. The storm had passed, and the warm October sun was burning with no hint of any clouds.

The experience of the previous evening seemed surreal and he found himself marveling that blood was still surging through his veins. He struggled to his feet but soon sank to his hind end from the exhaustion that drained every muscle in his body.

He pulled his knees up to his chin and wrapped his arms around his legs as he contemplated what he should do now. Putting his hands into his pockets to keep them warm, he felt a wad of soggy paper and pulled it out. It was his letter to Grace that he'd meant to give to Mr. Twain to post. Carefully opening it up, he could tell this one letter that would never get sent. None of the writing was legible. He tossed it onto the sand and pocketed the five-dollar coin.

Looking out over the expanse of the ocean he saw nothing but blue, both water and sky. The pounding surf muffled the sound of approaching footsteps.

"Well, young fellow, what in the world are you doing out here in the middle of nowhere?"

Charlie looked up to see the outline of a man standing over him, the sun behind his back, putting him into silhouette. He put his hand up to shade his eyes and could make out a rather tall, well dressed fellow. His cap tilted to the left of his head, covering a partially bald head. He sported a wide, handlebar moustache and piercing blue eyes.

"Who are you, mister?" inquired Charlie.

"The name is Orville. I was out for a stroll and noted you struggling to get to your feet. How does it happen you are on this beach with nary a house for a couple of miles either way?"

"I fell off a steamer in a storm last night. I thought I was a goner fer sure. Looks like I washed up here . . . wherever here is."

"My lad, you are a lucky boy, indeed. The hand of Providence has smiled upon you and you should be thanking your Maker for your deliverance."

"You sure talk funny, mister. Where am I?"

"Fate has put you on The Outer Banks of North Carolina. You are sitting upon the sand of the town Kill Devil Hills. To the south of here is Nags Hill and to the north, Kitty Hawk."

"Doesn't Carolina use any regular names fer places?"

Orville Wright chuckled. "Guess I never thought of it. What's your name, lad?"

"Fisher, Charlie Fisher."

"Well, Mr. Fisher, if you're up to it, walk with me back to my shop and we can get you something to eat."

The shop Orville was referring to was quite unlike anything Charlie had ever seen. It was more of a large barn, painted white and had two large doors that both swung outward. As he led Charlie into the building, he noted several tables along one wall that held a variety of strange looking machines. Several other contraptions lined an opposite wall that Orville explained were bicycles.

"I've heard of those things," Charlie said, "but I've never actually seen one."

What really caught the young man's attention was the oddest looking machine he had ever seen.

It was propped up on two tables. Two wing-like spans ran parallel to each other about eight feet apart and were separated by a series of eighteen iron bars. The spans were about four feet wide and covered with what looked like some sort of tarp. Running cross bar through the middle was a shorter version but without the tarp. Two long bars ran from the top of the long span to a pair of runners like Charlie had seen on a sled. At one end of the cross piece was a second much shorter span that resembled the longer one. At the opposite end was some sort of a motor.

Charlie thought the whole machine was held together with chicken wire, cables running from one end to the other.

"Wilbur," called out Orville, "we have a guest!"

Stepping out from behind the machine was a second man almost as tall as the gent who found him on the beach. He had a wide expanded forehead with a crown of black hair that spanned from one ear over to the other. He wore a set of greasy overalls that Charlie thought maybe hadn't seen a washing for quite a while. He shifted a wrench from his right hand to his left and walked towards Charlie.

"Hello, young man," said Wilbur. His voice was a bit deeper than Orville's but had that same clipped way of speaking. "Who might you be?"

"Charlie Fisher," he replied. "Wilbur, is it?" He extended his own hand and shook it.

"Yes, Wilbur Wright. I'm Orville's better looking brother."

"Pleased to meet you."

Orville then explained how he happened upon Charlie at the beach and gave a brief explanation of how he had come to be there.

"Sounds like you had an adventure, Charles."

Charlie felt a tinge of homesickness. Only his mother ever called him "Charles".

"I was thinking," said Wilbur, "that Mr. Fisher might be a bit hungry after his escapade, and we could have him join us in a repast. It's about time for lunch, anyway."

"If you don't mind me asking, what in heaven's name is this contraption?" Charlie walked over to the machine. "I ain't never seen nothin' like this in my life."

"Ah! A curious mind, Wilbur." Orville set the wrench on a table and joined Charlie. "This, Charles, is something we've been working on for years. It's a flying machine."

Charlie turned to the man in disbelief. "Excuse me, but did you say 'flying'?"

Orville spoke up. "We believe, Charlie, that man is destined to fly. We've had limited success with other models but have never been able to keep one in the air for any length of time."

Wilbur continued the explanation. "We still have some minor adjustments to make to our aero plane but I think that within a few months we will get this off the ground and into the sky."

"Well, I just about heard everything now. A flying machine! This I gotta see."

"Let's adjourn to the house and enjoy a repast," said Orville.

On the way the brothers engaged in conversation about altimeters, thrust, and chain drives that left Charlie just shaking his head.

Over a lunch of fried chicken and boiled eggs, the two men told Charlie of their many experiments with a propelled flying machine that had begun years before in their bicycle shop in Dayton, Ohio. They talked excitedly of differentials, aerodynamics, and wind over rudders.

They had built model after model in working towards the machine now sitting in their barn. The failure of one machine was followed by adaptations in the building of its successor. When the work on that one nose-dived, it resulted in a better one that followed.

Test after test, failure after failure, Wilbur and Orville Wright were guided by their determination of flying.

After lunch, they returned to the barn and continued their work while Charlie watched, occasionally fetching them a tool when they called for it. It was well after ten in the evening before they finally decided to call it a night. They offered Charlie a small cot in the back of the barn. Only Orville called it a "hangar". He gladly accepted and fell onto the bed, immediately plunging into a deep sleep. He dreamt of a gate coming loose from the fence and flying into the night sky.

22

Aaron

Mark Twain was deeply disturbed by the almost assured death of his charge. He felt responsible, in a way, for Charlie's demise and wished there was something he could do to assuage his guilt.

He finally decided that Charlie's intended bride should be made aware of what happened and wrote her a note. He remembered that the boy had mentioned her name as Grace Reynolds and she lived in Port Byron, Illinois. He addressed the envelope in his own broad stroke style of writing and, after some thought, included a promissory note of one hundred dollars that could be cashed in any bank of her choosing. With a heavy heart he posted the letter and wondered what that red-haired girl would do now.

October started the month with a biting, cold wind as the winter got a start earlier than usual. The occasional few flakes of snow whistled around the Reynolds homestead. Inside the house, Aaron, Hannah, Hattie, and Grace stood warming their hands over a Franklin wood stove. The black heater roared with a fire of a few logs Aaron had put into it. It served as heater, cook stove, and oven for the home. The bare furnishings of the three rooms constantly reminded Aaron of his failed promise of providing better for his family.

His job at the limestone mill was often not enough to purchase even a few necessities at the Port Byron Mercantile. He had long since been refused further credit at the general store until he could pay what he owed. Even the twenty-seven dollar debt was far out of his reach. The Reynolds family lived from day to day on the vegetables Hannah got from her garden, the eggs from the flock of ten chickens, and the milk of their one cow. When he did work at the mill it was for a dollar a day. From that dollar he could buy a little flour, some coffee, and perhaps a can of peaches.

"Becky," he said peering over the stove at his wife, "we have got to get some money somehow. I just ain't providin' fer you like I should."

"Now, you see here, Aaron Reynolds," she replied, "you stop that nonsense kind of talk. We've got a roof over our heads and a fire to keep us warm. You provide me and the young ones just fine."

"Someday, Papa," said Hattie, noting the sorrow in her father's voice, "I'm gonna make some money and I'll give it all to you."

"Me, too, Papa," chimed in Grace.

"Thank you, girls. You do your daddy's heart good."

After breakfast, Aaron pulled on his heavy jacket and stepped into the biting wind of an Illinois winter. Plodding through the snow towards the barn he heard a ruckus coming from the chicken coop.

Wolves were a continuing menace and Aaron started running for the coop on the other side of the barn. He sometimes carried his old Remington with him, but this morning it was still hanging over the mantle in the house, and he wouldn't have time to run back and get it. A pack of wolves could wipe out his entire flock within a minute. He scooped down and grabbed an axe that was embedded in a log near the barn.

Rounding the corner the squawking of ten chickens suddenly fell silent and he heard nothing but the growling and gnashing of teeth as he tore open the gate. The wolves had dug under the fence and were now having their own breakfast of chicken.

He barreled through the coop's door and came face to face with three wolves. Feathers were flying in all directions with every chicken he had, lying dead on the ground. The trio of animals all raised their heads at the same time to snarl at this new intruder on their meal.

The largest of the three took a step towards Aaron, baring his teeth back. The gray wolf focused on the eyes of Aaron who took a step back and raised the axe over his head for the inevitable rush towards him.

As if they had an unspoken signal amongst them the other two split in opposite directions to flank this enemy on either side. Blood was dripping from their jowls as they each made their move.

The wolf on the left made a leap for Aaron's throat, but the axe was just a bit quicker as it came down and split the animal's head in two. It yelped its death cry and dropped at Aaron's feet as the other two made their own jumps.

The lead wolf sank his teeth into Aaron's arm as the one on the right grabbed his leg. The thickness of the coat's sleeve managed to blunt the force of the wolf's bite but it was still strong enough to make Aaron think his arm had been broken. He shifted the axe to his left hand, and swung at the animal's tail but the wolf that was chomping down on his leg made Aaron miss and he fell in a heap to the coop's floor.

Both wolves released their holds and started for Aaron's throat. He raised his arm up to protect his head and the leader managed to get a hold of his wrist. The pain he felt of breaking bones was excruciating. He could see blood starting to gush from the wound as the wolf clamped down even harder causing the axe to fall to the ground.

Aaron tried to sit up and push himself so he had his back to the wall while kicking with his opposite leg at the wolf chewing on his leg. The leader saw his chance and let go of Aaron's arm to move in for the kill at the throat.

He felt the powerful jaws close on his throat as the wolf snarled through clenched teeth. In a rising panic, he felt bile rising up into his mouth. Aaron tried to scream, but the clamp on his throat caused only a muted cry.

Over the shrieks of the two animals about to end his life, Aaron heard the crack of a Remington rifle. The wolf at his throat released his hold and fell dead to the ground. A second shot ended the life of the animal on his leg.

Aaron looked up to see Hannah standing in the doorway of the coop, the rifle still aimed at the two wolves. Her silhouette against the blowing snow behind her would be a recollection that he knew would stay with him for the rest of his life.

That image of Hannah was his last thought before he passed out from a mixture of fright and a loss of blood.

Aaron's brain was in a fog as he struggled to climb back to consciousness. It was the throbbing of pain on his arm, his leg and throat that brought him back to reality. His first thought was of Hannah's silhouette. He struggled to open his eyes to see that it was, indeed, Hannah standing over him as she spoke to Grace.

"I want you to stay right here with him, Grace, while I go boil some water to clean those wounds."

"Okay, Mama," she replied, as Hannah left the room.

Grace turned to her father who was trying to sit up. "No, Papa. You lay right there. Hattie's gone to get the doctor. You've got to get patched up and every time you move like that, you're gonna lose more blood.

Aaron tried to speak but couldn't form any words that made sense.

"The wolf tore at your throat, Papa, so don't try to talk. Mama'll take care of ya until the doctor gets here."

Aaron nodded that he understood and reached out to take Grace's hand. He needed the comfort of a human touch to erase the thoughts flooding his head of that wolf coming at his throat.

When the doctor had gotten there an hour later, Hannah had bandaged him up as well as she could and had managed to get the bleeding stopped.

The doctor spent the better part of the next hour in stitching up the wounds, wrapping Aaron's throat and giving him a dose of laudanum for his pain. He finished his work, closed his doctor's bag as Hannah walked him to the door.

"Thank you, Dr. Rogers. How much we owe you?"

"That would be three dollars, Hannah."

"We ain't got three dollars but I can give you a couple chickens for your dinner tonight. Long's as you don't mind they got bit by a wolf first."

"That's fine, Hannah. Why don't you just give me the money when you can?"

"'Preciate it, Doctor. We don't like to be beholden to anyone but you're surely gonna get your money soon's my Aaron can get back on his feet."

"That might be a spell. He's pretty well bitten up. I'm mostly worried about that throat wound. He might never get his normal voice back, but we'll have to wait and see." He paused in the doorway. "Mind you, he shouldn't be trying to do much for at least a month. Don't let him talk and make him stay in bed for the next couple of weeks until those wounds start to heal. I'll be back around in a few days to check in on him."

"Thank you, Doctor Rogers. Now I gotta go bury me some wolves."

Aaron's recovery took longer than expected, and he was still confined to his bed after a month. Hannah, Grace, and Hattie all took on his chores as he healed.

When the doctor came by and took off the bandages from Aaron's throat, he asked him to try and say his name. He sat up and opened his mouth but nothing would come out.

"I was kind of afraid of this, Aaron. Your vocal cords have been damaged. The most you'll ever be able to do is a whisper, but for right now I want you to just stay quiet and not do too much. Get yourself a pencil and pad and communicate by writing down what you need to say."

Aaron dismally nodded his head, sinking back down into his pillow.

"Don't worry, Papa," said Grace, "I'll take good care of you."

Aaron smiled weakly and fell asleep.

The start of December was even colder than November as the wind whistled down the Mississippi gripping the town of Port Byron in a deep freeze.

The girls kept up their school work as well as they could, but stayed home more often than they plodded through the mile of snow to do their studies.

It was on one such day that Grace was instructed by Hannah to stop by the Mercantile where mail was posted for the town. They didn't often get anything posted to them so would only check whenever they needed to stop and get whatever supplies they needed with whatever money they had.

Grace walked into the general store and went to stand by the stove in the center of the room, warming her hands.

"Good afternoon, Grace. What will it be today?" asked Jeremiah Simmons, the balding owner of the store.

"Hello, Mr. Simmons. Mama asked me to check the post and to get however much coffee I can for ten cents."

The portly man turned to the pigeon holed boxes on the wall behind the counter and pulled out three pieces of mail and handed it to Grace. "And ten cents of coffee," he said, handing a brown bag to Grace. She was standing in front the candy counter where she usually ended up every time she walked into the store. "Hmmm. Seems that Grace Reynolds might be wanting a stick of horehound."

"Sure would, Mr. Simmons, but I don't got no extra for candy."

"Tell you what. Why don't you take two sticks? One for you and one for Hattie. Someday maybe you can come back and give me the penny you owe me."

"Gee, thanks," she replied, grabbing the two sticks of horehound from his hand before he could change his mind. She turned and made her way out of the store, brushing past a large man that had just entered. "Oh, 'scuse me."

She had run right into Duggie Hayes, who grinned down at her and licked his lips that sent a chill through her.

"Thet's all right by me, MISS Reynolds. Jest reliving that little kiss you gave me a spell back."

"Duggie, you know dang well you forced that on me," she hissed as she ran out of the store.

He followed her and yelled after the fleeing girl. "Yessir, shore would like to relive that moment. It was pret' near my favorite memory. Come on back here, Gracie . . . got sumptin I wantsta show ya." He pulled the braid out from his shirt and lifted it to his nose . . . something he did twenty times a day.

His horrible cackle faded in her ears as she hurried down the street through the snow.

When Grace got home she took off her coat and put the coffee on the table. She walked over to Hattie, who was sewing on a dress she was making for herself. "Mr. Simmons said to give this to The Hat."

Hattie was about to scream in protest at the hated nickname until she saw the horehound stick that Grace was holding out.

"Ooh! Horehound," she cried, grabbing the candy and completely forgetting why she was mad.

"Here's the mail, Mama," Grace said to Hattie who was standing at the stove, stirring a pot of porridge for dinner.

"Thank you, child. Now go in and check on your father. He's still having trouble eating so's I'm hoping he'll be able to take some of the soup."

"Yes, m."

Grace was able to get a few tablespoons of the porridge into her father who then closed his eyes and went back to sleep.

"Grace," called her mother from the kitchen. "Did you know that you got a piece of mail? Didn't you notice that when you picked it up at the mercantile?"

"A letter? For ME? I bet it's from Charlie," she yelled excitedly, running into the kitchen. She grabbed the letter from her mother, expecting to see Charlie's scrawl. She stared at the envelope that was addressed to Miss Grace Reynolds, Port Byron, Illinois. The return address said simply, Samuel Clemens.

"Mama, who's Samuel Clemens? And why's he writin' me a letter?"

"Gracious, child, the only person I know by that name is the writer Mark Twain. I have no earthly idea why he's writing you."

Grace tore open the envelope and read its contents.

November 2, 1903

Dear Miss Grace,

I am writing this letter to you with a heavy heart because I am the bearer of sad news. I know of no other way of telling you so I'll just tell it right out. I'm afraid that the young man you are engaged to, Mr. Charles Fisher, was lost at sea last October 30th.

"NO!" Grace dropped the letter to the floor and sobbed. "Oh, Mama," she cried, *"My Charlie is dead!"*

"Oh, darling, say it ain't so!" Hannah picked up the letter and continued reading as Aaron, awakened by Grace's scream, hobbled into the kitchen and sunk into a chair.

Unable to speak, he gestured to Grace to come to him.

Grace ran to her father and dropped into his arms, still crying. Hattie walked over and awkwardly patted Grace's shoulder.

Aaron pointed at the letter in Hannah's hand. His lips said, "Read it, Becky."

Hannah continued reading.

I met Charlie in New Orleans where he'd had an unfortunate accident. Apparently, he had been waylaid in the French Quarter and inadvertently missed his embarkation with Buffalo Bill's Wild West Show as it was going to Europe.

Charlie literally had no money, no possessions and was in dire need of a friend, which I promptly offered. I travel this country to supplement my income for my writing research and was in need of someone to attend to my personal needs. Charlie accepted my offer of employment and we boarded a steamer from New Orleans to Washington, DC, where I was to give a series of lectures.

Off the coast of North Carolina we encountered a massive storm that nearly sunk our boat. Charlie apparently went on deck and was hit by a huge wave sweeping him overboard and into the turbulent waters. I was watching from the bridge and witnessed the episode. Nothing could be done to save your young man and, for that, I deeply regret my role in bringing about his death. Had I not offered him employment he would still be alive. I shall live with that knowledge until my own dying day.

Enclosed, please find a promissory note for one hundred dollars. This represents Charlie's wages plus some extra for whatever memorial you wish to have for him.

Please inform Charlie's family of his passing. Again, please accept my condolences on the loss of your betrothed. Charlie spoke of you constantly and I feel like I know you, even though we've not met. Perhaps someday we shall.

Sincerely,

Mr. Samuel L. Clemens

Hannah looked into the envelope and pulled out a piece of paper promising the bearer, Miss Grace Reynolds, a total of one hundred dollars, drawn from a bank in Hannibal, Missouri.

"Oh, mercy, Aaron! This is a hundred dollars, made out to Gracie!"

Aaron, Hannah, and Hattie just stared at the piece of paper in her hands. Each was wondering if their financial woes were finally being put to rest. Grace continued wailing into Aaron's shoulder, unhearing of the rest of the letter and of their windfall. Hannah tucked the promissory note into her sugar tin. They would have a family meeting tomorrow to discuss the turn of events.

It took Grace another half hour before her sobbing turned to whimpering and finally to just the occasional sniffle. She was emotionally and physically drained. Aaron, in spite of his own weakness, lifted his daughter and carried her to her bed that she shared with Hattie.

Grace thought back to her grandmother's words that Charlie would return to her. *How could she have been so wrong? I never knew Granny to be mistaken. Now Charlie was dead and she couldn't imagine what her life would be without him.* Her emotions drained, she spent a dreamless night in the welcome haven of slumber.

23
Charlie

Hand me that wrench, Charlie."

Orville was tightening a bolt on the strange looking flying machine. Charlie handed him the tool and studied what the man was doing.

Orville and Wilbur, after conferring with each other, decided they needed an extra hand and offered Charlie room and board if he would assist them with their endeavors. Charlie readily accepted the offer, knowing he would never have another opportunity like this one to watch the two men do the impossible.

He was highly skeptical of seeing a man fly like a bird. The wonderment of it made him completely dismiss his recent brush with death.

"So does this machine flap those wings like a bird?" he asked.

"No, Charlie," replied Wilbur. "The concept of aerodynamics is the flow of air under the wings, lifting it into the air. To do that, it needs to take a running start to lift it off the ground. That's what the engine is for . . . to get it rolling far enough and fast enough to take flight."

"But what if it takes off and you lose power? Won't you come down too hard and crash the thing?"

"No. That is why we chose Kitty Hawk to make our test. The winds on the beach are particularly strong, and the sand provides a softer cushion should we come down faster than we want."

"Alright, but what controls the air going under the wings?"

"That's why we developed these smaller wings on the back of the aircraft," Orville interjected and explained patiently. "We control the lift by lowering or raising them. Our problem now is that we can't seem to get the weight in the middle just right. It's throwing everything off balance."

"Well," replied Charlie, "I don't rightly know much about what you're sayin', but why can't you move the seat over to the left a bit, move the engine to the right and that ways you can balance the guy flying it with the weight of the engine?"

Orville turned to Wilbur and looked at him with a look of revelation. Wilbur slapped his forehead.

"Yes! That's the answer. Charlie, my boy, you just solved something we have both puzzled over for the past year."

The two brothers turned back to the machine, talking excitedly about how to accomplish Charlie's suggestion.

The next two weeks were spent making the adjustments necessary. Charlie toiled beside the brothers and three other mechanics at least eighteen hours a day, eating and sleeping only when they were either too hungry or too exhausted to carry on.

By December 14th, they were finally ready to wheel their craft down to the rail off the slope of Kill Devil Hill. Four local men volunteered to help the brothers with the flight. One man whom

Charlie had befriended was John Daniels. The others he knew only slightly and couldn't remember their names.

Both of the brothers wanted the privilege of being the first to fly and decided to toss a coin. Wilbur's tails won out and he climbed into the pilot's bed, stretching out on his stomach. Orville started the engine and tempered the fuel intake for the right speed it would need to thrust it off the slope. Wilbur grasped the handles that controlled the cables and nodded to Orville on the right wing and Charlie on the left. They pushed it down the rail when the wind lifted the plane a couple of feet. Wilbur, however, had launched it at too sharp an angle and the plane dived nose first into the sand, causing the forward elevator to crumple under the weight of the craft.

Both Charlie and Orville rushed towards the plane to see if Wilbur had been injured. He raised his hand in frustration. "I'm all right. I'm all right."

He climbed off the pilot's bed and went to inspect the damage. They decided it was a relatively minor repair and wheeled it back to the barn where they spent the better part of the rest of the day making repairs.

The next day brought dark clouds heavy with rain, and the flight had to be postponed. This was followed by two more days of light rain and little wind.

On December 17th, the skies had cleared to a deep December blue. The winds were fairly strong and the temperature was just above freezing as they wheeled the glider back to the rail on Kill Devil Hill. This time, however, it was Orville that got the honor of flying. They set up a camera and asked John Daniels to squeeze the bulb at the moment of lift off.

Charlie's hands were cold and chapped as he took the left wing and waited for the signal to push. Wilbur got the engine started and moved to the right wing. Upon Orville's nod, both men gave a mighty shove and the glider moved down the rail. The aircraft held this time and propelled through the air for about twelve seconds before landing in the sand 120 feet away.

Buoyed by their achievement, they pushed the plane back into position and Wilbur now took the pilot's position. This time the aircraft flew 195 feet. The men were joyous and laughing at their success pushed the plane back into place. Again, it was Orville who settled onto his stomach, released the brake that held it in place and flew 200 feet in 15 seconds.

Giddy with excitement, they moved back to the rail for another run with Wilbur at the controls. He was in the air for almost a full minute, traveling 852 feet. This flight, however, ended when the plane took a hard landing, damaging one of the supports at the front of the plane.

They moved the glider back into place for another possible run when a strong gust of wind tumbled it backwards, narrowly missing Charlie who was standing behind. The crankcase broke into pieces as it hit the sand, snapping the remaining wing supports. John Daniels held onto the plane too long, throwing him onto a sand dune, injuring his leg.

While the glider had not lived up to their full expectations, the Wright Brothers ushered in an era of possible human flight with a powered flying machine.

The brothers were jubilant in their experiments and returned to their home base in Dayton just before Christmas.

Charlie, again, was alone, but on a cold Carolina beach with no prospects of what he should do next.

24

Grace

Christmas 1903 held no joy for Grace. Her family's attempts to comfort her always ended in a fresh round of tears. She spent days sobbing into her pillow and made no effort on Christmas day to join them for a roast pheasant that had passed through the sights of Aaron's Remington.

She had no interest in discussing the hundred-dollar windfall from Samuel Clemons, refusing to even leave the house and take it to the bank. Aaron's frustration at leaving the promissory note in the sugar bin for safekeeping led him to plead in his whisper to Grace to cash it.

His throat wound continued to heal to the point where he could at least whisper.

"Gracie, I know you're sad . . . at losing Charlie like he done." Aaron had to stop after every sentence to swallow before continuing. "We got . . . make his death mean somethin'. Wouldn't want you to sit around . . . mopin' over him like this."

"Papa, I can't. I just can't. It's like once I cash it, Imma sayin' I accept he's really dead. I'm not so sure he is cause nobody ever found his body."

"You don't know that." He sat pondering what to say next. "Tell you what. Let's cash the check . . . give some of it . . . to Charlie's family. Went over there a couple of days ago . . . told James. He was . . . heartbroken. I didn't tell them about . . . money but . . . be nice if you could take some . . . and give it to them?"

Grace wiped her tears with the sleeve of her dress, considering this act of charity. "Alright, Papa. I'll do it for his family. How much should I give them?"

"Mebbe 'bout twenty dollars. They could surely . . . use it, too."

The next day, Grace cashed the note, set aside twenty-five dollars and handed the rest to Aaron. "Here, Papa. Use it to what you will. I'll take this over to Mr. Fisher and then go visit Grandmother. She always makes me feel better and I'm gonna give her five dollars to help her."

"Bless you, child," he whispered. "Saved us a hard winter." He gratefully hugged his daughter close to his chest. "Cannot be more proud . . . of you than I am right now."

Grace plodded along the frozen horse trail north of Port Byron along the Mississippi, turning right onto a little traveled path into the forest. Aaron made her take the old Remington for safety from the wolves, just in case a few of them were still around. He'd taken her hunting several times and taught her how to shoot. At the age of thirteen, she was just about as good a shot as him and could hit the eye of a squirrel at a hundred feet.

About a mile into a stand of firs, she turned onto another path of hardened mud up to the Fisher homestead. She had been here a few times with Charlie but it was the first time without holding his hand, without joy in her heart. She walked up to the log cabin and climbed upon the porch.

With a new tear and a heavy heart, she raised her hand and gently knocked on the door.

25

Lucinda

After commiserating with Charlie's family about his fate, Grace shouldered the old Remington and took the road towards Coe, the tiny community where her grandmother lived. It was about two miles, and Grace intended to stay the night or even longer if her grandmother would only ask.

The cold wind cut through Grace, and she wished now she had worn an extra layer of clothing. She gripped the collar of her coat and raised it up over her face to cut back the icy tendrils of chill. She stopped to rewrap her scarf and better cover her ears.

The path was overgrown with weeds giving evidence of the lack of traffic to and from Lucinda's tumble-down cabin. The only visitors she ever received were from the Reynolds family. She found it more difficult with each passing day to attend to her needs. The long forgotten garden was untended and choked with milkweed.

Grace's knock on the door went unanswered so she pushed it open and it twisted off the frame. The leather hinge had finally rotted through and could no longer bear the weight of the door.

"Granny," called Grace, "are you in here? Where are you?"

The only sounds were the whisperings of the wind through the cracks of mortar. The cabin was empty.

Grace went to the fireplace and felt a faint warmth coming from the dying embers of wood. She had been here recently, but Grace could find her nowhere in or around the cabin. She didn't know what to think and sat down on the front step, drawing her knees up to her chin. She had to put herself into a place where Lucinda might have gone.

Making a snap decision, she got up, stepped off the porch and headed west, towards the river. Granny often would visit a ledge that stood high above the river. She called it her "thinking place." Maybe she had gone there to talk to her spirits.

As she climbed the trail to the ledge, she spotted a piece of a worn blanket that had caught on a shrub. Grace pulled it from the bush and lifted it to her nose, taking a huge whiff. The smell of jasmine identified it as definitely belonging to her grandmother. The path snaked through a small meadow. A dying apple orchard skirted the lea. She quickened her pace and finally reached the small clearing overlooking the Mississippi.

There, on an outcropping of rock, sat the huddled figure of her grandmother. Fearing the worst, Grace ran to the old woman and placed her hand on Lucinda's shoulder.

"Grandmother! Are you alright?"

The blanket covering her stirred and a pair of dimmed eyes looked up to see her granddaughter shaking her shoulder.

"O îyokîpî?" she wheezed through chattering teeth. "Why are you here, my child?"

"I came to see you and give you news of my Charlie. Why are you up here on this cold day? You will catch your death."

The old woman sat and coughed for half-a-minute, a glob of brown spittle coming from her mouth. "It is my time, Grace. I am no longer *wikȟóškalaka,* a young girl. Isaac is calling me to join him, and I go joyfully to once again be by his side. Even now I can see him across the water, beckoning me."

Grace turned and seeing no one, blinked back tears. "You can't go, Grandmother. I love you too much to let you go. I have too many things to tell you."

"I'm sorry, child. I have grown too feeble to be of any further assist to you. I have come here to say my final prayers and ask forgiveness from my father for leaving him so many years ago."

Lucinda paused to catch her breath before she continued. "What is this news of your *teȟila?*"

Grace quickly recounted the story of Charlie's death and, through her tears, told of her immense sorrow.

"Remember the bag of special herbs, Gracie, but do not use it until you absolutely must." Lucinda's eyes further clouded as she gasped for breath. She wanted to re-tell her vision of Charlie returning to her side but could no longer find the words.

A shaft of light opened on Lucinda, bathing her in a golden glow. She could see the shadows fleeing as Isaac reached down and took her hand. Filled with a new burst of energy, she felt her youth returning. Looking into Isaac's eyes, a glory filled her heart as she stepped to the other side, from darkness to an illumined brightness.

Lucinda now saw her father, also welcoming her with opened arms. His broad shoulders heaved with laughter as he enveloped her in warmth. She sighed a great happiness and was gone.

Grace sat and stared at the suddenly relaxed face of her grandmother and knew she had breathed her last.

Grace closed Lucinda's eyes and gently laid her back on the ground, covering her with the thin blanket the best she could. Placing a kiss on her forehead, she then pulled what brush she could to cover her grandmother's body to shelter it from hungry animals. She would run back down the hillside, get her father and together they would return to lay his mother to a proper rest.

"Oh, Granny," she cried. "Granny, I so love you."

26

Charlie

New Year's Day, 1904, was gray and windy. A stiff breeze off the Atlantic crept around the hangar's doors putting a deep chill into Charlie's bones. It only added to his loneliness and depression as he pondered what he should do. Go back home to his family and to Gracie or resolve the itch he had to discover more of what the world had to offer.

Making up his mind, he gathered all his belongings, meager as they were, and shoved them into a makeshift backpack. He scribbled a note to the Wright Brothers, thanking them for their hospitality, leaving it pinned to their work bench. Slinging the backpack over his shoulders he stepped into the bracing wind, closing the hangar's doors behind him. Hiking north, he had a bit more than two dollars in his pocket. He found a ferry at the tip of the outer banks and paid a nickel for passage to the mainland. He had always had a hankering to see New York City.

He walked for close to twenty-five miles before coming across a set of railroad tracks running parallel to a river. Living near Port Byron, Charlie was familiar with trains and often saw hoboes who would ride the rails drifting from one part of the country to another. He came across a small camping spot a hundred feet off the tracks with about a half-dozen men warming themselves by a fire.

Stepping into the middle of them, Charlie sized up the rough looking group and wondered if he had ventured into something he wouldn't be able to escape.

"Howdy, gentlemen. I smelled your pot of beans there and wondered if I could get a plate. I'm powerful hungry."

A very large man stood up to face Charlie. He weighed twice as much as him and was about a foot taller. The man's dirty clothing, unshaven face, and looming size intimidated Charlie, and he started to back away from the fire.

"Welcome, friend," said the man, whose soft voice belied his tough demeanor. He extended his hand for a handshake. Seeing the uncertainly in Charlie's eyes, his mouth turned into a crooked, kindly grin. "Pull up a log and hep youself. You've ain't nothin' to be 'fraid of."

Charlie's relief was evident as he grabbed the man's hand and shook it. "Haven't eaten in a couple of days and I'm getting' weak from hunger."

The man leaned down and spooned some beans onto a tin plate, offering it to Charlie. "Ain't got no fancy silverware for ya, so ya'll hafta eat with your fingers."

"This'll be fine. Thank you fer your kindness. My name is Charlie."

"Well, if you're figgerin' on becoming one of us, we don't use our names. I'm Skillet and this bunch of ornry critters are Boston, Lone Cat, Whiskers, Two-Shot, and that ugly cuss across from ya is Scar."

Charlie could see where the man got his name. A long scar stretched from his left eye, down his face, ending somewhere in the grizzled beard under his chin.

"Pleased to meet ya, gents."

"I bin Skillet fer so long, I sum times fergit my real name. Now you hafta get a handle. Whatta ya think, men? What's he look like to you?"

Scar piped up first. "Skinny fella. Looks like a Bean Stalk to me."

"Bean Stalk it is then," said Skillet. "Now sit yore arse down and tell us yore story."

After relating his tale, Scar chimed in. "Good heavens, boy . . . and you say you're only sixteen-yar-old? I bin ridin' the rails fer near on the past twenty-five yar and you've already lived more'n a life than I have."

"Got to admit, I'm a little surprised myself."

"Well, gittin' late," said Skillet. "Ain't ya even gotta blanket? Going to get pretty cold night and there's a hint of snow in the air. Here. Take this 'un. It's kinda thin but you'll make do." He tossed Charlie a blanket that hadn't seen a washing for a long time.

"Much obliged, sir." He tried to maneuver himself closer to the fire.

"Think nothin' of it, Bean Stalk. We'ns gotta take care of each other."

The man they called Lone Cat threw a sawed off section of a cross piece onto the fire. "Got some creosote on it so it'll smoke." The new wood was already giving off an acrid odor.

The men found their own spots pulling their blankets up around them and settled in for the cold night. Charlie fell asleep looking up at the vast array of stars stretching across the Carolina sky.

The next morning, Charlie woke up to the smell of a dark coffee brewing over the camp fire. Skillet tossed him a beat up metal cup and told him to help himself.

"Where'd you get water?"

Boston spoke up first. "Wagon rut ovah yondah." Charlie wondered at the strange accent. Maybe folks talked that way in Boston. "Melted snow just enough ta make a potful. The grit yoh get ain't from coffah grounds."

Charlie poured himself a cup of the dark brew and dug into his plate of beans, left over from the previous evening.

Finishing, they poured the rest of the coffee on the fire and started packing up their belongings.

"The next train will be headin' north in about quarter'n hour," said Scar. "We be jumpin' it iffen ya a mind to join us. We're on a long grade uphill and the train will slow down long enough fer us ta find an empty box car and pilin' in."

True to his word, Charlie soon heard a whistle of a train as it started its way up the hill.

The ragged group of men started climbing the embankment towards the tracks. Skillet held a hand out to Charlie to help him up the hill. "Stay close to me, Bean, since you ain't nevah done this here afore. Let me get into the rail car and I'll help you inside. Be careful cuz many a man has lost a life or a limb by carelessness."

The men made it to the tracks just as the Number 29 came into sight. It was starting to make its' way up the grade. The huge locomotive belched black smoke from its stack as the coalman shoveled scoops of fuel into the firebox.

"The sixth boxcar is open," shouted Whiskers over the din of the approaching train.

"I see it," answered Skillet. "Stay close, Bean." Charlie almost turned around to see who he was talking to before he remembered his new nickname.

The engineer paid no mind to the group of hobos standing by the track. He had been one himself in his younger days and was respectful of the life they led. Hopping trains was something he did himself before landing the job of driving one.

The engine pushed past the men smothering them in dust and smoke. Charlie found it hard to breathe in the acrid coal residue and flying coal ash stinging his face.

Engine, tender box, followed by twelve boxcars, three flatbeds loaded with timber, and a caboose made their way up the hill. Some of the smoke cleared out and Charlie counted six box cars until he saw one with an open door.

Whiskers followed by Scar, Lone Cat, and Skillet, grabbed the low handle of the door and pulled themselves into the empty car. Once Skillet got in he turned and held a hand out to help Charlie.

He made a grab for Skillet's hand but tripped on a timber and almost tumbled under the wheels. He quickly regained his balance and started running faster than he ever had in his life, keeping one eye on the ground for obstacles and the other on the outstretched glove of Skillet.

His heart pounding, Charlie made one last stab at grabbing Skillet's hand and clenched it tightly. Skillet pulled him into the box car, and he sprawled onto the floor trying to catch his breath. He sat up to watch as Two Shot was the last to attempt getting into the car. The man's face showed his exertion as Skillet reached out to pull him through the door.

Their fingertips just touched as Two Shot stumbled. Trying to right himself, the forward momentum was too much and the man fell on to the tracks, the box car's wheels slicing him in two. The sickening thump and the man's screams were something that would haunt Charlie to his own dying day.

All eyes were turned to the open space of the door, each man trembling with their own emotions, speechless at having just lost a friend.

After a full minute, Scar was the first to speak. "Lord, how many times has he hopped a train? Never missed. Not once."

A disquieting mood settled over the men in the box car, each to his own thoughts.

"Twasn't much a man, caint even hop a train." A voice from the deep shadows of the rumbling car cut the silence like a sharp blade.

"Who said that?" shouted Skillet, furious at the callous remark.

Out of the darkness stepped a man who outweighed Skillet by fifty pounds and had four inches of height. "I did, Skillet. So what?"

Skillet stepped back a couple of steps. "Goliath!" he spat. The huge man wore a pair of filthy overalls, a dingy white shirt, and a pair of shoes that should have been discarded years ago. "What gives you pause to run down a man after he dies?"

He had had run-ins before with the giant of a man standing in front of him and always came out on the losing end. He'd broken Skillet's arm in a previous fight and it had never quite healed right, leaving it weakened.

"He greased the rails, so what? Happens. Long time, no see, Skillet. Howse that arm of your'n?" he sneered.

Charlie looked around Skillet to see that the man he called Goliath carried a long axe handle in his hand, minus the blade.

"Who's the pipsqueak ya brung with ya?" he said, motioning towards Charlie.

"Nevah mind him. Ya got no right talking like that. Ya know that Two-Shot has jumped many a car. Jest stumbled, that's all."

"Well, looks like ya traded one pansy fer anothah." He walked around Skillet to take a closer look at Charlie. "Now that's a might pretty fellah. Youse up for some fun, little man?"

Charlie didn't know what the giant meant by "fun" but the way he said it, made him not want to find out.

Skillet stepped in front of his foe. "You leave him alone. He ain't botherin' ya none."

Goliath raised the axe handle and planted the end of it with a sharp jab into Skillet's chest. "Ya take one more step and you'll be left with TWO broken arms. Now ya git outta me way whilst you still can and let me gets acquainted with my pretty little banty heah."

Skillet's friends swarmed in to help him defend Charlie. "You have to take on all of us", growled Boston.

Without warning, Goliath swung his weapon and caught Boston on the side of his head, dropping the man into the straw on the floor. The others backed off while the big man swung the handle in an arc. "Anybody else want to interfere with my fun?"

Scar knelt beside the unconscious Boston and pulled him out of the circle of men. It was just at that moment that the train gathered speed going down the other side of the hill making every car jerk.

The motion caught Goliath off guard as he stumbled back towards the open door. Charlie make a flying leap across the floor landing just behind the giant. He stumbled backwards over Charlie, his heavy boot slamming into the boy's side.

Goliath's arms flailed wildly trying to grab the edge of the door only to disappear through the open door just as the train passed over a trestle.

He somersaulted ass over heels through the air into the cold river a hundred feet below.

Every man but Boston and Charlie rushed to the opening to watch their enemy make a huge splash. They watched as the motionless body sunk beneath the surface of the water.

Scar turned to help Charlie to his feet who was tenderly rubbing his side. "I think he broke a rib."

"Better a rib than what he was planning on doin', my boy."

"That was quick thinkin', Bean," said Skillet. "It gave me a world of pleasure seeing him go through that door."

Boston groaned on the floor and tried to sit up. A huge welt was forming over his eye. "What happened?"

"Young Bean here jest killed Goliath," said Lone Cat. His voice was high pitched, and Charlie thought it the first time he'd ever heard the man speak. Now he knew why.

"I didn't mean to kill him. I jest wanted him to fall down so y'all could get the best of him."

Scar did his best at trying to tend to the Boston's wound as the others settled into their blankets on the floor. As they lay there letting the train wheels make their rhythmic "clack-clack" they marveled over Charlie's dispatch of the giant Goliath.

"Never seed nothin' like it," said Scar. "Wonder if we need our Bean here a new name. "David . . . the Giant Killer."

"All the same to you," said Charlie, "think I'll stick with Bean." He gingerly rubbed his side. He didn't think the rib was broken but he would have a huge bruise in the morning.

Skillet chuckled, pulled his thin blanket up over his shoulders and fell asleep.

Charlie lay awake for a long time, listening to the wheels on the rails and staring at the open box car door. He'd killed a man and he didn't like the feeling. No sir. He didn't like it at all.

27

Grace

S tanding behind an oak tree, Duggie Hayes watched the pretty girl with auburn-tresses walking a path through the woods. His humiliation at the hands of John L. Sullivan continued to burn at his core. It only added to the hate he felt towards the bewitching girl now strolling in the midst of towering oaks. He had retrieved the braid from the school house where Grace had dropped it and strung it on a piece of string, looping it around his neck. Every day, he took it out of his shirt and smelled it.

Grace had blossomed from the freckle-faced child that fell into the moccasin stealing Mississippi River a few years ago, into a young girl that caught the eye of more than just a few teen-aged boys in and around Port Byron.

Many of them had gone calling at the Reynolds' doorstep in hopes of wooing the thirteen-year-old Grace. Those that tried went away disappointed. Grace simply turned down everyone with the one sentence she delivered to each of them. "Sorry, but I'm still grieving over my Charlie."

Grace stopped to rest on a rock as she hummed a tune she'd heard at Buffalo Bill's rodeo. It was her connection to the song that kept Charlie alive in her mind and in her heart.

The humming came to an abrupt stop as Duggie stepped out from behind the tree.

"Well, well, what do we got here? Little miss Goody Gracie without her precious Charlie to protect her."

Grace jumped up from the rock and grabbed a stick, holding it out in front of her.

"You get away from me, Duggie Hayes, else I'll poke yore eye out!"

Duggie took a step towards her, fingering the braid inside his shirt. "Now what's you want to go and act like that fer? I just wants a little kiss so you can see what a real man can do fer ya."

Grace took a step back and jabbed the stick at him. "I'ma warning you. You touch me and my pa'll finish off what Charlie and Uncle John started."

"I don' thinks it'll come to that, Gracie. Me and youse are like two little peas in a pod. We gonna go behind that tree and have us some fun."

Duggie reached out with a quick motion and grabbed the stick, wrenching it out of her hand. The sudden move startled her and left a splinter in her hand, causing it to bleed.

She cried out in pain and turned to run back along the path. A tree root caused her to stumble and she fell to the ground, skinning both of her knees.

Duggie caught up to her and grabbed the back of her frock. The flimsy material gave way and partially exposed her, which only inflamed his desire. He pulled her to the ground with one hand and reached for the twine holding up his pants with the other.

Grace pulled up her dress to cover herself and scooted on her butt along the ground. Her cries from her wounds and her embarrassment echoed through the trees.

"Now I gotcha just where's I wants ya. Now 'bout that kiss," he said as his pants fell to the ground exposing his intention.

Grace's eyes widened in fear as it was the first time she'd ever seen a boy naked. She screamed in terror as Duggie fell to the ground on his knees and grabbed her ankles, yanking her towards him.

Grace wasn't sure what happened next because Duggie's body all of a sudden fell on top of her. She grimaced in what she thought came next but he just lay on top of her, blood dripping from a wound at the back of his neck. A braid of hair fell onto her face and she couldn't begin to know what that might be.

His body then was lifted off the top of her, and she sat up to find a boy standing over both of them, his hand gripping a large stone.

"Harmon!" Grace exclaimed. "Oh, thank you, God, praise Jesus."

Harmon Lovell reached down and offered his other hand to help Grace get to her feet.

"Gracie, looks like you coulda used some help there. I was walking along when I heard your screams and I came runnin."

"Oh, Harmon! You don't know how glad I am to see you." She stepped around the prostrated hulk of the naked Duggie Hayes and gave Harlan a hug, forgetting her shame of having a boy getting a glimpse of her body. She pulled the dress around herself. "Can you walk me home, Harmon?"

"Surely can, Gracie. Sure hope he never finds out what hit him," he said, gesturing towards Duggie. "He would surely come round and give me what fer. I tain't fraid of him, you know. Just don't want him messin' with me."

"Well, he'll never find out from me, fer sure."

The two of them started back down the path towards home. "Harmon, what can I ever do to repay you the kindness you showed me? My pa, when he finds out, will prob'ly pay a visit over ta the Hayeses. He'll surely wants to do somethin' fer you, too."

"Aw, Gracie, that tweren't nuthin. I'm glad he got what's comin' to him. I know Charlie waylaid him once and I saw what your Uncle did to him back in town."

"Still . . . I would do most anything fer ya, iffen ya just ask."

"Well, there is one little thing, if you don't mind."

"What is it? Anything."

"Well, I'm a little embarrassed to ask ya."

"Come on, Harmon. Come right out and say it."

"Well, you suppose you could talk me up to your sister Hattie? I been trying to get the gumption to even talk to her but I get all tangled up in my words around her and end up sayin' nuthin."

Grace laughed. "Harmon, that's about the funniest thing I ever heerd. Hattie keeps asking why that nice Harmon Lovell doesn't come a callin'. She thinks it's because you don't like her much."

"Oh, Lordy! Really?"

"Once I tell her what ya did fer me, she'll have those stars dancin' in her eyes."

Harmon reached over and gave Grace's hand a squeeze. He had a big grin on his face.

Grace was still shaking from her scare and wondered what it was that Duggie had tied with a string around his neck.

28
Aaron

Aaron did, indeed, pay a visit to the Hayes farm after he heard Grace relate her story and what Harmon Lovell had done for her.

He rapped loudly on the door and then stepped back, hearing a motion inside the house and footsteps. "Yeah, jest a minute, dammit. I'm a comin', but this better be good, disturbing a man's nap."

The door flung open nearly hitting Aaron in the face.

"What the Sam Hill you want?" Jeremy Hayes growled, recognizing Aaron.

In his hoarse whisper Aaron tried to sound as forceful as he felt. "It's about yourn boy, Hayes. He attacked my Gracie and was trying to force himself on her when somebody come along and knocked him out."

Hayes roared in laughter. "So that's whut happened. Damn kid comes home and tells me he fallen outta tree. Well, so what? Boys do what boys do. Whut ya want me to do about it?"

"You tell that sum bitch to leave my girl alone, or I'm a gonna take a shotgun to him and sees that he'll never do it again."

"You threatenin' my boy?" Hayes screamed. "That little pig-faced redhead prob'ly egged him on. Too bad he didn't finish the job."

Hayes never saw Aaron's balled up right fist before it rammed his nose back into his head. The big man dropped like a sack of taters and lay still.

Aaron rubbed his hand, thinking maybe he'd broken it. "I mean it, Hayes. I'll gun him down. And don't think I won't do it, Duggie." He noticed the boy standing behind the door. "Tell your Pa when he wakes up that the next visit will be from the sheriff. Or mebbe me with that shotgun."

Duggie stayed behind the door, not sure if Aaron would do him like he'd done to his pa.

Aaron turned on his heel and strode back up the path, rubbing his hand.

Damn, he thought. I did break it.

29
Charlie

O ver the next few months Charlie and Skillet were the only hobos left of the original group as the others went different directions. Skillet spent time grooming Charlie in the ways of living on the rails. As a Road Kid, he looked upon Skillet as his mentor. He learned the way to find easy meals by the hobo system of identifying who would give a bowl of soup or sandwich and those who were to be avoided.

"Learn the signs, Bean," said Skillet. "Say you are hiking along a road and come upon a farm or a home. Iffen a green circle is on the picket fence, the people there will feed you something. A drawing of a cat shows ya that a nice lady lives there and is good fer a bowl of soup. Ya see a triangle, just keep moving because the owner has a gun so beware. Hobos have come through before ya and they've marked the spots."

Charlie wanted to keep drifting north because he wanted to see New York City. The most people he'd ever seen at one time was at Buffalo Bill's show. Other hobos they met at camps along the way would fill his head with images of what to expect. Gas lights, the new mode of transportation called a motor car, street after street of buildings higher than anything he'd ever seen before.

Hobos are different from tramps in that they would always accept work if it was available. Charlie was able to keep a few coins in his pocket by cleaning out stables, repairing fences, painting a barn.

By the time the two got to Pennsylvania, Skillet told him he was going to catch the next train that headed west. He had a sister in Ohio and he wanted to see her before he moved on towards California. He tried to convince Charlie to join him but the boy had his sights fixed on the big city.

"Bean," warned Skillet as he waited beside the rails for a train headed west, "be careful. Word has traveled about yore hubbub with Goliath. For whatever reason he had friends, and they might not take too kindly towards you. Approach camps with caution cuz ya never know when one of them jackals might take their revenge. Most hobos are good people, but there are also those who'd sooner put a knife in yore gizzard than look at ya."

A train tooted its whistle from over the ridge and Skillet got to his feet and grabbed his brindle stick. "Here comes the cannonball, Bean. Ya might want ta change yore name to avoid them that aim to do ya harm or ya'll end up in the boneyard fer sure. Change yore name to Banty. I like the sound of that."

The train was coming around the curve, and Skillet made his way up the bank. "Keep yore eye for them easy marks and ya'll do jest fine. Take care now."

Charlie waved good-bye to his friend and watched him grab the handle of an empty stock car. Skillet threw his brindle into the open space and pulled himself aboard. He stood up in the doorway and gave a two finger salute to the boy. Charlie watched as the train picked up speed and disappeared around a curve.

He was alone again.

Charlie continued his journey to the northeast, stopping at camps and introducing himself as Banty. He didn't want any more trouble than he already had and mostly kept to himself.

He realized he hadn't written Grace since the letter that had been destroyed from his desperate swim in the Atlantic. One evening he sat down with a pencil and piece of a brown paper bag and wrote a note.

> Dear Little Bit,
>
> Sorry I aint wrote much lately. I've bin workin my way up ta New York and once I bin there, I think I'll head on back ta Ilinoise and we can get on wiffen our life. I'm larnin alot bout life and how good it be to settle down with you and raise some young uns. Aint got much money saved yet but hope to change that luck fore I see you again.
> Love Yore Charlie

Charlie stopped by a farm house that had a green ribbon tied to the corner post and asked if he could work for a sandwich. The lady of the house told him she needed her back porch propped up before it fell off the rocks holding it up. If he would repair her porch she would give him a full meal with a nice slice of cherry pie and a cup of coffee. Charlie spent most of the morning doing the repair job and she fed him what she promised.

"Ma-am, mightn't you have an envelope I can send to my Gracie back in Illinois. She ain't heard from me in a while, and I want to let her know I'm doing fine."

"Certainly, young man." She went back into the house and returned with an envelope. "You give me a penny for the postage, and I'll put it into the post for you when I go into Altoona."

"Thank you, ma'am. That's mighty kind of you." He put the letter and a five-dollar coin into the envelope, addressed it, and handed it with a penny back to the lady. He headed back down the pathway and turned right, towards the north.

The woman took the letter to Altoona the next day for the mail train leaving that very afternoon.

ALTOONA MIRROR

Altoona, Pennsylvania

Weather for the Week of May 31, 1904: Hot & Dry

LATE BULLETIN

Train Derailment

KILLS FOUR IN

Plunge off trestle

OF MAIL TRAIN

Altoona, Pennsylvania

A mail train traveling west derailed over a trestle across Clearfield Creek near Ambry causing a loss of life to four souls, including the engineer, brakeman, conductor and coalman.

In addition to the loss of life railroad officials said that several bags of mail were destroyed.

They advised that anyone who posted mail from Altoona in the last seven days, it will not have reached its destination and should take steps to resend their post.

BREAK-INS REPORTED

Several break-ins were reported over the weekend at various businesses along Main Street.

Damage was sustained in stores along Pleasant Valley and Tennyson Road. Merchants are still assessing the dollar damage and whatever merchandise might have been pilfered.

The sheriff is continuing his investigation.

SOCIAL NEWS

Miss Bertha Blatt of the city has announced her engagement to Mr. Vern Marshall. The couple has not set a date for their wedded bliss.

Marilyn Joy Walker has set June 10th for a tea party at her home on Shawnee Avenue to celebrate the 50th wedding anniversary of her parents, Mr. and Mrs. Robert Walker.

Mrs. Sheryl Peterson is asking for volunteers to help clean the First Baptist Church. Anyone interested may simply show up on Saturday at the church on Hickman Avenue, ten o'clock in the morning.

An Ice Cream Social will be held at First Methodist Church following a revival meeting this Sunday evening. You need not be a member of the church and all are welcome.

Koch's Drugs has announced a special sale on trusses. Feel immediate relief and place your trust in a truss from Koch's Drugs.

NATIONAL NEWS

St. Louis, Missouri

The Louisiana Purchase Exposition, also known as the St. Louis World Fair was recently held in that fair city.

Entertainment, goods, culture, history and anthropology are all subjects to be covered.

The exhibition opened on April Thirtieth and will run until December First. It has been stated that more than fifteen hundred buildings were constructed and over seventy miles of roads and walkways just to show all of the exhibits.

The fair is to commemorate the One Hundredth Anniversary of the Louisiana Purchase made by President Thomas Jefferson.

The United States Postal Service is issuing different value stamps in conjunction with the celebration.

One of the features is a giant bird cage filled with many of our aviary feathered friends.

Other features include new food varieties such as a "waffle" ice cream cone.

Make plans to visit this marvelous celebration. It is unlike anything ever seen in the United States and promises to be an unforgettable experience.

1904 is a Presidential election year.
Please vote.

PENNSYLVANIA NEWS

A new book has been published titled "Pennsylvania at Gettysburg". It tells of ceremonies at the dedication of monuments erected by the commonwealth of Pennsylvania to Major General George G. Meade, Major General Winfield S. Hancock, and Major General John F. Reynolds and to mark the positions of the Pennsylvania commands engaged in the battle.

W.S. Ray is the printer out of Harrisburg. The book has two volumes.

RECENT DEATHS

Walter Higgins, 60, of Altoona. Corporal Higgins was a veteran of the War Between the States as a member of the Pennsylvania Third Calvary.

Sarah Bottoms, 102, of Williamsburg.

Penelope Johnston, 22, of Spruce Creek, who was here visiting her sister, Catharine Fahey.

Feel free to give us your opinions of world, state or local events. Write in care of this paper.

Cason's Meat Market has some beautiful cuts of fresh beef and pork. Remember our motto: "If it isn't from Cason's, it's not fresh."

30

Charlie

Charlie had just crossed the New York State border in a box car that was bound for Vermont. He hopped off at a water stop and walked the rails looking for a hobo camp. It had been over 24 hours since he'd eaten and even a plate of cold beans sounded good to him.

He found what he was looking for a mile from the water stop with a camp set up in a clearing about a hundred feet off the tracks.

Stepping into the midst of a circle of men, he introduced himself as Banty and came up from the Carolinas. They offered him a bowl of soup that had questionable chunks of something, he wasn't sure what. He was hungry enough that he downed it and was dipping into the pot for a second helping.

"Well, Banty, you shore enough ain't had much to eat goin' after that muskrat stew thet way."

Charlie looked into the bowl and suddenly lost his appetite. How much farther down must I go, he thought, before I get back to my Gracie? He knew the answer: too much of the country to see before he settled down.

One man got up to stoke the fire and as he was turning the logs over, he asked a question. "Anybody hear about Goliath takin' a header off'n a train down Carolina way?"

Charlie froze. He didn't want to show any reaction that he knew anything about it.

One of the other men spoke up. "I heerd it was someone named Bean that pushed him off into a river. Goliath may have been a jungle buzzard," he said referring to hobo slang identifying as someone who preyed on his own kind, "but didn't deserve no cross-up like thet. Musta been a mighty big man to take him down."

Another man across from Charlie spoke up. "Goliath was me friend and nevah did me no wrong. Evah catch up to the punk who done it, he be pushin' up daisies fore night fall."

Charlie decided to steer the direction of the conversation. "Yeah, I heard that this Bean was a huge man. Never heard of him before. Somebody prob'ly caught up with him 'fore now and done Goliath some justice."

The men around the campfire agreed that this Bean most likely had met his own Maker by now and they settled in for the night.

Charlie breathed a sigh of relief. He lay down on his back and stared up at the stars and the moon for a while. His thoughts turn from Goliath to Gracie and wondered if she had gotten his letter and was reading it right now under the light of that same beautiful moon.

The next morning, Charlie walked a dozen miles along the track until he came to a junction that appeared to veer to the east. He turned to the right and walked another mile before he came to a long grade up a high hill. He sat and waited. Day passed into night, night into day and by three o'clock the next afternoon he heard the whistle he had wanted to hear.

Before long, he had grabbed the handle of a box car door and pulled himself into the opening. The car was empty, and he settled into a corner, hoping the shadows would hide him from any railroad bulls that might be looking for unwanted passengers.

Two days of hot sun in a smelly boxcar only added to Charlie's miseries as his stomach continued to growl, warning him that he needed to find some nourishment and soon. His thirst was even worse as he had emptied his canteen the day before.

By the third morning he knew he would have to hop off and find water and food. He got up and made his way to the open door to find a glimpse of where he might be. Just as he got to the door a sign flashed by that Elizabeth, New Jersey, was but two miles away. He sat down with his legs hanging over the edge, watching the country side pass by. The train slowed as it headed into a rail yard, as tracks started branching off each other. Charlie counted two, three, six, and finally an unbelievable 24 sets of rails, some empty, some with other trains. Men were yelling instructions to each other, calling to the engineers on backing into staging yards where cars were to be dropped off and their contents off-loaded onto docks.

Not wanting to chance a run-in with a railroad bull he hopped down when it was safe to do so and walked towards a dock that had men working taking cargo into a warehouse.

"Hey, you there!" Charlie turned to face a man who was obviously in charge of operations as he was holding a clipboard full of papers.

"You hoboing, mister?"

"Nope," Charlie answered. He knew his clothes were probably a giveaway but took a chance. "Just looking for some work. I'm strong and can handle most anything."

The man eyed Charlie suspiciously and then decided to take him for his word. "Good! I'm short about three men right now and I can use you. What's your name?"

"Charlie Fisher, sir."

"Well, Charlie. I pay 50 cents a day and you'll get it at the end of your shift. See that feller at the end of the dock," he said pointing towards a man sporting a huge walrus moustache. "Go tell him that Mr. McDougall just hired you, and he will tell you what to do."

"Thank you, sir," Charlie responded and hopped up on the dock. Introducing himself, the man grunted and pointed to a box car. "Git on up there and start carrying those cartons into the warehouse. Just follow the others, and they'll show you where to put them."

Charlie spent the next ten hours running boxes, small machinery, and tools from the train cars into the warehouse where they would then be distributed throughout the country. He noticed one address on a box of tools that were bound for Moline, Illinois, and he felt a wave of homesickness come over him. At the end of their day, the men lined up to the paymaster and received their wages.

Charlie pocketed his 50 cents and asked where he could get a meal and a bed. One of the men behind him told of a flop house only a few blocks away and he headed in that direction after promising the paymaster he would return the next day.

He spent the next month, following the same routine . . . up at 4:30, going to a bodega for a sandwich, traipsing to the rail yard, and returning about nine that evening. By the end of May, he had saved almost twenty dollars which he kept tucked into an inside pocket he'd sewn into his shirt.

Charlie's work kept him so tired that he never found the time to find and explore New York City which was his main purpose of even being there. On the last day of May, he told the paymaster he would not be back. He had no more than the ragged clothes on his back and walked until he reached the shores of Newark Bay. He found a ferry, paid his nickel fare and boarded for the crossing that would take him to Manhattan.

Crossing into the Upper New York Bay Charlie never imagined seeing the sight that greeted him as the boat rounded the tip of the Bayonne peninsula. Staring down straight ahead of him was the Statue of Liberty. He saw the torch held high over her head and as the ferry crossed underneath its shadow, Charlie felt a shiver tracing a track along his spine. He'd heard of the construction and dedication a scant eighteen years before but never imagined he would ever actually see it. A green tint covered the entire structure from a patina that was oxidizing the copper beneath. Charlie thought he could make out people looking out from the torch and wondered what such a view might be seen from there.

As the ferry docked at the tip of Manhattan, Charlie stepped off and gave one last look at the lady holding her torch high. He turned and walked into New York City.

31

Grace

Grace's depression over Charlie's death was gradually lessening. She never took off the bag hanging around her neck that her grandmother had given her, except to bathe. Just touching it and feeling its texture was comforting.

She found solace in grooming her chestnut sorrel, Champion. The horse had a light, reddish brown coat, more closely resembling a palomino than a chestnut. Grace would often spend an hour just combing through Champ's mane. It relaxed her and gave her time to think of a life that might have been with Charlie.

She took long rides with Champion through the Illinois countryside, often running him at a full gallop. The horse seemed to enjoy those outings and ran down roads and through meadows with joyous abandon.

Sometimes Aaron rode with her and would challenge Grace to a race. He never won. His buckskin was strong and wiry, but could never match the speed of Champion.

"Gracie, that is a fine piece of horse flesh you've got there," he said in his raspy whisper after one such race. They were standing in the corral and wiping down the sweat from their horses. "I wonder if you might'n want to put him into a *real* horserace."

"What do you mean, Papa?"

"I saw a circular down at the mercantile that the Moline County Fair is coming up, and there will be a contest for riders to see who has the fastest horse. First prize is fifteen dollars. I bet Champion could give any horse he faced a real challenge." He stopped to drink a cup of water from his canteen.

"Papa, I don't know nothin' 'bout horse racing."

"Mebbe you don't but that horse is the fastest I've seen in these parts." He unhitched his buckskin's bridle and hung it on a hook of the barn door. "You put Champion in the race, give him his lead, and let him decide if he can outrun those against him."

Grace was warming up to the idea. "We could sure enough use the fifteen dollars, Papa."

"I don't want the money for us, baby girl. You win . . . the money is yours to do as you see fit."

"Really? I won't need to use it to buy flour, or coffee, or canned peaches?"

"Really! The money is yours. Mebbe you'd like a new dress or a bonnet."

Grace continued grooming her horse. "Wow! Fifteen dollars of my very own. What do you think, Champ? You want to run a race?"

Champion turned to her and snorted with a whinny.

Hannah was dead set against her daughter risking her life in a horse race. "Aaron Reynolds, there is no way I'm letting my youngest get on the back of a horse and chancing she will meet her death for a mere fifteen dollars."

They were sitting in the cool of the evening, rocking on their porch.

"Now, Becky, you can see how excited she is about this." He took a draw on his pipe and blew out a small wisp of smoke that dissipated into the spring air as he tried to come up with an argument in Grace's favor. "Look what it has done for her spirits. I actually heard her singin' to herself last night as she cuddled Miss Petunia. I ain't seen her do that since Charlie passed."

"Well, I got enough to fret about what with Henrietta's upcoming marriage to Harmon. It won't be much a ceremony without her sister there as her Maid of Honor because she's laying in the back room with a broken neck!"

"Sorry, Becky, but my mind's made up. I said she could race her horse and she is *going* to race her horse." His raspy whisper didn't carry much authority but his manner more than made up for it.

Hannah wouldn't talk to Aaron for two days she was so mad.

Two weeks passed and the family packed up the buckboard with a picnic lunch. Aaron took the reins as Hannah settled in next to him. She never said a word on the fifteen-mile trip, keeping her arms folded in front of her and her spine straight and rigid. Hattie rode on a pillow in the back to absorb the bumps, holding hands with Harmon whom she had invited along for the day's enjoyment. Grace followed on Champion, who seemed to sense the excitement. She occasionally bent forward and whispered into his ear, followed by a scratch and a pat on the neck.

As the buckboard pulled into the county fairgrounds, people were everywhere with children laughing and playing games, women huddled around tables piled with food, and men standing near a threshing contest trying to make themselves heard over the noise of the machinery. A great many people were gathered around a man who came in his new 1904 Oldsmobile automobile. It was the first time many of the fairgoers had ever seen this new mode of transportation and it seemed to be generating a lot of excitement. The man kept a rag handy to wipe down any hand prints from the many who wanted to touch it.

Grace made her way to the grandstand that fronted onto an oval racetrack. She passed her way through the gate into the center field looking for the registration table. Spotting a line of riders in front of a long table behind which sat three men, she fell in behind the last horse and rider. She clutched her dollar coin entry fee that Aaron had slipped into her hand earlier.

Finally, she heard, "Next" and stepped up to a ruddy faced man at the table.

"What do you want, girlie?" He had a bright red moustache that twitched on the ends when he talked.

"I want to race my horse, sir."

"Sorry, we don't allow no females onto the track. Might hurt themselves trying to compete with the men."

"No, sir. I aim to be in that race. Your rules say nothin' about no girls allowed."

"Move on out the way, girlie. Next!"

"No, Sir! My name is not *Girlie.* I'm Grace Reynolds and I'm registering my horse Champion to race."

"Now you listen to me, girlie. I ain't registering no girl, woman, or female of any kind to a race. This is a *man's* sport and I 'spect you don't have the right tools to be in a *man's* sport. Move aside afore I have you escorted offen the track."

"No, Sir! And don't call me Girlie again. You ain't got no right to tell me what to do cause the circular don't say nothin' about no women allowed."

Several of the men started guffawing behind her. "C'mon, Bill, get her outta here so we can get on with it."

"Yeah," piped in a chorus of other riders.

"Next thing, she be wantin' to vote."

"Women got no place being in a race. Should be up in the stands where she belongs, cheering on her man."

"Dammit, the race is gonna start before we even gets a chance to register. Let's get going."

Grace turned in a fury towards her detractors and tried to stomp her foot with as much authority as she could muster. All she managed was to raise a puff of dust. "I ain't gonna be in no stands and I ain't gotta man to cheer on. Why don't you so-called men go up into the stands and cheer *me* on because I got me a horse that's gonna beat the livin' hell out of all of you."

She turned back to the man they called Bill. "Now, here's my dollar entry fee, and you give me the number and tell me where to go with my horse. And you do it *right* now!"

"Oh, I'm gonna tell you where to go all right, girlie. Get your skinny little ass back on that piece of crow bait and skedaddle on outta here."

Grace had heard all she cared to hear and reached over the table grabbing the man by one end of his monstrous moustache and gave it a hard yank. *"Register me now!"*

The man's face registered complete surprise as he reared back in his chair, lost his balance, and tumbled into the dirt with a hard thump.

"What the hell?" He tried scrambling to his feet, only to fall on his face, breaking his nose. Blood started spurting from his face as the men around all started laughing at the spectacle of a hundred-pound girl besting a two hundred fifty-pound man.

"Dang," said one of them, "this is better than anything they got on the midway." He was doubled over in laughter as the rest of them joined in.

"Whut in the Sam Hill is going on over here?" A voice thundered over the laughter as a man strode up to the table. He had a red ribbon on his chest that said he was the "Head Judge".

Bill was trying to stem the flow of blood from his nose as he sputtered that "Thet damned female is trying to register for the race and told her no women allowed."

Grace stepped up to the judge trying to stretch herself to match the man's height. "And I'm telling you that there is nuthin' on the circular that says a woman can't register and ride her horse. Now here is my dollar, and I want my number."

The other men started joining Grace's side. "C'mon, Henry. Let 'er race. You get her dollar, she loses the race, and we can all have a good laugh afterwards."

Several of the other men shouted their agreement.

Henry tried to stifle his chuckle as he reached down and pulled Bill up to his feet. "Go ahead and register her, Bill, so we can get on with it."

"I ain't doin' no sech thing. I *quit!*" He went into the crowd of men gathered around the spectacle still holding his nose.

"All right, young lady," said Henry. "Give me your name, your horse's name, and your dollar."

"Grace May Reynolds! Champion!" she stated firmly and slammed the dollar coin down on the table.

The crowd of men started laughing again. "Champion? That mangy lookin' critter?" yelled one man. "That horse will be the last one outta the gate and left lookin' at the tail end of all those in front of him."

"Here's your number, Miss Reynolds. You're registered for the flat race at three o'clock this afternoon."

"Thank you, Sir. It's nice to see at least *one* gentleman in this crowd of jackals." She took the number and walked Champion back through the middle of catcalls and insults.

Once she was back outside the track, she took out her brush and groomed Champion's mane. She was trembling at her experience. She had never acted out that way before and surprised even herself when she thought back on the encounter. "I must be more like my mama than I thought," she whispered to her horse. "We'll show 'em, boy. You and me are gonna show 'em." She went to find her family but never said a word to any of them of what had happened.

At two o'clock, Grace said good-bye to her parents and Hattie.

"Gracie," said Aaron, as he placed his hand on the saddle horn, "remember to just let Champion run his own race. He's got heart and he's faster than any horse I've seen in a long time. I want you to enjoy the race, but mostly I want you to be careful. You've never done this before, and there are more experienced riders out there. Don't take any chances you don't have to."

"Okay, Papa. I'll be careful." She clicked her tongue. Girl and horse once again entered the gate, crossed the oval track and made their way to where other horses stood with their riders. Aaron, Hannah, Hattie, and the doting Harmon made their way into the grandstand.

She turned and tried to find her family in the stands but with a thousand people milling about trying to find their seats she couldn't spot them.

She heard a familiar, unwanted voice behind her. "Well, looky here. Why if it isn't my little Gracie Reynolds."

Grace whirled in her saddle to confront Duggie Hayes. "Get away from me, Duggie. I can't deal with you. Not today. Not now."

"What are you doing out here with all the menfolk? You best get up into the grandstand where you can cheer me on to win this race."

"You ain't winnin' nothing, mister. I'm into this race and I'm gonna do my best to win it."

"You? But you ain't nothin' but a female tadpole. How'd they ever let you in with the menfolk?"

Grace ignored him as she urged Champion forward. She reached inside her saddlebag and got out her number and pinned it to the front of her blouse.

Hayes roared with laughter. "Number thirteen. It's bad luck enough to have a girl in this race and then she draws number thirteen. Yore goin' down fer sure."

"*Riders for the flat race,*" bellowed a man standing on the track, using a cone shaped device that amplified his voice.

Grace had seen one of those before when she attended Buffalo Bill's show with Charlie. A twinge of sadness dampened her excitement at the thought of Charlie and never seeing him again.

"*Line up your horses for the start of the race. Remember, don't start until you hear the sound of the gun. Any rider doing so will forfeit the race and his entry fee.*"

Most of the riders jockeyed for a position nearer the fence to get a better start. Starting on the outside would be a disadvantage. Grace did not know this and, as a result, she ended up as the last horse at the outside starting line. Some of the other riders were still grumbling that a girl was being allowed to compete, but most of them just avoided her. Duggie managed to be about mid-point of the fifteen horse lineup. Every horse along the line seemed jumpy and some were nervously backing out, only to be goaded back by their riders.

"*On your mark. Get set.*"

The tension was rippling through every rider, every racer, when the explosion of the starting pistol roared. Every horse but the startled Champion leaped forward to make the one-mile circuit. Champion reared up on his hind legs in fright, almost dumping Grace onto the hard dirt track.

Grace dug her heels into Champion's side. He needed no more prodding, but was already seven lengths behind all the others. Grace saw that the other riders were navigating their horses towards the inside rail so she followed suit and fell in behind the line.

The roar of the crowd was deafening to everyone in the grandstand, but Grace tuned it all out as she grabbed a handful of mane. All she heard was the pounding of the hooves of her horse. Champion seemed to understand what was going on and quickly overcame the horse in front of him. Grace bent low over the saddle horn, knowing the wind resistance would be less. She could feel the heat rising from her horse as he pumped his legs. Grace imagined herself as just one with Champion, a single force pushing forward.

Champion passed two more horses, one of which being ridden by Duggie Hayes. He looked over at the girl and her rider, incredulous she was about to pass him. Using a whip, he lashed out at Grace, missing her but landing squarely on the rump of Champion which only resulted in a new burst of energy from the sorrel.

Grace managed a sideways glance to tell her that the horses were passing the halfway mark of the circuit. She could barely make out the people in the grandstand, all on their feet, all yelling at the top of their voices to make one solid roar.

Champion passed another horse, then another, and another. Grace was now just holding on for her life. She had never ridden this fast before and she was scared that Champ would lose his footing and fall, but he kept hammering his legs forward.

In the stands, Aaron was yelling as much as he could, encouraging his daughter. *"Go, Gracie! I know you can do it! Come on, Champion! Go number thirteen!"* His rasp gradually weakened until he lost his voice all together. Harmon chuckled to himself at seeing his future father-in-law going through the motions of yelling, but hearing nothing come out of his mouth.

Hannah couldn't bear to watch and turned her head down. She grabbed Hattie's hand as the girl winced in pain at how tightly her mother had latched onto her. Every once in a while, Hannah would sneak a peek at the long line of horses racing around the track.

On the track, Gracie had managed to make her way to the inside rail. Champion passed three more horses, leaving just five ahead of them. Suddenly, one of them stumbled and rider with horse went flying head over heels. Two of the other lead horses had to veer out of the way to avoid the fallen which gave Champion the chance to come up to within two lengths of the next horse and five behind the lead.

Rounding the home stretch, it was now a battle of three horses. Grace could feel not only her own heart but of that of Champion's pumping in his own broad chest. Huge snorts of air hissed from his nostrils as he overtook the second horse and was closing in on just one length of the lead. Froth from his mouth swirled back into Grace's face and she sensed a strange taste of oats.

Grace looked ahead and saw the finish line which seemed to be coming at her with dizzying speed. She clamped her legs even tighter into Champion's side and put her mouth up to his left ear.

"Now, Champ," she whispered. "We'll show them what a girl can do. I love you, no matter what."

The chestnut seemed to understand exactly what was needed and ran faster than he ever had in his life. The palomino in the lead sensed another horse coming up on his right side and hesitated for a second before charging even harder.

Suddenly, everything seemed to go into slow motion for Grace as the two of them galloped to the finish. Champion was now nose to nose with the palomino, and the race was a duel of two strong horses.

Grace was unaware of anything happening except the pulsating animal beneath her. No crowd noise, no beating of hooves, no snorting of air. They were one. They were girl and horse.

Slowly, everything came back into focus as she saw Champion's nose just a scant inch in front of the other horse. A deafening roar continued from the grandstand as the four competitors crossed the finish line . . . horse and horse, rider and rider.

Grace chanced a glance to her left and saw the palomino and rider slightly behind her.

She had won. She and Champion were, indeed, the champions, and her heart soared in pride as she let go of the saddle horn and raised her arms in glorious triumph.

A girl had just beaten some of the best riders and horses in Moline County.

32
Charlie

The seventeen-year-old boy from Fayette, Iowa, and Port Byron, Illinois, had never seen so many people in his entire life. When he stepped onto Park Row, he saw hundreds of folks hustling along the street, all seeming to be in a hurry to get to wherever they were going. Horses were in abundance with the occasional motor car wending its way through the masses of people crossing from one side of the street to the other.

He was amazed at seeing a vehicle moving down the Row that didn't have a horse in front of it. The automobile's driver sat in the open seat steering with some sort of round wheel. It was noisy, and the driver sometimes tooted a horn to alert a pedestrian it was behind him. Charlie didn't know why that would have been necessary when even someone hard of hearing could hear it from a block away.

He saw his first trolley as it nearly ran him down, jingling its bell as a warning to all in its path. It was travelling on a track down the middle of the street with people hanging off the sides, some of whom would occasionally hop off as others jumped on.

Folks appeared to be sitting inside and a stairwell went to the top where others were sitting.

Men in white coats were pushing barrels on wheels and would scoop up horse manure that had fallen to the street, although most horses had a bag rigged up on their hind quarters to catch the droppings.

On the street nearly every man he saw wore a long black coat and tall black hats. Women were similarly dressed with the occasional gray frock and bonnets with a ribbon tied around the top of the head. Seemingly, facial hair adorned all the male faces over the age of twenty-one. He was starting to grow his own beard and moustache, but it didn't rival what some of the men were sporting.

Newsboys stood on every corner hawking papers. The sounds of the city all merged into a cacophony of shouts, bells, horses clopping, noisy trolley tracks, and an excitement that seemed to have a life of its own.

Charlie could not believe the sight of trains that sat high on elevated tracks as they passed overhead, adding to the noise of the city. They thundered on their rails, coming around corners of buildings, and disappearing further down the street. He stopped a nicely dressed man and asked what that train was called. He looked at Charlie with contempt and noted his dirty clothes and the odor of an unwashed body, completely ignoring him and kept walking with just a bit more energy to his step, just to get away as soon as could.

"Well, excuse me, feller," Charlie called after him. "Please pardon my rudeness." He heard another man pointing out a train passing overhead to a fellow walker, referring to it as a subway.

As he walked, he took note of the buildings, each one appearing to be taller than the next. When he came across a structure that had the name Park Row Building, Charlie started counting windows up. When he got to thirty he saw two giant American flags flying from the top of dome like structures on the front corners of the building. People were streaming in and out, hurrying on their way, jostling each other as they passed. When someone accidentally bumped another, there was no apology, but each accepted it as the way it was done in the big city.

A man sporting a large moustache rounded a corner and bowled into Charlie, knocking him off his feet. "Watch where you're going, buster," the man growled. "Better yet, go down to the Bowery where you belong. For God's sake, man, take a bath." By the time Charlie got to his feet to challenge the man, he had disappeared among the throng of people.

He wondered about the Bowery and if he could find people of his own station there. Asking directions from a storekeeper he was told to walk through Chinatown to get there. "Just take St. James Place until you get to the Bowery. Follow the Bowery to Broome. Can't miss it. Be careful of Chinatown at night, young fellow. It isn't the best place to be after dark."

Just as Charlie passed under the arch that said "Chinatown" the sun was dipping behind the buildings. A Chinese jewelry shop had a clock that indicated the time was 7:15, so he picked up his pace remembering the storekeeper's warning. The sights, sounds and smells of the street, however, were intoxicating, and Charlie slowed down as he tried to take it all in.

The street was a hub of activity as the large majority of people he noticed were Chinese. He had never seen anything like these people in their various stages of colorful dress. Many of them wore pointed hats while others, even the men, wore their hair in long pigtails. One man's hair was braided and grew down past his backside.

Shopkeepers were chattering in a completely foreign language, women were poring over large bins of vegetables in front of a market, children played in the street chasing a rolling hoop with a stick. Every store had signs written in strange markings that resembled sticks piled against each other.

He passed one shop that had skinned dogs hanging from a rope. Charlie could not imagine why anyone would do such a thing when he suddenly realized it was a grocery store. The merchant would cut the dog from the rope and pass it to a customer who shoved it into her wicker basket. Charlie felt his stomach churning and almost threw up into the street but was able to suppress the gag and hurried along the street.

He decided to get into the middle of the throughway where a narrow path was kept open for wagons and horses. He passed a goat which seemed to be foraging for any garbage left at the curbside. People just stepped around the animal and went on their way.

Whenever he passed a cross street he tried to find signs that would lead him out of this din of people. One of those seemed to be lined on both sides with three and four story tenements. Long ropes stretched high overhead from one building to the one across the street, each laden with laundry drying in the still air. He tried counting the number of lines but when he reached twelve, he gave up and moved on.

Passing Canal Street, Charlie walked into what seemed to be some sort of parade. Chinese were ringing symbols and playing flutes as he came face to face with an undulating dragon. It threw a fright into him until he realized it was animated by eight pairs of legs belonging to people inside of it. The dragon was made up of flowing yards of silks as it weaved from one curbside to the other. It was followed by a band of Chinese banging pots and singing in their language in a strange melody. Charlie imagined picking it out with his violin but got lost in the timbre of tone.

Unable to continue down the street he stopped and watched as more dragons, more bands, more people paraded by. Once the last dragon passed he was able to continue down Bowery Street until he got into surroundings that seemed more normal to him. It had broad streets with fewer people, but he felt more comfortable with this scenery than that he had just left behind. Once he got to Broome Street Charlie noted a seedier part of town. It was now dark, and he saw many men and a few women sleeping in doorways. He knew he would never find a place to stay tonight so he kept walking until he found an alleyway with no people and turned that way until he came to a number of garbage cans.

Charlie could feel a deep tiredness in every bone of his body and he curled up behind the cans, laid his head on his arm and with the smell of rotting garbage in his nose, promptly went to sleep.

Morning was just breaking the dawn when Charlie felt something tugging at his legs. He awoke to find a bedraggled man leaning over him pulling at his shoes.

"Hey, mister, what do you think you're doin'?" He kicked the man in the rump, knocking him to the ground. The shoeless man jumped up and ran back out of the alley.

Now wide awake, Charlie got up and relieved himself behind the cans, keeping a watch for anyone that might see him. He stepped into the street as early morning people were starting their own day. He realized he was extremely hungry and was sorely in need of a bath. Walking down the street he saw a sign advertising a bath for five cents. Paying the man in front his nickel, he stepped behind a curtain, removed his clothes and stepped into the tub of tepid soapy water which had probably been used a couple of times before he had gotten into it.

After his bath he asked the man where he could get something to eat and was directed to a shop across the street. He crossed into the store to find long tables where other people were eating. He placed his order, paid his dime and received a sandwich of dry bread with a couple of slices of questionable meat and a cup of very dark coffee, which he found was at least hot. He asked a man across the table from him the date, who mumbled it was Tuesday, June 14th.

Finishing, he stepped back into the street and headed east toward the rising sun. He walked Broome Street until he got to Broadway, remembering that Mr. Twain had mentioned that during some of their discussions, so he turned left, walking three miles until he got to Times Square, where stood a rather odd shaped building that looked to be at least 30 stories. It was triangular in shape and the street split in two, Broadway going to the left and 7th Avenue to the right. Standing in its shadow, Charlie didn't think he would ever see anything that high in the sky. People were going in all directions, and the noise was almost deafening. Clanging trolley cars, people yelling at each other, horses whinnying, and the ever increasing presence of the motor cars. He had never seen such humanity.

Charlie reached into his pocket, fingered the few remaining coins and decided he probably should spend another night on the street before taking in more of the city. He found a small café, ordered a cheese sandwich and a glass of milk. He took it back onto the street, found an empty doorway and ate slowly, watching the traffic passing him by, both pedestrian, horse driven and motor car. He grew weary and fell asleep in a seated position.

He awoke with a start about four the next morning when a light shower made an attempt to sweep the streets clean, giving it a slightly better smell than the one from the evening before. He huddled back a little further in the doorway and dozed until the sun rose, casting long shadows down through the canyon of buildings. He got up, stretched, and decided he'd seen enough of Broadway and headed north on Seventh.

As he walked, he noticed the changing landscape and had gone about a mile when the road abruptly ended leading onto a huge grassy area. A sign indicated it was a place called Central Park, and he crossed the street. He found it a welcome sight to see such a large expanse of green after two days of dust, mud, and gray buildings and again felt a twinge of homesickness for the foliage of Iowa and Illinois.

He started walking a pathway which branched off into other pathways, but he stuck to the one which seemed to be the main trail. The further he walked into the park, the more he noticed the noise ebbing away into a peaceful silence, broken only by the strollers as they quietly talked to each other. The corridor took several twists and turns, and he guessed he must have walked at least another two miles until he came to a large lake.

Children were either floating makeshift ships or splashing in the water trying to ward off the day's heat as the sun rose in the sky. He saw that he had two choices . . . the path to the left or the path to the right and chose the latter of them which took him back to the edge of the park and a street with signage calling it 85th.

He decided to continue walking east on the road lined with homes that had actual green yards in front of them, bordered with white washed picket fences.

His peaceful walk was about to come to an abrupt end.

Captain William Van Schaick was at the helm of his passenger ship that morning on the *General Slocum* travelling south on the East River. The paddlewheel steamship had just picked up over 1,300 passengers, mostly women and children, who were on a church outing and picnic. Children running along the deck were excited as it was the first time they had ever been on a boat ride. Women were wearing their best finery, dresses made of heavy cloth. Their buttoned-up shoes made clicking sounds on the floor planks as they strolled along the decks, chatting with one another. The sunshine splashed on everyone aboard and held the promise of a fine day for cruising the river. The passengers paid a quarter apiece for their daytrip.

The *General Slocum* did not have a good reputation as it had run aground several times in the past and collided with other boats during its short thirteen-year life on the river. Named after a Civil War General and New York Congressman Henry Slocum, the ship was a New York City common site near the harbors and ports of the East River and the Atlantic Ocean.

Below decks on this day, an unskilled laborer by the name of Clyde Rollins lit up a cigarette in the Lamp Room, a storage area where lanterns used for ship lighting were kept. Here is where the lamp oil was stored, wicks were trimmed, and the lamps kept in working order. While smoking was discouraged, there was no rule against it, and Clyde routinely rolled his own smokes and satisfied his habit twenty times a day.

Lying on a bed of straw, Clyde drew on his cigarette while taking a break from his work. A steward called down to him from the main deck that the captain was calling for lamps in the pilothouse.

"Awright, awright! Hold yore horses. Bringin' 'em up in a minute." Clyde laid his cigarette on a table. He wasn't about to waste good tobacco and would be back to finish his smoke in a minute or two. Grabbing three lamps, he climbed the railing to complete his task.

A passing boat by the Slocum created a wake, and the ship bobbed slightly to the side, just enough for the cigarette to roll off the table onto the straw that was soaked in spilled lamp oil.

Clyde's return was delayed as the steward gave him instructions to collect other lamps from several cabins on the port side.

The cigarette continued to smolder in the straw until an ember burst into a tiny flame. The oil fed on the fire causing a slight explosion, landing other embers on the oily rags littering the floor. The room quickly became an inferno and flames licked at the walls, feeding on the rich mixture of fuel and wood.

A young black boy about twelve years old happened to pass by on the main deck and noticed the smell of smoke coming from below. He had been hired by the ship's company to assist the stewards for running errands. He ran to find his manager.

"There be a bit of smoke comin' from the Lamp Room down yonder. I think there might be a fire or sumptin."

The steward had caught this child in a lie twice before and told him to get back to work or he would take a boot to his rump.

"You say so, but I thinks you oughta taken a look."

"Get yore arse back to work. NOW!"

"Yassuh. Sure will do thet."

Below, the fire continued to burn and was eating through the floor planks as well as the walls. Flames had reached the ceiling and were now burning through the floor above it. The heat caused popping sounds as the fire ate through tiny pockets of air in the wood.

In the pilot house Captain Van Schaick was enjoying his own smoke. A cloud of brownish fumes almost made the eyes of his First Mate water, who had the helm.

"Damn fine day, Mate. Making good time and do believe we'll be back in port by late afternoon."

"Aye, sir," he replied.

"Keep the wheel, Mate. Believe I'll step outside for a breath of fresh air."

"Aye, sir." He wished the fresh air would come to him, but he kept quiet.

Van Schaick stepped onto the deck, holding the railing with both hands as he took in a huge breath of air, exhaling slowly before sticking the cigar back between his stained teeth. His mind drifted to the German pub a block from his launching port and the mug of ale awaiting him this afternoon when he heard a commotion from a deck below him.

"*Fire!*" somebody yelled, and Van Schaick saw flames licking out of the door leading to the lower deck and the Lamp Room.

"Oh, Gott! Es war so ein schöner Morgen," he mumbled under his breath as he realized his morning just turned from good to very bad.

Dashing down the steps to the lower deck, he grabbed the shirt of the first steward he could find. "What's going on, Steward? Where's that fire coming from?"

"From the Lamp Room, sir! No one can even get close to the door, the fire is so hot!"

Passengers, drawn by the screaming of others, were rushing to the fore to see what all the commotion was about. When most of those nearest the rail saw what was happening, they also started screaming, and a panic swept over the crowd like an ocean wave.

Women were screaming for their children, some clutching babies to their bosoms and tried to turn back to the safety of the inner decks. The movement started a stampede and people were being trampled underfoot, adding to the din of noise and flailing bodies. Children, caught in the terror, were stomped, killing more than a few in the process.

As the fire found new fuel to consume it climbed quickly to the upper deck, and those who were unfortunate enough to be closest were also trampled from the horde pushing behind them.

Van Schaick ran back into the pilot house and gave orders to head to ground the ship on North Brother Island up river. The helmsman in his own panic turned the ship to port, the opposite direction of the Captain's orders.

Rushing back to the rail, Van Schaick saw the screaming passengers trying to put life jackets onto their children. The ship's owner, however, had never seen safety as a priority, and the jackets and life preservers had rotted and were falling apart, rendering them useless.

Women were throwing their children into the water and jumping in after them. The heavy dresses they were wearing were made even heavier from the water, and they sank before they could get to their screaming children, most of who could not swim and slipped under the waves to their watery graves.

Charlie's New York City stroll came to an abrupt end when he reached the docks on the west side of the East River. He wasn't sure which direction he should take now and decided to turn left to see where it would take him.

As he got to a street called East 92nd, he heard a commotion coming from out in the water and was shocked when he saw a ship about fifty yards off shore that had flames and smoke leaping high into the sky. Others on the dock were gathering and pointing but none were making any effort leading to a rescue.

People were jumping off the ship into the water but when they failed to come up again, Charlie knew that folks were dying out there and he had to do something.

Quickly shedding his shoes, jacket and shirt he took a running jump and leaped off the dock into the water. It might have been June, but the cold water sent a shock through his body as he remembered what happened when he was thrown into the sea from the *Carolina* when he was serving Mark Twain.

Gasping for air, Charlie began swimming strong strokes towards the ship. The tide was moving out and it helped him move more quickly. Within five minutes he was within fifty feet of the ship as it was churning about in the water, even as the flames were reaching the paddlewheels. He was sickened as he saw people who were in the water drawn into the paddles and beaten to death.

Charlie saw a little girl desperately trying to keep her head above water and reached her within five strokes. Grabbing her by the shirt collar, the child turned and grabbed him around her neck.

"Don't struggle, honey," he panted, "just relax and let me do the swimming."

She relaxed but was crying for her mama. "You let me get you to shore, darlin', and I'll come back out and see if I can find your mama."

That seemed to relax her, and Charlie starting swimming back to the dock when he heard a gurgling cry come from behind him. Looking back he saw a frightened boy about four-years-old clutching to a half-dissolved life preserver. Charlie reversed his direction and went back to the child.

"Grab around my neck, son. We'll get you back to shore in no time." He whispered to the girl, "Help me keep him safe, honey, so he doesn't struggle." The girl seemed to understand and tried to comfort the panicked lad through her own tears.

Charlie's efforts to stay afloat were taxing his own strength but within five minutes he reached the dock where two men jumped into the water and relieved him of his weight of two children. Life preservers were thrown down from others on the dock to pull them up to safety.

Charlie ignored his screaming muscles and made another trip towards the *Slocum*. Twice more he pulled children from under the waves and got them back to the shore. He knew he could probably make one more before exhaustion would force him to quit. This time he found a teenaged girl who also grabbed him in a panic.

Her struggles pulled them both under the water before Charlie could grab a breath. Her flailing arms kept him from getting back to the surface and alarm crept into his heart as he realized the girl would drown them both. The water softened his blow as he ran a fist to her chin, knocking her unconscious. She went limp, and he was able to get under her and push her back up. His lungs were exploding, and with one more push of his legs he broke the surface and drew in a huge breath of air. Nothing had ever tasted so sweet.

Charlie's muscles simply would not surge with the adrenaline he felt with the first three trips, and he took his time treading the water back to the shoreline where waiting arms took the last victim from him.

Charlie collapsed on the dock and heaved with fatigue, looking up at the circle of faces above him, their voices excited with adoration of this hero. Five people would grow up to live their own lives because of him.

33

Aaron

Grace's win at the county fair's horse race considerably raised her spirits. She took exceptional pride in knowing she had beaten Duggie Hayes and had no more run-ins with him since then.

It was Monday, June 20th, and she was in the kitchen peeling a bowl of potatoes. Hannah was frying eggs at the wood stove, Hattie was working on sewing, and Aaron was in his usual place at the dinner table with a cup of coffee and the latest newspaper from Moline that he had picked up at the Port Byron Mercantile.

"They had a big ship fire on the river back in New York City. Good Lord! Over a thousand souls perished on a steamboat called the *General Slocum,* mostly women and children."

"Oh, those poor people," cried Hattie, looking up from her sewing. "What happened?"

"The captain, a Mr. Van Schaick, I hope I'm pronouncin' that right, instead of headin' to the shore so people could jump off, steered it up river to an island, garranteein' that more folks would die."

"Sounds to me like that man ought to be strung up from the nearest tree," said Hannah.

"More people died than were saved. One fellow jumped into the river from the shore and saved five children all by hisself."

"Sounds like a hero, Papa," said Grace.

"The young man says he's no hero and wouldn't even give his name. Said anybody would have done the same."

"Still say he's a hero, Papa."

"Reckon so, reckon so. Hey, says here that Teddy Roosevelt is coming to Moline on a campaign stop, sailin' down from St. Paul, Minnesoty. The Republican Party is going all out to make sure he gets a second term."

"Those politicians will say anything to get elected," countered Hannah.

"None the less, might go down to the dock and see the ship. Mebbe he'll be out on the deck and we can wave to him as he passes by. They've got a schedule here on towns he'll be seeing from the ship. Looks likely he'll be going by Port Byron, let's see, sometime around noon on the morrow."

"Can I go too, Poppa?" asked Grace, plopping another potato in the bowl.

"Shore can, Gracie. Everybody can go."

"I got enough chores right here to keep me busy. Don't need to see any tomfool politico," said Hannah. "Hattie, set the table. Eggs are almost ready and the biscuits are about to come out of the oven."

The next morning, President Theodore Roosevelt stepped out on the dock from his stateroom.

"Good morning, Mr. President," chirped his private secretary, Louis McHenry Howe, who was enjoying his morning cigar.

"Good day to you, Mister Howe", he replied as he pulled at his walrus moustache. "What's on our agenda this day?"

"We have one last campaign stop in Moline before we catch a train back to Boston, sir. Unfortunately, we may be delayed a bit because of a malfunction in the engine room and we'll have to pull into a dock near Port Byron on the Illinois side. We should be no more than an hour, but you might like to get off ship and stretch your legs a bit."

"How big a town is this Port Byron?"

"Very small, sir. It runs around 700 people."

"Well, even a town of 700 people will vote so why don't we just stroll the street and see if we can drum up a few?"

"Yes, sir."

Aaron had finally talked Hannah into joining him on their half mile trip into town. He climbed onto the buckboard with Hannah and Hattie, while Grace followed on Champion. He picked up the reins and by ten, they were pulling up in front of the mercantile.

"Aaron", said Hannah, "long as we're here I need to pick up some flour and a pound of coffee. How's our credit?"

"Paid up, Becky, thanks to our windfall from Mr. Twain." He grimaced and immediately regretted his answer when he saw tears well up in Grace's eyes. "I'm sorry baby girl; that was the completely wrong thing to say."

Grace never said a word but dismounted her horse and started grooming him from behind so no one would see her weeping.

Just when she thought she was getting over the hurt, something would give a reminder of her loss.

"Aaron, I swear," said Hannah. "Please think before talking."

"Sorry, Becky."

At that moment, a ship's horn pierced the stillness of the day and the family turned to see a large steamboat coming down the river. Other people had also gathered along the dirt street to see if they could catch a glimpse of the Rough Rider, a nickname he gained from his service in a war in Cuba just six years before.

"I declare," said Aaron, "do believe it's headed into the dock. Paper didn't say nuthin' 'bout stopping in Port Byron."

"It's coming right for us, Papa," said Hattie. She wished she had invited Harmon along. They might have gotten to see the President.

The large ship pulled into the dock and laborers were casting ropes to tie it off. A cheer went up from the crowd as they recognized the man himself stepping off the gangway. People pressed forward as they hoped to shake his hand.

"Top of the day to you, good citizens of Port Byron," his voice boomed. "It's a blessing to be in the great state of Illinois."

Aaron was one of those moving in to maybe say something to him when he tripped and fell right into the President's arms.

"Well now," said Roosevelt, "I didn't expect this warm a welcome."

"Sorry, Mr. President, I tripped, see, and didn't mean no harm."

"Quite all right. Just wanted to make sure you're not an anarchist." Roosevelt was still leery of people who disagreed with his policies after the assassination a few years before of William McKinley. As his Vice President, he ascended to the top spot.

"No, sir, I'm a Democrat."

The Republican Roosevelt roared with laughter. "Well, some say that's almost as bad."

"My wife back there on the buckboard, she's got no use for politics, but I follow them pretty closely."

"You have a fine looking family, sir. What's your name?"

"Reynolds. Aaron Reynolds. My wife Becky and Hattie and that carrot top standing by her horse is Grace."

Roosevelt walked over to the buckboard and patted the smooth nose of Champion. "I consider myself to be a good judge of horses, Grace, and that is one fine steed you have."

"Thank you, sir. His name is Champion and he won the first prize for beating out fifteen other horses in a race at the County Fair." Her heart burst with pride as she talked about her horse with the President of the United States.

"I can certainly see why. Now if you'll excuse me, I need to meet more of these fine Port Byron citizens."

"Yes, sir," she said, as Roosevelt walked into the crowd, shaking hands and asking people to vote for him.

Later, when the family had returned to the farm, Aaron was still talking about meeting the great man himself.

"Aaron," said Hannah, "he's just a man like anyone else. You carry on like he's the Risen Lord himself."

"Mebbe I'll switch to being Republican."

Hannah just shook her head and turned to begin fixing supper.

34

Grace

Grace's education in Port Byron's one room school came to an end at the age of fourteen. The school wasn't equipped to extend beyond the eighth grade, and the teacher, Priscilla Donnelly, was not qualified to be an instructor to the upper grades. She wasn't even supposed to teach the elementary levels, but the city fathers couldn't afford an Education graduate so they hired Miss Donnelly for a few dollars a week.

While Grace was friendly with all of her classmates, only one could be counted as a true pal . . . Sarah May Hayes. Duggie's sister was two years younger than Grace, but they often walked home together chattering about the usual teenage gossip.

While the two girls were unlikely friends because of Sarah's older brother, they both shared the same middle name and, for whatever reason, it drew them together.

Sarah had been horrified at Duggie's persistent unwanted behavior towards Grace. "Is it wrong to hate your own brother, Gracie? He constantly teases me and sometimes hits me, saying that a girl has got to know her place."

"Why don't you complain to your father?"

"He's even worse. He sometimes makes me stay home from school just so I'm there to fix his lunch. I can usually get to school when he's still passed out from drinking all the night before. I've been lucky to get home before he even wakes up. Otherwise, he'll take the switch to me." She pulled the back of her dress down to reveal large welts, some fresh, others that were older. "It's like that all the way down my backside. Does your pa wallop you like that?"

"Oh, Sarah, I'm so sorry. No, my papa would never hit me. Mama sometimes threatens to, but she never does."

"You don't 'spose I can come live with you, do you?"

"I'd like nuthin' better than to have my bestest friend living with me, but all I got is a small bed in the loft over the kitchen, sharing with Hattie. The other two rooms are the kitchen and a bedroom where Mama and Papa sleep. It's so small you have to step outside jest so's you can turn around."

As they were talking they passed by an abandoned farm house sitting on a lane back off the road. It was the old Taylor place and the legend was that Jacob Taylor, back in the 70s, went crazy and took an axe to the whole family while they slept in their beds. All ten of the family members were buried in the shadow of the two-story house. Tales were told how that when they were buried in their shallow graves, the men tasked with the chore couldn't tell whose head belonged to which body. Ranging in ages from five to twelve, severed limbs were just thrown into several boxes and buried amongst the roots of the tall oak tree where the murderer had hung himself after massacring his family.

The house had gone unoccupied from that dark day and was falling into disrepair. Vines, untended, were growing up the side

of the outside walls where they had broken into windows and
wound their way inside. The front porch had missing boards and
one of the posts holding up the portico had collapsed, causing
the overhanging roof to slant dangerously to one side. The chimney, long unused, was dropping bricks to the ground which was
overrun by weeds. To see the house from the front produced fear
in man and child alike as the upper windows resembled gaping
black eyes and the darkened entry door seemed to beckon any
unwary victim to enter into its mouth and be eaten.

Grace, as a much younger child, knew of the stories told by
her pa about the massacre and would always run past the broken
down gate whenever she passed. It gave her the chills just looking
at the tall oak tree that stood there. In her mind she could see old
man Taylor still twisting at the end of a rope.

Now that she was older, she felt that maybe the story of ghosts
roaming the rooms of the dilapidated structure were just that—
stories. Her mother constantly lectured that the only spirit that
counted was the Holy one found in the Bible.

She stopped abruptly at the gate and looked up towards the
house, an idea forming in her mind.

"Sarah, I don't know that I can do much about your pa, but
maybe we can get Duggie to back off from you."

"What do you mean? How?"

"Let me work some things out in my mind before I tell you."

When they got to the turnoff up to the Hayes farm, Grace
shuddered when she saw Duggie leaning up against a tree, smoking some corn silk.

"Well, there's my sweet little Gracie, coming to see her man,"
he called out, choking on a lung full of smoke. "Seems you and

my kid sister are just about best of friends. I guess that makes us kind of related lovers."

"The day I cuddle up to you," she retorted, "will be the day I dance on your grave."

"Ah, now, is that any way to talk to your future husband?"

Grace seized upon an idea and smiled. "If you can prove your so-called manhood two weeks from today, I will come right up to you and kiss you full on the lips."

"Grace," exclaimed Sarah, "don't do it. He'll take advantage of you fer sure."

"I know what I'm doing, Sarah," she whispered. "Leave it to me."

"What do I have to do?" Duggie was already licking his lips in anticipation.

"You have to go into the old Taylor place and pick up something from each room and bring it back to me. I'll be waitin' for you outside."

He blanched at the thought of going near the house because of the stories and felt a chill tracing a path up and down his spine. He wiped a tear dripping from his damaged eye. "Do what again?"

"You heard me. Go into the house at midnight in a fortnight, get some article from every room and return to me with your treasure. You do that, and the kiss is yours, given freely. Let's see how big a man you are. You couldn't even get past my Uncle John Sullivan, so let's see how you do with this."

Bile rose in Duggie's throat at the mention of the punishing blow at the hands of her uncle. His bluster got the better of him.

He took another drag on the corn silk cigarette, threw it to the ground and mashed it with his foot.

"Okay, dammit! Two weeks from tonight, you be here and I 'spect you'll be gettin' a lot more than just a kiss!" He sauntered up the path, hoping his shaking knees wouldn't give away his fear.

Grace said her goodbyes to Sarah and by the time she got to her own gate, she had formulated her plan but knew she would have to have help. She hurried up the path and sought out her pa.

Two weeks later, Grace and her father, with the help of Hattie, had all the pieces in place. Aaron admitted to himself he was having fun with the project and was delighted that Grace's mind was kept busy, keeping her depression at bay. Indeed, she was actually enjoying herself and kept imagining the scenarios that were going to take place inside the Taylor farm house this very night.

Aaron, Grace, and Hattie pored over their plans every night at their kitchen table. Hannah thought it was all foolishness but didn't object to it. Aaron and Hattie would be inside the house at the appointed time and would set things in motion as Duggie entered. They made a list of supplies they would need to make things work. A heavy chain, several lanterns, an axe, a gallon of red paint, a white sheet of gossamer silk, and rope were all items that needed to be collected. He captured a raccoon and killed it so that by the time the event was to take place, it would be sufficiently decayed and odorous. Hattie was to be inside the house with Aaron. Every detail was reviewed several times so each person knew their part in the plan.

They were ready. Aaron and Hattie slipped into the house an hour before midnight to make sure things were set up properly. Aaron sat on the stairs leading to the second floor and pulled out his pipe, tamped in some tobacco and put a match to it. As he puffed on the pipe, he blew curls of smoke into the air. Taylor, when he was alive, was always seen with a pipe in his mouth. It was as much a part of his face as his nose and whenever people told stories of the murders, they always made reference to the ever present pipe. He kept his lantern turned low so that it wouldn't be seen from the outside.

Hattie waited upstairs but even she was frightened by the sinister mood of the house. The three of them had been into the house several times during the two weeks, always during daylight setting up their plan, so she was used to the surroundings. But now, at this hour, sitting in the dark, she felt her own misgivings at being in the murderous dwelling, even for an hour.

A few minutes before midnight, Grace and Harmon Lovell walked up to the front steps with their own lanterns. She wanted Hattie's beau to be there as a witness. She heard voices coming from the trail in the darkness.

"I tole you, Sarah, I didn't want you comin'. When I gets my kiss I don't want nobody else around because I'm fixin' to get just a little bit more than a peck on the lips."

"Well, I promised Grace I would be here and I never break a promise. So leave me alone."

"She prob'ly won't even be there and made me come all the way over here jest so's she could stand me up."

"Oh, she'll be here alright. In fact, there she is now."

The brother and sister walked up to Grace who had placed the lantern on the ground so that light shining up on her face gave it a rather sinister appearance. Duggie took his own lantern and held it up, softening some of the shadows.

"Well, here I am, little man," she said, giving added emphasis to the word 'little'.

Duggie brushed off the slight. "What's he doin' here?" He gestured at Harmon.

"Witness. You cheat and everybody in Moline County is goin' to know about it."

"I ain't gonna cheat. Hope you got yore lips all nice and puckered fer me cuz I'm goin' to collect."

"Frankly, I'm surprised to see you here, Duggie. Fact is, I could hear your knees knocking all the way down to the gate."

Sarah giggled and Duggie turned to his sister with a facial warning that implied she best be quiet or he would give her what for when they got back home.

"Here's the rules," said Grace. "You have to get something from every room. There's three rooms upstairs and three rooms downstairs." Duggie didn't question how she knew that. "People say that the house is just as it was left on the night of the murders so you shouldn't have any trouble findin' something to bring back to me. And just so you won't get stuff from just one room and come back out, you'll go to the window of each room and shine your light so I know you ain't cheatin.'"

Duggie's face fell because that was exactly what he planned. He knew he couldn't back down now, especially with Harmon and Sarah there to blab that he didn't do it.

Grace swung the lantern back and forth making eerie shadows. "Since I know you ain't gonna make it, little man, I've got no worries about you collectin'." As an afterthought, she added, "And if you don't make it through the whole house, you have to promise to never touch Sarah again. Be on your way now."

"Hah!" he snorted. "Don't you worry. It won't take me no time a'tall to be through and down here to collect me reward."

Duggie turned and stood at the bottom of the steps rising up to the front porch. He could feel every nerve in his body screaming, urging him to turn and run back down the path. He took a big gulp of the air just as the full moon passed behind a cloud. He raised his lantern high and took his first step. The boards creaked under his weight and threatened to break. He took one more step and thought there was no way any kiss was worth the fear he was feeling at that moment. He swallowed his misgivings and reached for the gaping door. The knob pulled off in his hand but the door swung open anyway.

He turned back and looked at Grace who shooed him in with a wave of her hands. He hoped his eyes wouldn't betray how he felt.

Aaron heard the voices outside and whispered upstairs to Hattie. "Here they come. Be ready." He took a huge lungful of pipe smoke and exhaled it as he quietly backed up the steps.

Duggie stepped into the foyer, holding his lantern high to get a feel for the house. A large parlor was to his left and two doorways were on the right down a hallway. Just as he stepped into the parlor to retrieve his first souvenir he caught a faint whiff of pipe tobacco smoke. He, too, knew the stories of Jacob Taylor's ever present pipe. Pausing, he fought the urge to back out of the room and run out of the house.

Swaying the lantern back and forth he caught sight of a table that had a lace covering. He wadded it up and stuffed it into his pants. He went to the window and swung his lantern back and forth to let Grace know he had gone to the first room. One down and five to go.

Stepping back into a hallway, fear gripped his privates as he heard something that sounded like a chain slowly being drugged across the floor above him.

"Oh, God! Oh, God! Oh, God!" he whispered to himself. "This damn place really *IS* haunted."

He continued to the next room on his right which appeared to be the kitchen. A table, laden with dust, someone had scrawled the words:

$$\text{help}$$
$$\text{me}$$

Duggie closed his eyes tight as a chill traced its way up and down his spine into his now shriveled manhood. Tears formed in his eyes and he started gasping for breath. He couldn't stop now, he just couldn't.

Backing out of the kitchen, he knocked over a chair that had a seat cushion on it. He grabbed it up and ran to the window and swung his lantern back and forth.

Two down. Four to go.

He stopped at the entry to the next room and placed his hand on the frame, panting and gathering up whatever courage he had left. The faint odor of pipe smoke still lingered in the air. Stepping inside, he held the lantern out in front of him, trying to make out shapes in the darkness. Again, the sound of a dragging chain but this time it was accompanied by the slow clomp of steps.

Clomp, chain. Clomp, chain. Clomp, chain.

Peering into the room, he detected a new odor . . . one of rotting flesh. A great buzzing sound was added to the "clomp, chain". Flies started buzzing around his head and as he frantically waved them off, Duggie's dinner churned in his stomach, and he vomited into the doorway, adding to the stench.

Holding his nose, he entered the room, found a song book on the piano in the room, stuffed it into his pants and hurried over to wave his lantern through the window. He backed out of the room where he was able to release his nose and took in a huge lungful of less toxic air.

He wasn't sure he would be able to make it to the stairs, let alone climb them. Just as he placed his hand on the newel post, he heard a muffled female scream coming from one of the upper rooms.

"No, Papa! No," followed by a loud thump.

Duggie froze. He couldn't go forward. He couldn't go back. Sweat beaded on his forehead, running rivulets down into his eyes. He sniveled through his broken nose and wiped both sweat and tears from his face with his dirty shirt sleeve. He stood there for a full two minutes, holding onto the newel with a tight grip, his fear gripping him in his lower intestines as he listened for more sounds.

Hearing none, he tried to convince himself that his imagination was running away with him and he hadn't actually heard anything, had smelled nothing, and had not actually seen any flies. "That's it," he whispered to himself. "My mind's playin' foolery on me. Ain't none of them things really happened."

Once he had convinced himself of the imaginary events, he took his first step up the rickety stairs. With every step of the way, the boards creaked with a squeal, threatening to drop him back to the main floor. Reaching the top of the landing, he looked down the narrow hallway and saw three rooms, one on the left which must have been above the parlor and two on the right. These must be the bedrooms, he thought, where Jacob Taylor took an axe to his wife and children. A new dread gripped him as he approached the room on the left. He turned the knob and pushed the door open, his lantern held high.

Nothing seemed out of the ordinary in this room until he noticed three beds lined up against the far wall. Spattered on the wall were great splotches of a dark red. Sheets and blankets on the beds were covered in what appeared to be dried blood. Again, he felt bile rise in his throat and he nearly threw up again. Holding it back he grabbed a girl's doll, not noticing it had blood across the front of its dress. Had he examined it more closely he would have seen it was nothing but red paint. He hurried to the window and waved the lantern back and forth.

Four down. Two to go.

He was starting to gain confidence as he turned and re-entered the hallway, anticipating the liberties he would take when Grace put her lips to his. He felt a stirring below his rope belt and grinned. This was going to be easier than he thought.

The first room on the right must have been Jacob and Hilda's room as it had only one bed, washstand, armoire and a dresser with a mirror smudged with years of settled dust. Flashing the lantern around the room the mirror caught his warped reflection, and nearly dropped it until he realized it was just himself staring back at him. He grinned at how foolish he must have looked and noticed a hairbrush on the top. He grabbed it, stuffed it in his pants and went to the window to flash the signal.

Down below, Grace and Harmon were amazed that Duggie had made it as far as he had and she started getting uneasy. "Oh, you don't think he's going to make it do you, Harm?"

"I don't think so, Gracie. It's that last room that is going to prove his undoing."

Duggie was now pleased with himself at having conquered this so-called haunted house. He even whistled to himself just to hear a normal sound as he advanced to the final room. One more room to go and he would go throw his treasures at Grace's feet and move in for the kiss which he knew would involve a whole lot of groping on his part. He could see Grace's soft curves in his mind and how his hands would explore each and every one of them.

Reaching the final door, he swung it open and stepped inside. He held his lantern high over his head and noted four beds, two on each side of the room.

The only thing different in this room was the lantern on the floor beyond the far bed. Duggie caught a glimpse of a figure, rising up from the bed. The silhouette froze him in terror. Aaron, standing behind the door, splashed a cup of water on the hot glass of Duggie's lantern, shattering it, dousing the fire and leaving the room darkened except for the lantern on the far side.

Hattie held her head at an odd angle hoping it gave the illusion of just hanging off her shoulders; She held up what looked like a bloodied hand, pointed at Duggie and screamed, "Why, Papa, why?"

Aaron threw the white sheet of gossamer silk across the room. Duggie convinced himself it was a spirit drifting across the room as it gently shimmered slowly to the floor. The darkness of the room made it seem like the cloth passed through the floor boards.

"No, Daddy! No! Oh, God, somebody help me!" Hattie cried.

Aaron reached from behind the darkness of the door separating him from Duggie and threw an ax, imbedding it in the frame just inches from Duggie's head.

Duggie's self-confidence dissipated within a second as his kidneys let loose with a gush of urine, saturating the front of his pants. He screamed and backed out of the room, stumbling and falling as he did. He got up, still screaming and groped his way down the dark hallway towards the stairs.

Out in the front yard, Harmon had taken the rope and flung it over the lowest branch of the oak tree. He had tied off an effigy of a man. His straw filled bag for a head had the face of a man with eyeballs hanging from their sockets. He placed his own lantern below to give it an eerie appearance.

He, Sarah and Grace were muffling their laughter from the screams coming that seemed to fill the house.

Inside, Duggie was gripping the stairway railing, still screaming. Halfway down, he tripped on the rotted carpeting and tumbled the rest of the steps to the bottom. His face bounced off a stair step and re-broke his nose. His mouth filled with blood. He jumped up and lurched towards the door illuminated by the moonlight from outside.

His feet never touched the steps as he jumped off the porch, tripping a second time right at the foot of the giant oak. As he stood up, the legs of the effigy hit his face. Looking up into the grotesque face, Duggie didn't see that it was just a made-up man. What he saw in his mind was the body of Jacob Taylor, swaying at the end of the rope.

Still screaming, Duggie's bowels emptied themselves, and he stumbled out of the yard, his blinded terror not allowing him to see Grace, Sarah, and Harmon standing there with somber expressions. He fled the yard leaving behind the stench of released urine and excrement.

Stepping out of the house, Aaron and Hattie joined the three outside as they all howled with laughter.

Grace hoped she would never see Duggie again. She couldn't have been more wrong.

35
Charlie

Charlie was growing weary of the praise for his actions on the East River. He hated being the center of attention unless he was on stage with his fiddle. He was thankful for the offers of food, cash, and more comfortable places to stay than a flop house in The Bowery. Women were actually coming up to him and offering him a warm place to sleep that hinted there might be more benefits than just sleep. He graciously declined those kinds of offers but readily accepted a week in a nice hotel here and then another week there. He ate in some of the finer restaurants, outfitted in nice clothing from a haberdashery, and was given a brand new pair of boots to replace his holes-in-the-soles shoes. New Yorkers were practically throwing money at him and he accumulated over $250 within a month's time.

He avoided reporters who wanted to interview him and make him a national hero. He never divulged his last name to anyone and was happy to explore New York City alone. He learned how to use the new subway, took a ferry ride out to the Statue of Liberty, and rode an elevator to the top of the Flatiron Building, the tallest structure at 20 stories in the city.

In September, he was offered a full month's stay at The Wolcott, a new hotel that had only been open since March. The front desk insisted on knowing his last name, so he told them it was Charles Joiner, his mother's maiden name. He asked that it not be revealed to anyone. Given a room on the top floor he could see Central Park, twenty blocks away. He marveled at how much he could observe from his window.

In mid-September, he was crossing the lobby when he heard a commotion near the entry way to the hotel's restaurant. Wondering what all the din was about he saw several reporters surrounding a man, attired in a white suit, white top hat and white shoes. He immediately recognized the figure and walked up behind him.

"Hello, Mr. Twain," he said. "Nice to see you again."

Samuel Clemens turned and for a moment his face changed from one of total confusion to a look of joy.

"*Charlie*? Is that really you, Charlie?"

"Yes, sir, it's me."

"But . . . but I thought you were dead. I saw the waves swallow you up during that storm off the Outer Banks. How . . . how do you come to be standing here?"

"Well, I was about to entertain the idea of having breakfast. Would you care to join me?"

A few of the reporters recognized Charlie as the hero of the *General Slocum* and immediately moved in to pepper the two men about how they knew each other.

"Not now, boys. I'm about to sit and break bread with this fine young man." He turned to address the maître d'. "Jacques, give us a table for two in the back and keep these fellows out of here."

"Certainly, Mr. Twain." With that he blocked the reporters from entering and led the two to a choice table near the rear of the room.

"Okay, Charlie," he said when they settled into their chairs. "Start from when I last saw you drowning in the storm and how you came to be in New York City dressed in fine clothes."

Over the next two hours, Charlie, with just a question or two injected by the author from time to time, recounted his journey. He told of being washed up on the beach of Kitty Hawk, meeting the Wright Brothers and assisting them in getting their flying machine off the ground, hopping the rails from North Carolina all the way to New York. He even told him of the death of Goliath. Twain grimaced at that part of the story. Charlie ended with his tale of rescuing five children from the *General Slocum* and receiving countless offers of money, hotel rooms, and clothing from adoring New Yorkers.

Charlie had never talked so much in his life but was so grateful at seeing a familiar face that he had barely touched his meal.

Twain sat back in his chair, lit a huge cigar and blew out a spiral of smoke. "Charlie, that is the most fantastic tale I have ever heard. I'm not sure I could have come up with a novel to encompass your life. I would consider writing one about you if my agenda were not so full at the moment."

"How about you, sir? What have you been doing for the past year?"

Twain told him of his book tours and lectures and how he had hired a new assistant that hardly came to the same quality of care that Charlie had given him during the short time they were together. "Nonetheless, he is a fine boy and I have been grooming him in the finer aspects of life. You know, when I thought you had died, I felt so guilty at being so helpless in rescuing you, I sent a note to your lady. What was her name again? Grace, was it not?"

"Yes, sir. Grace Reynolds."

"I sent her a bank note for one hundred dollars, hoping that would assuage my guilt, but it never helped ease my mind."

"I can pay you back, sir. I have money now."

"No! Absolutely not, Charlie. You need your cash more than I do, so you hang on to it."

"Well, I wrote her a letter from someplace in Pennsylvania so she knows I am alive."

"That's fine. Charlie, I am so glad to see you alive and well. It has eased a burden from my heart. I am due to give a lecture in about an hour so I must be off."

"Please don't tell the reporters my name, sir. They've been hounding me somethin' fierce and I just don't want the attention. I ain't no hero. I only done what anyone would have."

"Make no mistake, Charlie Fisher, you ARE a hero and your humility only reinforces my estimation of your character. Your secret is safe with me. Godspeed and I wish you well."

The two men stood and embraced before Twain took his leave. Charlie sat back down to a plate of cold eggs and thought about his plans. Constantly peppered with requests to reveal his last name he knew it was time to say good-bye to New York City.

36
Hattie

At the age of seventeen, Hattie was more than ready to be married. Her romance with Harmon Lovell was a quiet one, but the couple dearly loved each other and they were eager to start their life together.

With the wedding set for the Spring of 1905, Aaron and Hannah decided to build a larger home on their farm and offered the newlyweds their old one.

As the months passed, Grace was showing signs of coming out of her dark mood as she began to finally accept Charlie's death two years prior. Her horse Champion played a large part in her therapy as she groomed him daily, talking to him, and asking his advice on how her life should proceed.

Lack of cash predestined that Hattie and Harmon would have a very small wedding, attended by just family and a few close friends. The home Aaron was building was taking shape very nicely. Land was cleared of trees using the lumber to form a four room log cabin, complete with a dog-run and separate kitch-en. The dog-run was merely a breezeway setting apart the main house and the kitchen in case of a fire. That way, it wouldn't consume the whole house.

With the foundation and wooden flooring in place, Aaron placed the logs on top of each other, packing them with a new technology based cement on the outside sealing up any cracks, providing solid reinforcement to the overall structure. Once the walls were up, windows and doors were cut and work began on the roof. Aaron was able to obtain several sheets of tin which he overlaid on the supporting beams, securing them with huge nails forged from the Port Byron blacksmith.

By wedding day in April 1905, glass windows had been installed, curtains put up, furniture moved in and a blaze set in the new fireplace. Smoke drifted lazily into the sun-kissed sky where fifteen people gathered in the front yard for an outdoor wedding.

As the guests settled onto several bales of straw, the circuit rider minister and the groom took their places in front of the porch of the new home. As the crowd awaited the new bride, a handsome young man with a guitar strummed a melody for her entrance.

Aaron had hired the musician for fifty cents after hearing him play at a barn dance a month prior. The man's music seemed to fit his name perfectly . . . Isaac Harmony. Just over six feet tall, his sandy hair fell over his forehead just to the top of dark eyebrows. Grace was transfixed as she looked upon Isaac's features. She felt a stirring she had not felt since she had fallen in love with Charlie.

She immediately felt remorseful for her reaction as he played his guitar. But Charlie was dead, wasn't he? She was feeling lonely, and this new emotion confused her terribly. Shouldn't she feel loyal to what she had with Charlie? Wouldn't Charlie want her to carry on with her own life?

Her thoughts and conflicting sentiments were interrupted when Hattie appeared from the house on the arm of her father. Her gown was covered in white lace that she and her mother had worked on for six months. Her veil completely covered her face and when she stepped in to stand beside Harmon, she could barely contain her own excitement. Months of planning were coming to fruition as she and Harmon would be joined in matrimony.

Aaron took her arm and placed it on Harmon's, stepping back and sitting down beside Hannah who was dabbing her eyes. Isaac finished his melody on a nod from the minister and walked over to the guests. The only place he could find to sit was beside Grace who had a bale all to herself. Her heart quickened when he gave her a warm smile. She demurely smiled back and scooted over to the side to make room for him.

"Hello, Miss Reynolds," he said, placing his guitar on the side of the bale.

Grace blushed and smiled back at him. *Oh, Lord,* she thought, *not only does he know my **name** but his voice is as warm as his eyes.* She tried to concentrate on the wedding but couldn't help stealing a sideways glance at the handsome fellow next to her. Her heart was beating abnormally in her chest, and she couldn't control her breathing. She hardly paid heed to the vows being said in front of her.

She came out of her daze only when Isaac stood up and grabbed his guitar. Apparently, the words, "I now pronounce you man and wife" had been uttered, and the rest of the guests stood up and applauded as Hattie and Harmon kissed. Isaac was playing some sort of ballad as the new bride and groom passed between the guests, accepting congratulations.

Grace stood up and joined the applause, but her attention was focused on the figure standing beside her as his fingers slid across the frets and made a beautiful melody from the strings. Charlie had been completely removed from her mind as she became light-headed and felt herself falling back down on the bale.

Isaac never missed a lick on the guitar but turned and looked at her quizzically. She looked back up at him into his brown eyes and immediately fell in love.

"Grace. *Grace!*" A voice brought her back to consciousness as she turned and looked at her mother. "Grace. Honestly, child, I said to get up and go serve from the punch bowl. The reception is waiting."

"Oh, uh, sorry, Mama. I didn't hear you."

Hannah saw Grace staring at Isaac and immediately surmised what was happening with her youngest. She smiled and wondered if she would be planning another wedding within the next couple of years.

Grace took her place behind the punch bowl table and started ladling into the cups, never taking her eyes off Isaac, often spilling more onto the red-and-white checkered oilcloth than was making it into the cup.

When the reception had passed, Hattie and Harmon took a buggy into Moline for their honeymoon. All of the guests, save Isaac, had departed as Aaron, Hannah and Grace started the clean-up. Isaac offered to pitch in and was helping Grace with tasks that didn't need his assistance. Hannah nudged Aaron's elbow and nodded toward the two young people who were now engaged in a deep conversation. It was apparent that Isaac was just as taken with the red-headed fifteen-year old girl as she was with him.

When everything had been put away and no more chores were to be done, Aaron invited Isaac to stay for supper which he readily accepted. Aaron and Hannah sat on one side of the table laden with fried chicken, mashed potatoes and gravy, green beans and left-over wedding cake while Grace and Isaac sat opposite, a bit closer to each other than necessary.

The dinner conversation revealed that Isaac had moved with his parents, four brothers and three sisters to a farm just outside Port Byron from Davenport. He had plans on continuing his education as a businessman, going to college in Le Claire. To do that, however, he had to save his money. College had to remain only a dream for a year or two. Farm work, odd jobs, and music engagements would fund that dream.

Grace just had to know. "How many girls have you met since you moved here?"

"*Grace!*" exploded Hannah. "Mind your manners with personal questions like that."

Grace's blush nearly blended into the color of her red hair. "Sorry, Mama. Sorry, Isaac."

"That's Okay, Mrs. Reynolds," replied Isaac as he turned to Grace. "None I really cared about until today."

Grace nearly choked on a mouthful of potatoes and gravy. Isaac pounded her on the back to help her get air. She got up and ran out of the kitchen in embarrassment.

Isaac scrambled to his feet in dismay. "Oh, surely hope I didn't say something wrong, Mr. and Mrs. Reynolds."

Aaron chuckled. "No, 'spect, Isaac, that you only hit an itch that was a long time needed scratchin'."

Isaac looked confused and could only say, "Huh?"

"What I'm sayin' is that I think it might be a good idea for you to scratch that itch but for right now, it's probably best you head on home. I truly hope you'll come callin' again real soon."

"I'd like that, Mr. Reynolds. I truly would."

Grace, now that she had her own bedroom all to herself with Hattie gone, was not seen again for the rest of the night, trying to sort out her feelings. She tried to picture Charlie's face but couldn't seem to remember his features. A new face kept crowding into her mind.

37

Charlie

Dear Little Bit,

Well, here it is the middle of July 1905 and I been in New York City for several months. I growed tired of all the big city life and I left it all behind a couple of weeks ago.

I ran into Mr. Twain in the city and he said he had wired you a hundred dollers becuz he thot I was drownded. I ashored him I was very much alive and had helped the Wright boys get their flying machine into the air down there in North Carolina. I offered to pay him back the 100$ becuz I was alive but he said fer me to keep it as I needed the money worse than he did. I'm sorry iffen you thot I was dead, but now you know I'm alive, you can stop fretting.

I come into some extra dollars becuz sum folks were greatful to me for savin some children on a boat fire. Wasn't much a big deal to me but I guess the kids can have a full life now. I done what anyone woulda done.

I'm sorry to hafta tell you this but I kilt a man awhile back. He was coming afta me on a train down in Pencilvenya I think it was. Hope I speled that right. Anyway he was fixing to do me harm and I had no choice but to put an end to his evil ways and thots. I'm hopen you don't think any less of me cuz of it.

I left New York and made my way up to Boston. It's not as big as N.Y. but still just as busy. Too busy to soot me. I did get to see something called baseball. A man throws a ball to another man holding a bat and the batting person tries to hit the ball and get to one of three bases before getting put out. Each team gets three outs before turning it over to the other team. The Boston Americans were playing the Cleevland Naps. The Americans won the game. I rilly enjoyed it.

When I left Boston I hopped a train up to New Hampshir and that's where I am now. It sure is a pretty place with all the trees and forests. I found a boarding house in a little town called Concord. I always wanted to see the great lakes and that is where I'm headed tomorrow.

Well, I aint ever written such a long letter but want you ta know I am fine and I think about you ever day. Wished I was there to give you a hug. I'm enclosing a five dollar note for you to put aside for our wedding when I return.

Yore Charlie

Charlie posted his letter the next day on his way out of Concord.

Three weeks later the letter arrived at the Port Byron Mercantile which also served as the post office. Ezekiel Thomas was emptying the mail bag onto a table he used to sort letters before putting them into the different slots for residents to pick up.

Ezekiel didn't notice that one of the letters fell into a crevice between the table and the wall.

The letter was addressed to Miss Grace Reynolds, Port Byron, Illinois.

38
Grace

"G race, would you do me the honor of letting me take you to the barn dance Saturday night?"

Grace and Isaac were sitting on the porch swing on a cool-for-July evening. She couldn't shake loose the thoughts going through her head of Charlie standing up before the barn dance crowd playing his fiddle and his toe tapping to a square dance. She hesitated before speaking, "I think maybe I would like that, Isaac."

"And iffen you don't mind, I'll take along my guitar, play a few tunes and dedicate them to you."

"Oh, that's sweet. But you have to save some of the dances for me." She looked across at him, struck again by his handsome features. The moon was shining just off to his left, quickening her heart at the soft glow. "And don't go dancing with no other girls either," she added.

"Grace, there ain't any other girl there that would even tempt me."

"You do have the nicest way with words, Mr. Harmony."

She started playing with her name in her thoughts during the silence that followed. "Grace May Harmony. Grace May has Harmony. Gracie Harmony." She closed her eyes with a sigh. Another thought edged its way into her head. "Grace May Fisher. Little Bit Fisher. Gracie Fisher."

"An Indian Head Cent for your thoughts." Grace was startled out of her brief trance, practically forgetting where she was.

"Oh! I'm sorry! I . . . I was thinking that I . . . I can't wait until Saturday night."

Isaac broke into a smile and on an impulse, leaned over and kissed her.

Grace was so taken aback that the only thing she could think of was reaching out, taking his hand and kissing him back. A few moments passed before they broke away from each other, but she never let loose of his hand as she sighed.

Standing in the window behind them stood Hannah and Aaron, watching. "I do believe, dear husband," she whispered, "that our little girl has come out of her depression."

She took Aaron's hand in her own and squeezed it as the moon continued to shine and the swing still swayed as they watched a boy and a girl, wondering if they were falling in love.

39
Charlie

Archibald Anvil was a Civil War veteran in the First Regiment of U.S. Volunteer Sharpshooters, Company E. A likeable young man he joined the Union Army when he was just 15 years old, lying about his age because he wanted to see action. His Sharps rifle and his ability with it got Archie into the Army, impressing the man signing up volunteers by knocking a squirrel out of a tree from 300 feet.

He was excited when he found out he would be in the Second Battle of Bull Run in Manassas, Virginia, August, 1862, under Major General John Pope. Through miscommunications and inept commanders, the Union Army sustained heavy casualties with many taken prisoner and sent to the Confederate prison camp of Andersonville in Georgia.

When seventy-five men stepped off from the box car that carried them to the camp site they were immediately assaulted by the foul odor coming from the beyond the sixteen-foot stockade wall surrounding twenty-six acres of a swarming mass of humanity. Marched through the gate, Anvil and his fellow prisoners could not believe the utter hell into which they were to be imprisoned.

The gaunt men who used to be stalwart were now walking skeletons, bones clearly defined under pale skin. Men taken there fully expected to die and hundreds did, many committing suicide to end their incredible suffering.

Anvil endured this for three excruciating years until the War Between the States ended with General-in-Chief Robert E. Lee surrendering his sword to Ulysses S. Grant, Union Army Commander at Appomattox in Virginia.

Three years in Andersonville left Anvil a bitter, broken man as he made his way back to New Hampshire. It took three years before his body returned to the form it had when he enlisted, but health problems continued to plague him and he was no longer the likeable man he used to be and now shunned all friends, neighbors, and family. He preferred to live alone on his farm outside Henniker, a small hamlet west of Concord.

In the thirty years following Appomattox he was seldom seen and considered a recluse. He was growing lonely and by 1895 he decided he needed to take a wife to tend to his needs. A neighbor a few miles from his farm had eight sons and seven daughters. One of the girls was just thirteen-years-old when Anvil bargained with the father to let him have one of the girls for twenty bushels of corn that the man needed to feed his hogs.

Annie Comstock was reasonably attractive but lived so far away from neighbors it was quite unlikely she would attract the attention of any of the young men in the area. Her father saw an opportunity to have one less mouth to feed and have fodder for his sows in the deal. It was a win-win for him and for Anvil. Not so much for Annie.

Anvil lived up to his name. He was a hard man and not much taken with the foolishness of romance. As far as he was concerned there was no need to make the union official with a preacher. Annie's first night in the Anvil home was filled with pain and embarrassment as the forty-six-year-old man and the thirteen-year-old girl consummated their joining together on a mattress of corn shucks and lice.

In the ten years hence she had given birth to six children and she was tired beyond description. At just twenty-three, she looked far older. Her youngest was a daughter, three years old named Bessie, a delightful child who was the darling of the household . . . for everyone but Archie.

Archie's attitude towards people continued to coarsen. He blamed Annie for getting pregnant when he could barely make ends meet on his un-productive farm and giving him yet another setting at the table that he couldn't afford. All the children lived in fear of their father, and his tirades against them always ended with Annie taking the brunt of the abuse in trying to protect her brood.

Nearby farmers would sometimes offer to bring over a side of beef, a bag of potatoes or something that would help the struggling family, but Archie shunned all such overtures. He wasn't going to admit to anyone that he needed help or assistance and, as a result, the house was full of malnourished people, clad in rags, and often sick from their environment.

One October day in 1905, Archie was digging a well. He had used a witching stick that told him water flowed under his farm. He saw it as an end to his problems and worked furiously digging a hole. Deeper and deeper he went as his two oldest sons, aged nine and seven, pulled up buckets of dirt and threw over the fence into a pasture as they worked into the late afternoon.

Charlie was enjoying the early onset of fall as New Hampshire was turning into a blaze of orange, red, and yellow foliage. He had had enough of hopping trains and just walking greatly appealed to him. He had passed through Concord the day before and wanted to get further south before winter set in. The idea of tromping through snow did not hold any charm for him, and New Hampshire had the reputation of deep snows sweeping down out of Canada.

He was trying to conserve whatever money he had left from the gifts he'd received for his rescue of five children from grateful people in New York City. Whatever work he could pick up along the way helped.

He passed a town called Henniker when he saw activity on a small farm. He turned into the broken down gate and spotted a man climbing out of a well. Farm animals milled throughout the dirt yard trying to find a blade of grass to nibble . . . cows, hogs, chickens, and a dog who was furiously trying to get at a flea on his rump.

Several children in ragged clothes were playing in front of the house. A woman was on the porch of what could only be described as something above a hut but not quite a shanty. She appeared to be patching up a pair of overalls that already were being held together by other patches.

Charlie strode up to the man and said, "Howdy."

Anvil turned to the stranger and grumbled, "Wha' the hell you want?"

Charlie was a bit taken aback from the demeanor of the farmer in front of him. "Sorry to interrupt your work, sir. I'm just passin' through and was wonderin' if I could do some work for you to get a bite to eat. I've dug a few wells myself in my day and could be of some help to you."

"Get the hell off my land. I don't need nobody's help. Got my young'uns to give me all the help I need."

"Well, no need to get all quarrelsome about it. I'm just lookin' for a bite. I'll be on my way then."

"Good."

As Charlie turned to go back to the road he glanced over at the woman who mouthed the word, "Sorry".

He tipped his hat to her. "Ma'am."

Anvil's voice grew even angrier towards him. "Stop talkin' to my woman and get yore arse off my property."

Charlie ignored him and continued back to the road.

Anvil then directed his venom towards Annie. "Keep yore eyes to yourself, woman, and stop tryin' to lure ever man you see. I'll give you the worse horse whippin' yet iffen I ever catch you at it again."

"Sorry, Archie, didden mean no harm by it."

"Frederick, get yore ass back over here and take this bucket out to the fence."

"Alright, Pa." The boy scampered towards the well.

Anvil stepped back on the ladder and descended back into the hole. A hog started rooting near the hole and knocked the bucket of dirt at the edge into the well. It tumbled into the pit, hitting Anvil squarely on the top of the head, breaking his neck and knocking him to the bottom where he lay motionless.

The children and Annie all rushed to the well not knowing if Archie had managed to avoid the bucket. The closest was Bessie who tripped and fell into the hole, dropping twenty feet, hitting a supporting beam and landing on the body of her father. Her breath was knocked out of her as she gasped for air.

"Bessie!"

Annie's scream caught Charlie's attention, and he turned to see six children and the woman rushing to the edge of the well. He ran back onto the farm to see what happened. The children were crying and Annie kept screaming for Bessie.

"What's going on?" Charlie yelled at Annie trying to make himself overheard from the loud commotion.

"There! There!" she pointed at the well. "My husband went into the hole and my daughter fell in on top of him."

Charlie stepped up to the edge and peered into the darkness. All he could see was dust rising up from the hole and what appeared to be a supporting beam about ten feet down hanging precariously and about ready to give way. The makeshift ladder was busted from the weight of the bucket on its way down as it fell.

"Hey, Mister! You all right?" Charlie paused to try and hear something but all he heard was the panting of a child trying to catch her breath.

Charlie called out again but still received no response from the man.

"Can you climb down there," asked Annie, "and get my baby out?"

"No. First of all, the ladder is busted and secondly, that support beam will give way if anybody puts any weight on it. That would drop it down for sure and that wouldn't be good."

"We gotta do something! *Bessie!*" she screamed again.

"Mama," came a feeble cry.

"Quiet!" hissed Charlie. "I hear your child crying."

"Oh, Gawd! Oh, Gawd! Oh, Gawd! My baby is alive. What about my husband?"

"No. All I get is her crying. Now be quiet and let me think."

Charlie knew there was no way he would be able to go into the hole, even if he had the ladder. Throwing a rope down could prove fatal, both to the little girl and to her father. There was no guarantee he would be able to tie on to the rope and even by doing so it could dislodge that support beam.

"Okay. Here's what I want you to do. Get all these kids out of here. Send the oldest for help and one of you get me a shovel. I'll have to dig a second hole away from this one and then tunnel over to where the little girl has fallen. *Go! Get!*"

"There ain't nobody gonna help us. My husband has chased off any neighbor that came calling."

"Do as I say! I can't believe anybody wouldn't stop and help for the life of a child. *Get going!*"

Annie instructed the boy named Frederick to run to the next farm and see if they would help and went to get a shovel from the barn.

"Tell that farmer," yelled Charlie after the boy, "to get as many men as he can and bring ropes, shovels, wheel barrels and a mule with a hoist and pulley."

"Yes, sir," said Frederick as he ran as fast as he could back to the road.

Charlie grabbed the shovel from Annie's hands and started digging furiously about five feet away from the well. He only hoped the ground was not rocky slowing his work. That hope was dashed when the shovel clanged on a rock. He started digging around it and finally uprooted the six-pound stone from the ground. It wasn't long until he was soaked with sweat. His heart was racing, his adrenaline pushing him as he took large stabs with the shovel, occasionally running into a rock which was always dislodged easily.

Annie passed him a drink of water whenever he requested one, and the children helped by carrying the dirt away from the second hole.

By the time he was three feet down he heard the sounds of several buckboards coming up the road. He turned to see three wagons full of men rushing onto the farm. Annie was amazed to see this outpouring of aid from neighbors who had always been shunned by her husband.

The men in the wagons hit the ground on the run and all started talking at once until Charlie held up his hand to quiet them. He explained what he knew: that Anvil had been hit by a falling bucket and his three-year-old daughter had tumbled in after him. No sound could be heard from him, but the little girl could be heard crying. He explained that dropping a rope into the hole was not possible because of the danger of it caving in on top of the two at the bottom.

"I'm digging a second hole down to the approximate depth of the well and we can then tunnel across to reach them."

Three men jumped into the hole Charlie had started, and he got out to rest. He instructed the others to help carry the dirt and rocks away. "We need a hoist and pulley built over the new hole," he said, "so that we can pull up the dirt as they go deeper into the ground. A couple of you go and find three stout ten-foot poles that can be erected into a triangle over the top."

Two of them grabbed axes and hurried into the timber behind the barn as others pulled rope and the pulley from the wagons.

He turned to Annie, "Ma'am, you and the young 'uns stay back out of the way. Bring as many pails of water you can find so the men can fend away their thirst. If you got the food, start making sandwiches."

Just as he said that, a fourth wagon pulled into the yard with several wives of the men who had arrived earlier. They started pulling out plates and bowls of food and setting them up in the wagons circling around the well.

Annie hustled her children back up to the porch and stood amazed at the outpouring of compassion from her neighbors, knowing in her heart that she didn't deserve it.

Hour after hour passed as the men took shifts in digging down into the earth. The pulley and hoist were erected over the hole, and buckets were being lifted to the surface and carried away from the work. Soon a small hill of dirt and rocks was building in the center of the yard.

By nightfall lanterns were brought out as the work continued. A man at the original well reported that he no longer could hear the child's cries that brought choked tears from Annie.

"Don't worry, ma'am," said Charlie. "It's probably because she just fell asleep. No more dirt has fallen into the hole and the support seems to be holding so far."

A couple of the women came to console Annie and to assure her the men were doing all they could to help Bessie.

A man was hoisted out of the hole and Charlie stepped in to take his turn. "It looks like we're about twenty feet down and we're ready to start the tunnel over," the man said. "But we have a new problem. There's water seeping into our new hole and it's getting muddy down there."

Charlie nodded grimly, grabbed a lantern, and signaled to be lowered into the hole. As he reached the bottom, he stepped into three inches of water and could see more creeping up past his shoes. He started digging a new hole towards the well, knowing he had to get through five feet. Another man dropped in beside him with a bucket to haul up the new dirt.

"While I'm digging," said Charlie, "you haul up water as well as dirt. We don't have much time before we are submerged." He dug furiously making a hole about three feet in diameter. Charlie was short in stature, weighing no more than 150 pounds. He wasn't sure he would be able to drag the husband through the hole, if he was even alive, but he knew the little girl could be saved.

Spade after spade, new dirt was loosened and passed back through the connecting hole. Charlie was dead tired, but refused to let his muscles dictate his fatigue. Each stab of the shovel brought him closer.

"Hurry up, mister," cried the man behind him. The water's up to my knees and still rising."

Charlie didn't waste any breath on responding, but pushed himself beyond what he thought he could endure. He had to be close now and there was no time to stop and rest.

Dig. Push dirt back. Dig. Push dirt back.

"Water's between my knees and hips," hollered the man.

I know, thought Charlie. Shut up. I'm doing the best I can.

But it was just the boost he needed as he pushed the spade with one mighty heave and felt the wall of dirt give way. He had gotten through. A welcome whoosh swept over him as the cross circulation of air from the well helped him breathe a bit better.

"I'm through," he yelled back. "I made it!"

Men at the top of the well heard Charlie and relayed the message to others. "He's through! He's through!"

Everyone rushed excitedly towards the two holes. "Stay back!" someone yelled. "We don't want things caving in on them!"

Charlie enlarged the hole as he felt water creeping along his legs from the rescue hole. "Pass me the lantern," he yelled.

The man crawled as far as his body would allow him with the lantern pushing it past Charlie's knees. He grabbed it and worked it up to the lip of the tunnel and peered in to see Bessie just waking up and rubbing her eyes. She was lying on top of her dead father.

"I want my Mama," she said.

"Alright, sweetheart. You crawl over here towards me and I'll take you to your Mama."

Bessie started crawling towards Charlie when the supporting beam above her finally gave way and started crashing towards the bottom.

Charlie heard the crack of wood and knew he had only a split second to grab the child and pull her to safety. He dropped the lantern plunging the hole into total darkness.

Grabbing her by her ragged dress he pulled the child roughly into the tunnel just as wood, rocks and dirt crashed down, burying Anvil in what would be his final resting place.

Charlie knew he didn't have much time because the water now covered three inches of the tunnel. He frantically pulled Bessie back into the rescue hole and handed her off to the man standing waist deep in mud and sludge.

Clutching the child to his chest, he yelled to the top to pull him up, and he rose slowly as the girl whimpered that she wanted her Mama.

At the top he handed the girl off and yelled to get that rope back to the bottom to pull up Charlie.

Just as the rope again descended to the bottom, water surged into the hole as it burst open from an underground river. Within a few seconds Charlie was completely submerged in a raging torrent of water and mud. He barely had time to grab a lungful of air before the unrelenting wall of water cascaded into the hole pushing him violently upwards. As he rose he felt the descending rope and desperately grabbed it. Shooting out of the hole in a geyser of water, Charlie's head barely missed the overhanging pulley support, and he landed with a body punishing slam into the pile of dirt that had come from the hole.

Every man, woman, and child, with the exception of Annie and Bessie, rushed towards Charlie fully expecting to find a dead man.

Charlie, who'd had the wind knocked out of him, lay motionless on the mound of dirt as water continued to shoot geysers
from both holes drenching everyone within fifty feet of the new
twin wells.

They all gathered around Charlie, thinking he had drowned
in the onslaught of water, jumped back in fright as he suddenly
sputtered and opened his eyes.

"*He's alive!*" someone yelled, and the crowd broke into applause
and "Hoorahs" as someone helped him to his feet.

Still dazed, Charlie could only gasp, "Well, that weren't no fun.
What happened?"

"You saved her, mister. You saved the little girl," said a woman. Everyone was pounding him on the back and trying to
shake his hand.

"Oh, good," was all he said modestly. "Glad I could help." He
turned to Annie who was clutching Bessie tightly to her chest.
"Sorry 'bout your husband, ma'am, but it was him who saved
your daughter when she landed on top of him."

"Thank you! Thank you! Thank you! Say thank you to the
man, Bessie."

Bessie looked up shyly at her rescuer. "Thank you, mister," she
said in a whisper and then buried her face in her mother's chest.

Charlie reached out and placed his hand on the little girl's
head. "You're welcome, sweetheart. I'm glad you're okay."

40
Isaac

The family had come to accept that Grace was coming out of her depression over the news of Charlie's death. After all, no letters from him and the eyewitness report from someone no less the stature of Mark Twain was proof enough for the Reynolds family.

There also was no doubt about the intentions of Isaac Harmony. The musician seemed to have captured the heart of the 15-year-old Grace. They spent as much time together as they could, and Hannah got to the point that she knew to fix enough food for the family dinner as it might have to include one extra person.

Isaac knew he had to appeal to the parents as much as he did for their daughter. He assisted Aaron with chores on the farm that required the strength of a man who was used to hard work. The eighteen years he spent growing up on a farm in northern Illinois had hardened his muscles and his endurance.

He often relieved Aaron behind the plow, would jump up whenever Grace or Hannah entered the room, and rush to seat them at the dinner table. His manners, his speech, his very demeanor were all characteristics of good husband material.

He was respectful of his relationship to Grace, having only held her hand and never attempted to kiss her again after that evening on the porch unless it was invited. Grace was never one to shy away from anything, but Charlie was never that far from her mind. She was afraid that if she got too heavily involved with Isaac, she would be disrespectful of Charlie's memory.

So Isaac was kept at arm's length, but there was never any doubt of her attraction to him. Lying in her bed at night, unable to sleep, her thoughts were in constant turmoil. The thoughts would finally give way to sleep only to be caught up again in dreams. One such dream seemed to be recurring where she was married to Isaac when Charlie appeared at her door. The hurt she saw expressed in his eyes turned the dream into a nightmare where the two men fought each other in a deadly battle that ended with the murder of one of them. This always ended with Grace waking up screaming and in a drenching sweat. More than once, Hannah would get up from her own sleep and spend the rest of the night holding Grace, comforting her.

The courtship continued for months, and Isaac came to be as much a part of the family as he was to his own. He had designs on possibly marrying Grace and often smiled to himself as if he had an inner secret. He needed to make himself appear as a potential husband.

On a warm spring day in early 1906, Grace invited him to go to the spot where she had found her Grandmother Lucinda a few years before. Isaac picked up his guitar, thinking he might serenade his love and maybe do more than just hold hands. They climbed the hill to the top and sat on a rock overlooking the Mississippi River as butterflies flitted among the jasmine flowers.

Grace was deep in thought and Isaac sensed that, staying quiet as she prayed in her mind, calling to Lucinda's counsel on what she should do about her future. Isaac reached over to hold her hand, but Grace drew back, folding her arms into her lap.

Isaac spoke just one word. "Sorry."

She did not acknowledge she had even heard him. Isaac picked up his guitar and started strumming a gentle melody.

Grace thought back on all the stories her grandmother had told her. For whatever reason, one of the stories came into her head.

Many moons ago the Sun lived in the sky making her daily sweep from the East into the West. Every day She would stop when it was at its highest peak to have dinner with her daughter.

She always complained about the people on Maka, *the earth because they would never look directly at her and would always scrunch up their faces into a squint.*

"Look how ugly those people are," she said to her brother the Moon. "See what their i'toye, *faces do when they look at me?"*

"I think they are a oiyokipi oyate, *handsome people, because they always smile when they look at me at night."*

But the Sun wanted her revenge so when she stopped to have dinner with her daughter, she burned fiery hot, enough that it would kill people on the earth. The people became concerned that soon no one would be left because of the heat so they decided to kill Sun.

Two Sachems from the Great Lakota Tribe and the Great
Cherokee Tribe made up a medicine and drank it down under the
darkness of night so Sun wouldn't see them. The powerful medicine turned them into wamduška, snakes. One became an Adder
and the other a Timber Rattler. They would wait until Sun visited
her daughter at noon and try to bite her. The Adder waited by the
doorway to Daughter's house and when Sun appeared, he rose to
strike but Sun's rays were too hot and blinded him so that he only
spit out a yellow poison, as it does to this day when he tries to bite.
This scared Timber Rattler and he slithered into the forest without
trying to bite Sun.

The two tribes now needed new Sachems so they anointed
men who said they would try to kill Sun. They, too, made up a
strong medicine. One became a large horned beast and the other
a Copperhead. The tribes figured the beast would certainly be big
enough and strong enough to kill Sun, but Copperhead got too
impatient and curled up at the door of daughter's house, ready to
strike Sun when she entered for her dinner. Daughter came out to
see where her mother might be and the startled Copperhead struck,
killing her.

When Sun found her daughter dead she became very saddened
and disappeared into the house, spreading darkness over the land.
The tribes were now concerned because they had no Sun to warm
them during the day and grow their crops. They conferred with
each other and decided they would have to bring the daughter back
from the Spirit World. They decided they would send ten men, each
with a branch from a taŋpacaŋtaŋka, sycamore tree.

The men traveled to the Spirit World and would stand in a circle.
When Daughter entered the ring, a man would touch her with his

blessed sycamore branch. She circled around the ring until each man touched her with his branch. When the last man touched her with his branch, she fell out of the ring and they grabbed her and put her into a box. They slammed the lid tight so she could not escape. Other ghosts never seemed to notice what had happened.

On their journey back to the Alive World, Daughter started crying to be let out but the men ignored her. First she wanted water, then she wanted something to eat and her last plea was to crack the box a little so that she might have a breath of fresh air as she felt she was suffocating.

One of the men felt pity, and opened the box just a bit. He heard a "whish" sound like you hear from a du'ta, *redbird. He quickly closed the box before any of the other men could see what he had done.*

This is how we have the du'ta *and when you hear the Redbird's cry you know she is happy to be out of the box, able to breathe.*

The men, upon returning to their land, found Sun anxiously awaiting because she wanted to see her daughter again, as she always prepared a fine dinner and Sun was hungry. When the box was opened, it was empty and Sun was very grieved. As she wept, her tears fell upon the earth causing a Great Minitaŋ, *Flood. The people were afraid they would all be drowned so they prepared a big feast for Sun. They all danced around a circle and sang their best songs.*

Sun soon opened her eyes and saw what the people were doing for her so she stopped crying. She was so pleased that she forgot her grief and smiled.

Grace came out of her trance, vaguely aware that Isaac was quietly playing his guitar. She turned and smiled at him, leaned over and kissed him on his cheek.

She thought she had finally shed herself of her grief.

41

Charlie

O nce again, Charlie found himself embarrassed at all the attention he was receiving after rescuing Bessie from the well. He felt the praise was entirely unjustified. After all, anybody would have done the same.

Charlie reluctantly accepted Annie's pleas to stay for a couple more days before he continued his journey back to Illinois. He was anxious to get back to Grace and the life he envisioned with the girl he truly loved.

He found Annie to be a very charming woman. She almost seemed relieved to be freed from her husband's violent nature. She no longer lived in the constant fear of being beaten merely because the potatoes were lumpy or she couldn't keep a crying baby quiet.

Charlie could see that the meager property could be improved into a livable, sustaining farm. The front porch was falling down, the corral needed work, and the adjacent well he'd dug to get at Bessie could actually be used for drinking water if he could figure out a way to seal off the tunnel between the two. Anvil's corpse was contaminating the source and would either have to be removed from the well to be of any use or dig a new one. He built a cap over both holes to keep the water contained.

He set up a place where he could sleep in the barn and then set about his projects to help Annie reshape the home into suitable living conditions. Every morning, every evening he would sit at her kitchen table and eat whatever she could manage to put in front of him. Bessie found Charlie to be the exact opposite from her brutal father and seemed to be under his feet during all of his waking hours.

Annie had never had any romance in her life, and the only men she knew were her father and Archie. She looked forward to the times when Charlie walked into the door for his meals and soon took to paying more attention to how well she looked, combing out her hair, staying scrubbed and wearing her one and only nice dress, a rather drab piece of material that was enhanced by a few scrap pieces of lace she had in her sewing basket.

Two weeks after the well incident, Charlie was still at the Anvil farm and was reasonably close to finishing his list of things to do that improved the home. As he crossed the threshold for his supper that night, long after the sun had gone down, he was greeted by the aroma of fried chicken, hot biscuits, and cooked greens. Looking around for the usual batch of children that were always running around, he was stunned by the silence of the house.

"I put the children all to bed, Charlie, so you could enjoy a little peace and quiet," she explained while smoothing out her apron.

"Ah, I was wondering." He noted that Annie had loosened her hair from its' usual bun and was falling on her shoulders. It had an auburn glint, not as red as Grace's hair, but she still reminded him of her.

"Your supper is ready," she said as she held the chair out for him. Charlie caught the faintest hint of rose water as he settled down.

"Thought I might join you, iffen it's alright with you."

Charlie looked up at her and suddenly saw her in a new light . . . one he hadn't seen before. "I reckon I'd like that, Mrs. Anvil. Please sit."

"Charlie, you've been calling me that for the past two weeks. I'd take it for a real fancy if you'd call me by my given name. We're friends, ain't we? So call me Annie."

"Annie it is," he replied, grabbing a piece of chicken.

"I can't tell you how much I 'preciate you staying on and helpin' me out."

"Well, your hospitality has been most welcomed. These are mighty fine biscuits."

When they had finished their meal, Annie invited him out to sit on the newly repaired porch. "Sech a nice fall evening. 'Spect we'll be seeing snow fore long," she said after they settled into a pair of rockers.

Charlie had recently taken to smoking a pipe and pulled it out, tamped some tobacco into the bowl and put a match to it. He drew in a lungful of smoke and exhaled, watching it drift into the October air.

Annie tried to choose her words perfectly, but blurted out, "It's gotta be cold mean out in that barn. Why don't you stay here in the house tonight where it's warm?"

Charlie turned and looked at her with a questioning look on his face. "Now I've seen the inside of your house, Annie. There's only two rooms for sleeping. The children's and yours. I'd have to bunk down under the kitchen table."

Annie bit her lip, fighting for the right words. "Well, I was thinkin' maybe you could stay in my room." She felt herself blush a bright red.

"With me," she added, looking him in the eye.

Charlie took a long look at Annie's soft curves. Her open neck dress revealed just a peek at what lay underneath. The only woman he had ever kissed was a red-headed girl that he could see even now, pictured swinging on her gate. He'd had plenty of opportunities in his three years of travelling. Opportunities never taken.

"Annie, I told you about Grace back home. She's waiting for me, and I think maybe I'll stay in the barn tonight."

Annie sat silently for a few minutes before she spoke. "I'm sorry if I offended you. Didn't mean nothin' by it. I jest get so lonesome for a kind word or caress. Never got any of that from Archie." She dabbed at her eyes. "Guess I'll go clean up supper dishes and go to bed. Good night, Charlie."

"Good night, Annie."

Annie couldn't sleep. She tossed and turned, mulling over and over in her mind the handsome features of the boy sleeping out in her barn. *"After all,"* she reasoned, *"he's only seventeen. I'm twenty-three. I ain't much to look at."* She turned and cried into her pillow. *"I'm just so **dang** lonesome."* She made a decision and got out of bed.

Charlie, too, couldn't get to sleep. The barn was cold, the cow in the next stable over had just dropped a smelly pile into the fresh straw, and a hen that just hatched a brood of chicks was quietly clucking over them as they cheeped, nestling under the wings of their mother.

His thoughts were not just of Grace, but by the memory of that open necked dress. He had never been with a woman, never wanted to, except for Grace, until tonight. He listened to the sounds of the barn and finally sleep came to him.

He didn't hear the barn door as it creaked open but became suddenly aware of someone lifting his blanket and crawling in beside him.

"I just want to snuggle, Charlie," Annie whispered into his ear. "We don't got to do nothin'." She spooned into his back and put her arm under his. Charlie reached up and took her hand and held it close to his chest. She felt warm, and he became equally aware that she was a woman and he was a man.

Charlie never said a word. He just held her hand and felt her heavy breathing as it steadily became more apparent she had fallen asleep.

He no longer had any thoughts of Grace as he, too, drifted into a dream. It was filled with soft curves and the faint aroma of rose water.

42

Isaac

Well, cousin, it looks like that little filly is falling for me. You're right about one thing, though. She sure is a pretty thing. I think maybe another week or two and I'll pop the question to her. I've got Charlie Fisher pushed so far out of her mind that the taking will be easy. Might even get to bed her down before the wedding."

Isaac pulled on his pipe and passed it to his companion, sitting opposite him on a hay bale. The man accepted the pipe and took a deep inhale of smoke, slowly blowing it out. "Told you it would be easy. Now remember, we got to set up a time and place. When the moment's jest right, I'll come in and be happy with seconds."

Duggie Hayes passed the pipe back to his cousin, lay back and dreamed of the moment when he would get his revenge on Grace and her whole family. He only wished Charlie Fisher was alive so he would know what he'd done to his precious little love.

43

Charlie

Annie woke up at the sound of a rooster crowing and it took her a moment to wonder why she was lying on a pile of straw in the barn. She dreamily remembered and rolled over to snuggle in closer to Charlie, hoping he would change his mind and give her the closeness she so desperately needed.

All she got was an armful of air. Charlie had already gotten up and must be tending to his chores, she thought. She suddenly realized that the sun's rays were creeping into the barn's doors and she would have six hungry children up and expecting their breakfast. She got up, brushed off the straw clinging to her dress and made her way to the house.

By the time Annie was ladling scrambled eggs onto six plates, Charlie was three miles away, heading southwest. His brain was clogged with the memory of Annie's body nestled in with his and how he had almost given in to the temptation of what she was offering. The closeness of her breasts against his back had almost been too much for him to endure.

He had to push those thoughts out of his mind. He was sorry he didn't get to say goodbye to Bessie because the child had been clinging close to his side constantly. One time, a few days earlier, she had called him "Papa", and it melted his heart. "Sorry, Bessie," he whispered to himself.

Right now he had to keep pushing himself to get away from the deep snows that would soon cover the state. There would be snow further south but not at the depths New Hampshire received.

When he came across rail tracks that went South/North, he followed them, hoping for a southbound freight train. Two days later he got lucky and hopped a train on the Concord line. Occasionally hopping off for food, making switches between lines, and seeking out a day job to earn extra money, he soon found himself near Harrisburg, Pennsylvania, after crossing the state of New York.

Charlie spent most of the time with his feet dangling out the doorway of a boxcar. He knew his father had been born in Harrisburg and thought it would be interesting if he could find some relatives in the area before heading due west to Illinois.

Days turned to weeks, weeks to a month as Charlie rode the rails south into Pennsylvania, often jumping off whatever train he was on to find work. It wasn't hard to find some farmer who needed extra help ploughing a field, cutting hay, mending fences and, on two occasions, digging a well. For his efforts he received fifty cents a day.

Stowing his earnings into a sock he kept tied with a string around his neck, he rarely spent any of it because the farmers would provide meals or a place to bunk down in their barn.

Quite a few times he caught the eye of a daughter. Charlie's handsome features and hard-working nature made him a target for marriage-aged girls. He always managed to avoid unwanted overtures for his attention.

He'd just crossed the Pennsylvania border when he hopped off a freight and went looking for work. At the third farm he approached he found a farmer toiling in his field raking hay. Charlie asked for, and received, a job finishing the field. He figured it would take about three days if he really put his shoulder into it.

"Name is Clayton Constantine. Come on up to the house for supper when it turns dark."

Charlie grabbed the man's rake and went to work. At dusk, he washed up outside the barn and went to the house for his meal. Entering the kitchen, he walked right into a blonde girl who, without a doubt, was the most beautiful creature he'd ever seen.

"Oops, sorry, ma'am. Didn't see you standing there."

"Well, that's a fine howdy-doo, here I am fixing your supper, and you don't even see me." Charlie's legs felt weak and his pulse started pumping. Her voice was as smooth as any honey he'd ever seen come out of a hive.

"This here is my daughter, Clementine" said Clayton. "My wife passed on a year back, and she's kind of taken over as woman of the house. The rest of my young 'uns there at the table are Claude, Carl, Carla, Cassie, Caleb, and the baby down there is Beth."

Charlie turned up an eyebrow at the child's name.

Clayton felt he had to explain. "Yep, I know what you're thinking, but I couldn't think of no other girl's name that started with a C."

Charlie thought, "You couldn't think of Constance, Catherine, Cynthia, Christine," but he kept silent.

"Well, I'm pleased to meet each and every one of you. My name is Charlie, and I'm passing through on my way to Harrisburg."

"Whatcha gonna do in Harrisburg, Mr. Charlie?" Clementine's voice seemed to take the air out of the room. Charlie had to grab the back of a chair to keep from stumbling. He wasn't quite sure if it was from being so tired from his day's labors or from the presence of the honey blonde standing at the stove as she turned over a pork chop in her frying pan.

"I'm . . . I'm . . . well, I'm going to look up some kinfolk, uh, 'cuz my daddy came from Harrisburg, and I want to see if any of them were, uh, were, still living, um, there."

Charlie felt like an idiot. His words were coming out wrong, and he felt like he was mumbling. He tried not to stare at the girl but just couldn't help it.

"Nevah been to Harrisburg," she said, "fact is, I ain't been no place in all my sixteen years. I went into Mansfield once last year, but it's just a little bitty place and weren't much to see once I got there. Sit down, Mr. Charlie, and let me serve you some chops, taters and gravy, and collards."

Charlie was thankful for the invitation as she brushed up against him and forked a chop out of the frying pan and put it on his plate. "Thank you, ma'am."

Clementine looked down at him and gave a warm smile. "Now none of that 'ma'am' stuff, you hear. You call me Clementine, or Clemmie." She continued around the table dropping a pork chop onto each of the children's plates.

"Kin you cut my meat, mister?" Charlie turned to the little girl named Cassie and noticed she had a withered right arm. "I only got me but one arm."

"I sure can, little one," he said as he took his knife and portioned the chop into several tiny pieces.

"Cassie was borned with a arm that don't work none," explained Clayton.

"Well," replied Charlie, "the good Lord gave you one good arm and a pretty smile, so I'm thinking you'll do just fine."

Cassie beamed and placed her good hand on Charlie's arm. "Thank you, Mr. Charlie. Nobody's ever told me I had a pretty smile afore."

After the meal was finished, Clementine washed the dishes, and Charlie grabbed a towel and dried them. "You don't gotta do women's work, Mr. Charlie. Go sit out on the porch a spell."

"After a fine meal like that, Clementine, I think I have to help the hands that prepared it." He reached out to take a plate from her and his hand fell over hers and, for just the briefest moment, the two stood frozen in place. She turned to look at him and gave another one of the smiles that seemed to come from somewhere inside her. "Uh, oh, sorry, didn't mean to seem fresh," Charlie blurted.

"You weren't, Charlie." It was the first time she hadn't used the title 'Mister' in front of his name.

She took the dirty water in her pan and poured it into a slop bucket. "I have to put the little ones to bed. Go on outside on the porch and mebbe I'll join you in a bit."

"I'd like that, Clementine. I'd like that very much."

Fifteen minutes later, the screen door opened, and she came outside, took off her apron and placed it over the porch banister to dry in the night air. "Pa has already gone to bed, too, so I reckon it's just the two of us." She settled into the rocker beside his and gently rocked back and forth.

Charlie couldn't think of anything to say, but finally broke the silence.

"A fine evening but I smell some rain in the air. Hope I can get that hay into the barn before it happens."

"You sound like you're a traveling man, Charlie. You been to any big cities?

"The biggest city I've ever seen . . . New York City. I was there several months back."

"*New York City!* Well, I do wish I could see me that. Tell me about it."

For the next two hours, Charlie found it very easy to talk to this beautiful girl. He told her about Buffalo Bill, New Orleans, Mark Twain, the Wright Brothers, and his journey into the city of New York.

"I never in my life ever thought people would build one layer of a building on top of another layer. I saw some places there that had twenty floors. And people? People were everywhere."

He left out the part of his story about saving lives in the East River. "Then a spell back I helped people pull a little baby girl out of a well."

"You have got to be the most interesting person I know, Charlie. I imagine you're quite tired. Best if you get to bed before the sun rises." Clementine got up from her rocker, reached down, and patted his hand. "Good night."

"Good night, Clementine. Reckon I'll see you at sunrise."
Charlie got up and watched her disappear into the house, lingered for a moment and turned to the barn.

Again, Charlie struggled with his emotions as he tried to fall asleep in the hay loft on a mattress of burlap and straw. Clementine's face kept merging with that of Grace and back again. He knew Grace was waiting for him because he had written two letters telling her so. He pictured her in his mind but Grace's red hair kept turning into blonde and her face changed into Clementine's. He finally fell asleep two hours before he was to get up and take his rake into the hay field.

44

Grace

G race had gone from a skinny pig-tailed tomboy to her sixteenth year as an auburn-tressed, beauty sought by every like-aged boy within ten miles of the Reynolds farm. She was not vain in any sense of the word, but when she looked into the reflection of her hand mirror, she secretly marveled at what had happened to her face and body since Charlie had left on his journey with Buffalo Bill.

She wondered what Charlie would have thought of her now. She still mourned his death but with the attention of all the boys, her relationship with Isaac and her farm chores, the memory of his face receded in her mind.

She was still drawn to the rock on a cliff towering above the Mississippi near where her grandmother had passed away in her arms and often visited it to talk to her. She felt a connection to her grandmother that no one else would ever understand. It was during these times that she could talk to Lucinda and have conversations with her. She never felt the need to use the bag hanging from her neck.

In late October 1906 she couldn't shake the feeling that something was amiss, but she was unsure of what could be troubling her. Her relationship with Isaac seemed to be going well. She had finally accepted that Charlie had died. Something, however, was nagging at her, and she was at a loss as to what it might be.

She made a decision and would seek the wisdom of her Lakota heritage. Grace again made the trek to the rock and sat, feeling the breeze and promise of an early snow on her face. Taking the bag from her neck, she followed Lucinda's instructions. She had brought a canteen, cup and a bowl with her as well as matches. She had scooped up water from a spring along the path into the canteen. She built a campfire and warmed herself from the chilly wind.

Taking out the lock of hair from the bag, she put it to her nose and for nearly half an hour inhaled the essence of her grandmother as memories swept over her, recalling the many times she sat at Lucinda's knees, hearing stories of Indian spirits, of sacred formulas using plants and seeds from the area and tales of Lakota practices, their wisdom and knowledge of an almost forgotten culture.

Finally, she put the hair in the bowl and cupping her hands over it she put a match to the lock. The wind was blowing rather strongly and it took three tries before the hair ignited, leaving a small pile of ashes in the bottom of the bowl.

Adding the herbs to the ashes, she poured a cup of water into the bowl and placed it on the fire, watching it come to a slow boil. She poured the concoction into the cup, stirring it with a small twig. Holding it to her lips she blew on it to help cool it down, inhaling the steam which seemed to immediately make her light-headed.

With a bit of trepidation, she took a sip, then two and finally swallowed all the contents of the cup as she leaned back on the rock and waited for something to happen. The awful taste gave her face a pinched expression.

Suddenly, Grace was hit by a stomach spasm that doubled her over. She tried to brace herself on the ground, but it was as if the earth abruptly disappeared under her and she felt herself falling into a deep chasm. She tried flailing her arms but they were dead to her and she couldn't even feel her legs.

The moon, the sun, the planets, and the stars all whizzed by her in what seemed like an eternity. She felt herself land on what must have been an asteroid but strangely she felt no pain. She tried to sit up but nothing worked. The bitter taste of the brew she had taken lingered in her mouth but the stomach spasm seemed to have passed.

She struggled to open her eyes as they fluttered with a great heaviness. When they finally opened, she found herself still sitting beside the same rock where she had cradled her grandmother as she died.

A white glow encompassed her as she whimpered, wondering if her grandmother had somehow killed her with the potion.

"Welcome to my world, *Mitakŏja ke.*"

"*Nĭkusĭki!*" Grace immediately remembered the word for 'grandmother'. She sat up and rubbed her eyes against the bright light.

"I have sensed that you were bothered and would soon come to visit me. Tell me, child, why you are so troubled."

"Grandmother, I am saddened by something you told me long ago, that Charlie and I would be married and have four children. But I got a letter telling me that he has died, drowned in the ocean. It was from a man who saw him disappear beneath the waves. Since that time I have met a new man who says he loves me. Perhaps it is HIM that you saw me being married to."

"Child," said Lucinda as she stroked Grace's hair, "sometimes *Wakaŋ Taŋka* works in mysterious ways. My vision of your *teȟila* appears clouded, and I cannot say for certain why this is so. Let me tell you a story."

"When I walked the earth, my eyes were growing dim towards the end. Light comes from above and allows the heart to see clearly. It is in that tiny space of the heart that the Great Spirit resides. Know the center of your heart where it is pure and good. I now walk with your grandfather in this Spirit World, and my happiness is endless because of the purity given me by *Wakaŋ Taŋka*. This Great Spirit is our Most Holy One. There is also *Tuŋkashila*. He is known as the Son of God. In your religion he corresponds with the one called Jesus. The daughter of God is Earth and draws her powers from the four directions. These Holy Three hear all our prayers and send our voices to God. We cannot begin to understand the mysterious powers of them, only relate what we feel in our hearts.

"The white man has said we must embrace their religion, but it is too hard for us to understand all the different faiths. These attempts to 'save' us from our sins, however, was addressed by a great chief among us, Sitting Bull, since passed at Wounded Knee. He counseled that all Indians pray to God for life and to find good in our own way. We want this from God and we pray to him, but the white man did not believe us. We say nothing against his God and he should say nothing against ours. We both pray to only one God, the one who made us all."

"But, *Nïkusïki,* what does this story have to do with what is troubling me?"

"I am coming to that, *Mitakŏja ke.* You are still as impatient as you were when I walked the *maka.*

"I have told you in the past of the ritual of smoking a pipe. This was a gift given to the Lakotas by God. It must be filled with tobacco, blessed, and then lit in the correct way. The Spirit is within the smoke and when it is blown out it rises up to God and soothes Him. This is a purifying ritual and allows us to offer up our prayers to His holiness. He will hear us and we will hear him.

"Women are not allowed to participate in this ritual, only among the chiefs, elders, and important members of the tribe. When I was young my father would hear my supplications and those of his two wives. He would then come and tell us what the Spirit was saying to Him.

"In the time before I met and married your grandfather, I was infatuated with a young warrior from a neighboring Lakota tribe. He was the son of their chief. This man did not share a mutual affection and seemed to ignore the feelings of a young girl, even the girl of a tribal chief. I asked my father to intermediate on my behalf. He smoked a pipe with this warrior and sent a silent prayer to *Wakaŋ Taŋka.*

"Later my father said the answer was clouded and could not give me an affirmation that my beloved would ever feel the same about me as I about him. He could only say that it would work out in the end and my **true** *teĥila* would eventually emerge.

Unfortunately, he was not pleased on who that would be . . . your grandfather, Isaac."

"Isaac is the name of the boy who is courtin' me. Do you think that is a sign he is the one I am to marry?"

"I can only say that if your Isaac is the one for you, *Wakaŋ Taŋka* will give you the answer you need."

Lucinda spoke for another hour with Grace, relating stories she felt would help her on her journey.

"I fear that our time together is coming to an end, *Mitakŏja ke*. We cannot meet again in this form, but you are assured you can talk to me anytime you wish and you will be heard."

"Grandmother, do not leave me. I have much more to ask you."

"It cannot be, child, I must go. Please remember this: Always turn to the purity of your heart to find the answers you seek. It does not require many words to speak the truth."

With those words, Lucinda became a wisp and dissipated into the pines above.

Grace slumped back against the rock and slumbered a dreamless sleep. She awoke an hour later, feeling completely refreshed.

As she made her way back down the hill she pondered her grandmother's words. *Always turn to the purity of your heart to find the answers you seek,* she had said.

Grace wondered about her other parting expression. *It does not require many words to speak the truth.*

What had she meant by *that*?

45

Charlie

"**K**in you walk me to school, Charlie?"

He had been staying with the Constantines for two weeks as Clayton kept finding other jobs that could really use the help of a second man. Not that he objected any since he got to see Clementine every day.

"Well now, Cassie, you've been walking yourself and your brothers and sisters to school every day since I got here. How come you want me to walk you today?"

"Cuz some of the boys are always teasing me 'bout my arm and they call me names like One Arm or Leftie. It makes me mad, and I try and fight them but just get pushed down into the dirt. They're just plain mean! Mebbe you kin have a word with them."

"Doesn't your teacher put a stop to it?"

"Mister Devon ain't no better. He don't say nuthin' and tells me to start acting like a lady. I hate him! Pa says he's too busy to go have a talk."

"Well, we can't have none of that now, can we? How about it, Mr. Constantine? Can you give me an hour off so I can go have a talk with this Devon person?"

"I don't know, Charlie. We need to get out and mend fences today. I'm getting tired of my cows wandering off into the timber."

"Won't take me but an hour and I'll work extra late tonight."

"Awright, but get back here soon's you can."

"C'mon, kids, show me where you get your schoolin'."

Clementine stood on the porch and watch the procession down the path with the older children leading the way and Charlie bringing up the rear with Cassie riding piggy-back. She was starting to feel a real attraction to the handsome boy. "Sure is good with children, Pa."

Clayton looked up at her and saw something in her eyes that he knew would be coming along some day. He just grunted and went down to the barn.

The walk to school took twenty minutes and when they got there, Charlie set Cassie down on the ground and told her to join the others who were whooping and hollering before the bell rang. He wanted to observe what would happen with her when she went to a bag swing. She couldn't ride it because of her arm but stood watching her brother Carl jump onto it and start swaying in circles.

An older boy came up behind Cassie and jerked her pigtail. "Outta the way, ya one-armed pipsqueak. You can't swing if you can't even hold onto the rope!"

Cassie started crying and Charlie stepped out from behind the tree. He grabbed the bully by the strap of his bib overalls and pulled him right up into his face.

"Well, looky here! Seems we got a real man who likes to make little girls cry. That what a real man does? Make little girls cry?"

"Mist . . . Mister. I didn't mean nothin' by it." The boy's voice had a higher tone by three levels. "I . . . I . . . who are you?"

"I'm the man who's going to hang you from the highest tree I can find. You thinkin' you can make little girls cry from up there?"

"I . . . I . . . I'm sorry. I ain't gonna do it no more."

"I'm not so sure you ain't lying right to my face."

"No . . . no . . . I . . . I ain't lying. I swear to God, mister."

"All right. So here's what's gonna happen. I am appointing you as Cassie's protector. You're gonna step in whenever she gets bullied and you're gonna stop it. You're gonna be Cassie's very best friend. We understand each other?"

"Yes, sir. Oh, please, mister. I gotta pee."

Charlie let loose of the boy's straps and he fell to the ground. A large wet spot covered the front of his pants."

"Not so tough now, are we? Who's the baby here? You can't even hold your water!"

"See here! What's going on out here?"

Charlie turned to see a mousy little man bounding down the steps of the school house. He ran out to Charlie who was standing over the bully.

"Your name Devon?"

"I am Mr. Cyrus Devon and you are trespassing on city property. What right do you have coming here and pushing children to the ground?"

"Well, Mr. Cyrus Devon, you must be the man who refuses to help the little ones against the bullies the likes of this one." Charlie poked his finger right up to within an inch of Devon's nose. "If I have to come back here because you fail to enact discipline here, I ain't gonna be as nice as I am right now. Put your right arm behind your back."

"I will do no such thing, young man!"

"I said put your arm behind your back or I'll do it for you."

Devon saw the fire in Charlie's eyes and slowly put his arm behind his back.

"Now you leave that arm right there while I thrash you!"

"But I won't be able to defend myself."

"Dang right you can't. And neither can that little girl defend herself from boys two or three times her size. You catch what I'm sayin'?"

Devon's belligerence turned to a hint of fear.

"I asked you a question, Mister!"

"Yes, I understand what you're saying."

"Good! I better be hearing no reports of someone pushing around Cassie because *you*, Mister Cyrus Devon, will put a stop to it. Repeat what I just said so's I know I won't have to knock you down."

"I will not let anybody push around Cassie."

"What will happen if you do?"

"I suspect you will come back and 'thrash' me, as you put it."

"Damn right I will. Good day, sir!" Charlie turned and walked back out of the school yard, giving a wink to Cassie, who stood in awe at what she had just witnessed.

"I love you, Charlie," she whispered just loud enough for him to hear.

At the supper table that night, Cassie related to the whole family as to what happened that morning.

The children sat gape-mouthed at the story. Clementine brushed away a tear as Clayton just grunted and asked Carl to pass the taters.

Clementine knew she had found the man she wanted and decided she would waste no time in making her intentions known.

46

Grace

G race, we've been seeing each other for a couple of years
now and you know how I feel about you. Will you
marry me?"

Isaac Harmony was walking an autumn leaf path through the
woods behind the Reynolds farm, holding Grace's hand. The fall
colors had reached their peak and it was beautiful October day.

Isaac had a great many girlfriends outside a three-mile circle
of Port Byron so the odds of Grace ever meeting any of them
were not great. He had seduced at least three of them within the
past year with the promise that each of them was the only girl he
would ever consider marrying. Each of them had given in to his
beguiling charms, and one of them was now carrying his child.

"Isaac," answered Grace, "you know I think the world of you.
I really do. I was kind of wondering when you would ask me. I
been hesitant up to now because I still have feelings for Charlie."
She took out a hanky and dabbed at the tears in her eyes. She
wasn't sure if it was because of Charlie's death, her grandmother's
miscue of them marrying, or if it was the handsome boy now
holding her other hand and his proposal. "I have prayed about it,

for sure, and I knew I would have the answer for you as soon as it was asked."

Isaac turned on his best smile and got down on his knee. "Marry me, Grace. I love you and you're the only girl I've ever wanted to be my wife."

"My answer, Isaac, is . . . yes. Yes, I will marry you and give you children and keep your home for you." Her eyes were now freely dropping tears on her gingham.

"You just made me the happiest fella on earth." He got up, held her hand they started walking again.

They were coming upon an old barn that had been abandoned for years and Isaac pulled her towards it. "Let's seal our love for each other, Grace. Come inside with me."

They stepped into the shadows of the barn which had the smells of old hay, long since unused horse stalls, and the excrement of pigeon droppings. Isaac pulled her towards a mattress of hay lying inside one of the stalls. He drew her close to him and gave her one of his most wonderful kisses.

Grace melted in his arms and allowed herself to be lowered onto the hay. She wrapped her arms around Isaac and returned him kiss for kiss.

In the hay loft above lurked Duggie Hayes who watched with much anticipation. He wiped his drooping eye as it leaked, reminding him just how he had gotten it. His cousin Isaac had done just as they had planned and had drawn the red-haired girl into the barn where they would each take turns.

Isaac continued kissing Grace as his hand inched its way to the top button of her dress. Grace sensed what he was doing and grabbed his hand and pulled it away.

"C'mon, Grace. We're gonna get married anyway so what difference does it make if it's now or after the wedding?"

"I don't want to, Isaac. I mean, I do, but it'd be a sin."

"Let's have some fun. The Lord will forgive you."

"No, Isaac. I can't. I won't." Suddenly a thought crowded into her mind.

"Always turn to the purity of your heart to find the answers you seek, Mitakŏja ke."

Grace's eyes flew open hearing her grandmother's voice in her head. She felt hay and dust settling on them coming from the loft. She looked up and her eyes grew wide as she recognized who was watching from above.

"Isaac, Duggie Hayes is up there watching us. Get off me!"

Turning to the loft, he motioned with his hand. "Come on down, cousin. We've got her where we want her."

"Cousin?" Grace's mind started racing as she realized what was happening.

"It does not require many words to speak the truth."

"Yes, my dear little Grace," panted Isaac. "Duggie is my cousin, and we got you here to have fun for me and revenge for him." He crawled on top of her and fumbled with the top of her dress.

With one mighty shove of her knee, she caught Isaac by surprise. He cried out in pain and rolled off, clutching his groin.

It was right at that time, as Duggie came scrambling down the loft ladder, that one of the rotted rungs gave way, breaking his leg as he fell the remaining ten feet, landing on top of Isaac.

Grace rolled away just as the two tangled bodies went completely slack, both knocked out from Duggie's fall. She jumped up and stood panting over the two unconscious men. Her fear turned to anger as she drew back her foot and added more injury to Isaac's crotch.

"I'll bet the Lord will forgive me for *that*, you bastard!"

She turned and raced out of the barn, tears streaming from her eyes.

47

Charlie

C harlie was thoroughly flustered. The red-headed girl back in Illinois was waiting for him but, right now, in this moment of time, a beautiful honey blonde in Pennsylvania had made her intentions clear regarding Charlie's future.

Each passing day, Charlie promised himself he would quietly leave the next morning. The next day, however, saw him getting up, doing his chores, and then spending the evening hours on the front porch of the Constantine home, rocking and talking until nearly midnight with the stunning sixteen-year-old named Clementine.

She had gotten into the habit of ending the evening with a kiss on his cheek as she withdrew to go inside. He didn't know what kind of scent she was wearing, but it always managed to linger in the air for a few minutes after she retired.

Indian summer had passed and November brought a chill. On an evening giving a hint of frost, she surprised him with a kiss fully on the lips. Caught by surprise, Charlie closed his eyes to enjoy the moment. As the kiss lingered longer than a mere peck, Charlie opened his eyes and was shocked at seeing it was Grace on his lips. He sputtered and withdrew, blinked, and suddenly it was Clementine again, her blonde hair falling onto his face.

"Charlie, what's wrong?"

"Uh, nothing, uh, I was just caught by surprise, that's all."

"Didn't you enjoy it? I certainly did."

"Well, yeah. I mean, uh, who wouldn't?"

Clementine took his hand and gave it a soft squeeze. "I can stay out a little longer, Charlie, if you want me to. We can move our rockers a little closer together."

"Uh, don't get me wrong, Clemmie. I'd love to, but I've got a long day tomorrow. Your pa wants to start bringing in plenty of firewood for the winter." He got up from his chair and moved to the steps. "I guess I'll see you for breakfast."

"Oh, Okay, Charlie. We can continue this conversation tomorrow night."

"Good b . . ." Charlie almost said goodbye because he knew what he had to do. "Uh, good night, Clemmie. That . . . that was real nice."

"Good night, Charlie."

Charlie went back to his space in the loft of the barn and laid down. He couldn't get the image of Grace appearing in front of him, kissing his lips. There was only one thing he could do. He took out a piece of paper and his stub of a pencil and started writing.

The next morning, Clementine pulled out a pan of biscuits and took a chunk of butter and a jar of honey from the larder. She placed them on the table and decided to go out and wake up Charlie with another kiss.

Walking up to the barn door, she saw a scrap of paper stuck on a nail. She pulled it off and started reading.

Dear Clemuntine.

Yore kiss really rattled me last night and for a brief moment I wuz takin in by it and yore promis of more. Yore a delite-ful girl and I will always cheerish yore frenship over the past sevral weeks.

But I jest can't leed you on becuz I got me a beautifull red-haired gal back in Illinoise whose waiting for me to come home. I fell in love with her the furst time I ever seen her and her name is Grace. I cannot and will not betray her. Sorry for jest leavin like this but I dont think I could resist yore charms anymore.

Charlie

48

Aaron

T he people of northwestern Illinois could not remember the last time they had a snow storm as bad as the one on New Year's Day, 1907. Snow started falling on the Eve and it quickly became apparent that this one was unlike any other they had ever experienced.

By noon the next day there was over a foot on the ground, and it had shown no signs of letting up. It caught everyone by surprise, including those on the Reynolds farm just outside of Port Byron. Aaron shoveled a path to the barn and the hen house only to see it close up again from howling wind and drifts up to six feet high.

He managed to get the horses into the stable and piled hay around the walls in an attempt to provide some protection from the cold creeping in through the cracks. The temperature had dropped to fifteen degrees below zero. Fortunately, he had cut enough firewood two weeks before that would keep the house warm. He moved his flock of chickens into an extra pen in the barn giving them some measure of shelter as well.

By dusk he wearily tromped into the kitchen and pulled snow encrusted gloves off his hands and tried to thaw them out by the stove.

"Becky, I don't think I'll ever be warm again. It's incredible out there and shows absolutely no sign of letting up. The snow is blowing sideways, and you can't see your hand in front of your face. We got enough vittles to keep us going for a week or so?"

She hurried over and helped him out of his heavy coat. "We'll be all right. Where's Grace? She went out half an hour ago to tell you to come on in."

"Grace? I never saw her. Lordy, she out there in this storm?

Hannah's face reflected alarm. "Aaron, you've got to go find her. She can't survive in this. She only wore a thin coat when she went out."

"Good God!" he exclaimed, pulling his coat and gloves back on. He ran to the door but had a hard time holding it against the wind. He finally was able to slip through and close it again but not before a couple of plates blew off the shelf over Hannah's prep table and smashed on the wooden floor.

Once outside, he strained his eyes against the blowing snow to get some sense of what direction she might have taken. He stepped off the porch but slipped on a patch of ice, falling with a heavy thud to the ground, hurting his shoulder. Painfully, he got up and, bracing himself against the howler, made his way step by step towards the barn.

"Grace! Gracie! Where are you, child?" He couldn't even hear himself yell so he knew she wouldn't be able to hear it either. His throat had never fully healed from the wolf attack so it was not as loud as he wanted it to be.

He reached the door of the barn and pulled it open and slipped inside where it was a bit quieter. *"Gracie! Are you in here, girl?"*

The only sound was the wind whipping around the barn and through the cracks. Making a quick decision, he went to Champion's stall and put a halter over his head, looping a three-foot rope through the straps. He wound the rope around his gloved hand and led the horse to the barn door.

"Okay, big boy. We have to go out there and find your Gracie." Champion perked his ears forward hearing her name and looked about to see if she was behind him.

Aaron led the sorrel into the blizzard, holding tightly onto the rope. "Can you find her, boy? Can you find Gracie?" He started towards the hen house, thinking she might have taken refuge there. Halfway there, Champion resisted and pulled Aaron to the left, away from the house and barn.

"C'mon, Champ! Let's check the hen house."

The horse would have none of it and leaning into the gale, pulled the man away from the barn. He got up to the horse's ear and yelled into it, "Okay! I can't fight you and you seem to know where you're going. Take me to Grace, Champ! Find Grace."

Champion pulled Aaron fifty yards up towards the timber line behind the house. Snow had drifted to twice Aaron's six-foot frame but the horse plunged right into the drift, slowly plodding, breaking a path into the trees. It took ten minutes for man and horse to come into a clearing just short of the stand of timber. Champ stopped and tilted his ears first in one direction and then another before turning to his right and walking into the forest.

The wind was subdued to the point where they could walk more easily but two feet of snow on the ground still hindered their progress.

Every few feet, Aaron would yell Grace's name as loud as his voice would allow him. He prayed to God that Champion could sense where he was going.

Champ gave a loud whinny and pulled Aaron up to a mound of snow that seemed elevated above the two-foot level. He pawed the ground and gave a loud burst of air from his lungs, blowing snow off the form, revealing a dark brown coat.

"Oh, God! Gracie!" Aaron frantically dusted the rest of the snow off her body and picked her up in his arms. Grace was unconscious and her face had a bluish tint. He rubbed her cheeks wishing color to come back into them. He knew he had to get her back to a warm house or she would die.

He picked her up and put her across Champion's back. He climbed up behind her and leaned over to the horse's ear. "Take us home, boy. Let's take Gracie home."

Champion seemed to understand and worked his way back out of the timber into the howling blizzard. The path they had broken through the huge drift was already closed back up and, again, the sturdy animal worked his way through finally reaching the barn yard ten minutes later.

Aaron urged him back to the house. He yelled to Hannah who came running out, taking Grace down from the horse. Aaron jumped off and the two of them dragged the comatose girl back into the warmth of the fire.

"I'm going to take Champion back to the barn. Don't let her get too warm too quickly or frostbite will be even worse than it is now. I'll get a bucket of snow and you can rub that on her skin. Get some of that hot soup into her but only a little at a time. I have to take Champ back."

With that he went back out and led the horse back to the barn. He led him into the stall and gave him a bucket of oats. He stood caressing the horse's muzzle and felt tears falling onto his cheeks.

"You saved her life, boy! You saved her *life!* You are truly a hero and a champion." He spent a few more moments rubbing him down and then returned to the house.

Grace was still unconscious, but Aaron noted color was returning to her cheeks as Hannah tended to her.

"I think we have some extra prayers to offer the next time the preacher comes through, Becky."

"Thank you for saving our daughter, Aaron."

"All the thanks has to go to Champion. He found her."

49
Charlie

Charlie hopped a southbound Pennsylvania Railroad express not knowing it would soon be involved in one of the biggest train wreck disasters in Pennsylvania history.

He managed to grab the handles of a boxcar five cars behind one that was loaded with dynamite and settled himself in the doorway, legs dangling before the countryside that was speeding by at 25 miles an hour. He sat and wondered about his life over the past few years. He had just turned twenty and he was weary of travel. He wanted to get back to Illinois and see Grace, marry her, and start their family.

His boxcar carried five other hobos who seemed a bit unfriendly so he mostly avoided them. From their conversations he gathered the train would arrive in Harrisburg later in the afternoon. He knew absolutely no one in the city but hoped he could find other Fisher relations that knew his father James. His parents had migrated to Iowa in the early 70s seeking a life in the new frontier, but he wanted to get a handle on his own ancestry.

The train had slowed down somewhat, and Charlie stood up, hoping to find a safe spot to jump down and make his way into the town.

A half mile down the track, a northbound freight train was flagged by the crew because of a shifting engine. The express engineer slammed on his air brakes which was too much of a strain on the air valves and a rubber hose blew out. The middle of the train started to buckle just as a second express travelling in excess of 40 miles an hour side-swiped the buckled cars on the adjacent track.

Charlie lost his balance in the suddenly slowed train and fell back inside the car.

He hauled himself back up and rushed to the doorway, just in time to hear a huge explosion and witness a brilliant flash of white light as the boxcar with the dynamite ignited, spreading fire through passenger cars and boxcars alike in both directions. The resulting wreck and explosion buckled cars behind. Charlie could see that the car he was riding in would soon be part of the disaster. He knew that if he leaped to the ground, he would surely be crushed. He dived into a pile of hay that was at the farthest end of the boxcar and landed in a tangle of arms, legs and bodies of his fellow riders.

Charlie lost consciousness for just a few moments, but when he opened his eyes again, he was aware of a wall of fire just outside the car door. Explosions continued to rock the train, and the sounds were mixed with the screams of many people. He struggled to his feet and holding his arm up in front of his face to ward off the tremendous heat, he tried to peer into the flames to see if he had any means of escape. He felt the hair on his arms starting to singe.

Fearing that the car he was in would soon ignite into flames, he felt he had no choice but to leap as far as he could away from the train. He backed up to the opposite side of the car to give himself a running start and made the jump that he was afraid would end his life.

As he leapt through the inferno he had no idea if he would even be alive by the time he hit the ground. Behind him he heard the screams of the hobos who were suddenly trapped by a wall of fire that ignited the hay in the car.

Charlie's leap into the unknown did, indeed, save his life as he landed on a strip of ground that was free of any obstacles. He landed on his feet and went into a roll that helped cushion his rough landing.

He was temporarily dazed, but jumped to his feet and turned to see what had caused the initial explosion. Train cars were buckling against each other, rails were ripped from their ties while glass, metal parts, and pieces of human bodies scattered as far forward as the locomotive.

The screams brought back the memory of the women and children aboard the *General Slocum*. He ran to the nearest passenger car, leaping over flaming pieces of metal and bodies already burned beyond recognition. The heat and the inferno kept him from even getting close to the car. He knew instinctively that the people inside were beyond rescue.

He decided to reverse his course and ran to the cars that were behind the one he had been riding. He just narrowly missed being felled by a burning telegraph pole as it toppled to the ground.

He twisted out of the way and continued to the next passenger car. It was not yet on fire so he leapt onto the steps, grabbing the pull bar and swinging himself up onto the platform.

He tried opening the door to the car, but it had been jammed from the derailment. Peering into the window he saw the car's passengers piled on top of one another as they frantically tried to escape. There was no way he would get that door open. He turned and quickly scaled the steps on the side of the car to the top. He found a bracing rail running the length of the car. He backed his rear end to the side, reached down between his legs, grabbed the rail and jumped backwards.

Charlie's momentum swung him in an arc with his feet perfectly placed as he kicked in the side window, shattering the glass but leaving a space large enough for him to continue the swing. He landed in the lap of a man who lay twisted with his head turned in the opposite direction. There was no question he had died of a broken neck.

Pieces of glass nicked Charlie's face and arms, leaving a dozen wounds that started seeping blood. Charlie didn't care about the men in the car. He would leave them to their own devices in escaping. He was more interested in any children or women who wouldn't have the strength to get to the rear of the car.

Indeed, there were four crying children, one a baby still in the arms of his dead mother. She died from a stray piece of metal that pierced her throat, narrowly missing the child. Charlie tried to take the boy, but the mother's death grip made it difficult to pry him loose. His hands kept slipping from the woman's blood, as well as his own, as it dripped down over the child. A man was scrambling by, and Charlie grabbed his arm. "You, mister, help me with this baby."

The man's eyes were glazed over and was obviously going into shock. He kept stumbling forward. Charlie knew he couldn't depend on him so he continued working the mother's arms until he finally freed the infant.

A woman then staggered down the aisle, and he pulled her aside. "Here, ma'am, please take this baby and make your way to the rear because you ain't gonna get out the front."

The woman nodded her head, which was bleeding from her right temple. She took the baby and carried him off the train.

Charlie turned to see if anybody else needed help. Two little girls, dressed alike, were crying from across the aisle. They looked like twins, adorned in pink camisoles stained a darker red from cuts on their faces. They were the first identical twins Charlie had ever seen in his life. A woman was sitting across from them, likewise in shock, but Charlie thought he could make her understand before the train might catch fire.

"Ma'am!" She looked up at him, unfocused on the voice coming from this stranger. "Ma'am," he repeated. *"You got to get your girls off the train afore it catches fire!"*

She looked up at him and her eyes suddenly came to attention. She looked around and reached out to her daughters, gathering them into her bosom, holding them tightly. One arm hung loosely at her side, broken.

"Ma'am! You gotta get off the train! Now!"

She was suddenly aware of the pain from her arm and tried to get up from her seat, only to fall back, crying out. She looked down and saw the broken bone exposed to the air.

Charlie knew she wouldn't be able to get the girls out so he grabbed them both up, one under each arm like a sack of potatoes and lurched towards the rear, stumbling over a couple of bodies. He made it to the rear, went through the door onto the platform and jumped off the steps, nearly tripping and falling. He caught himself and put the two girls down, admonishing them not to move. He returned for their mother.

When he got back inside he saw the mother coming towards him, holding her arm that swung at an impossible angle. He rushed to her, put her good arm over his shoulder and worked them both back to the outside. He jumped off first, then held his arms out to her. She tripped on the last step. Weighing no more than a hundred pounds, Charlie was able to catch her. He carried her over to where the twins sat crying in the middle of the chaos.

"Ma'am, you've got to get your girls away from here before this whole place turns into a furnace." She nodded and guided the girls away from the train.

Charlie remembered he had one more child to get off the train and climbed back on as a couple of men came tumbling out. He worked himself past them and re-entered the car. He was met by an acrid cloud of smoke that stung his eyes. He felt no tiredness as his adrenalin kept pushing him forward. He knew the child was towards the middle of the car, lying between the seats on the floor. The smoke was thicker here and he could only feel his way, stopping between each seat, groping blindly around the floor for the boy, not knowing if he were dead or alive.

After the fourth try he wondered if he had only imagined the child. His lungs were screaming for oxygen, but he decided to try one more row. He was in luck.

Charlie's fingers wrapped around the very small ankle of what had to be the child. He grabbed up the boy and held him tightly to his chest as he made for the exit one last time. Or what he thought was the exit.

In the confusion of screaming people and a wall of smoke, he had gotten turned around and tripped over the bodies of the panicked people who had tried to escape out the front and now lay five deep in front of the door. Charlie heard the boy whimper as he fell on top of him so he knew he was still alive. He got back up, grabbed the boy again and reversed his direction.

In what seemed to be several minutes, but was actually less than thirty seconds, he made it to the rear door and stepped out, where the smoke was not as heavy and he could get a gasp of new air before his lungs burst.

Charlie was in mid-jump when the car exploded, hurtling man and child twenty feet away from the train. The force of the blast twisted them in mid-air and both landed in a heap on top of a burning railroad tie. Charlie rolled off the lumber but could feel his pant legs were on fire. He released the child and sat up, beating at the flames.

As he watched from where he had landed, he could only watch helplessly as car after car erupted in flames. As he got to his feet, he felt every muscle screaming in agony. As quickly as the adrenaline had taken over his body, it just as rapidly left, and his exhaustion overwhelmed him. He looked around and saw no sign of the children or women he had rescued. All that remained of the accident now were the flames rising from the string of train cars that had folded into an accordion shape. He could still hear the cries of people begging for help.

He picked up the little boy, who appeared to be no more than two years old. Turning he worked his way through the wreckage, not really knowing where he was going.

50
Aaron

Spring had come early in 1907. Aaron took Hannah's hand and walked her out to the front porch of the home he built for them when Hattie had gotten married. He stood at the top of the front steps and drew in a lungful of fresh air. Yellow daffodils were proudly spreading their golden petals and soaking in the warm rays of the sun.

"Great day to be alive, Becky! Let's just sit for a spell and enjoy what the Lord has given us." They sat down in the two rockers, silently watching the sun as it dipped slowly towards the rise of hills that marked the border of their property.

"What are you thinking about, Aaron?"

"Actually, I'm thinking about Grace. She seems to be coming out of her depression after her encounter with those two scalawags from last fall. I had high hopes for that boy."

"Well, I am equally dismayed. I always thought I was a pretty good judge of character, but my judgement took leave with Isaac. She had gone into her room for a week and wouldn't come out unless she had to go to the outhouse. First, she loses Charlie and then him."

"I ain't seen hide nor hair of either one of them ever since and hope I never do because I can't be responsible for what I might do. Sure would hate to be hauled off to prison for killing a skunk." He took out his pipe, tamped in a pinch of tobacco and put a match to the bowl. He drew smoke into his lungs, holding it for a moment and then blew it out, watching it swirl lazily until a slight breeze caught it, sending it into the night air.

"Well, the dishes are washed and put away, and I am dead on my feet," she said as she rocked. The creaking of the floor boards below them had a settling cadence lulling them into their own thoughts.

"I'm also a wonderin' what might have become of my life if I hadn't walked into that bank so many years ago."

Hannah smiled and gave his hand a squeeze. "I'd like to think you would have come in some other time, seen me and fallen over yourself, trying to get to my window."

"Might of at that. Yep, might of at that," he chuckled. He turned to look at her with a quizzical glint in his eyes. "You know, you never have told me anything of your life with your pa."

"Good reason. Too painful to think of it. Let it be, Aaron, just let it be."

"Sorry. Didn't mean to stir nothin' up." He took another long draw on his pipe. "I love you, Becky. I truly do."

"Now don't you go and get all sappy on me, Aaron Reynolds. You've given me a good life, two wonderful daughters, and a roof over my head, food on my table. I couldn't have asked for a better life, or a better man."

Aaron could feel his face getting red. He and his Becky had had this conversation before and he never got tired of hearing her praise. He closed his eyes to draw on his memories of his life with her. He grew suddenly still.

"Aaron, it's getting late and I'm getting a chill. Let's go on in and get ready for bed 'fore we come down with the ague." She turned to him and saw his pipe fall from his mouth down onto his shirt.

"Aaron, you're going to burn a hole in your shirt again. Why can't you be more careful? Aaron?" She reached over to shake him awake. "Aaron?"

A sudden chill gripped her as she jumped up and shook him by his shoulders. "Aaron Reynolds, you stop this right now. This isn't funny."

Aaron slumped forward in his rocker.

"Aaron!"

51
Charlie

As he walked away from the gruesome wreckage and the screams of people faded in his ears, Charlie was barely aware of the emergency wagons rushing past him. He was tired, homesick, and disheartened with everything that had happened to him since he left for his adventure with Buffalo Bill.

The small boy he was carrying clutched Charlie tightly around his neck as he cried for his mother. The child's wailing awakened him into reality.

"I'm sorry, son. I wish I could have saved your mother, too. Oh, Lord, what am I going to do with you?"

The words had a quieting effect on the lad and his sobbing subsided into whimpers. Charlie continued his walk out of the railyard and entered a broad mud-filled roadway carrying men on wagons pulled by mules or oxen. They were all headed to the accident to see what they could do.

Charlie knew he could no longer think of only himself. He had a child now that desperately needed his help.

"What's your name, son?" He wasn't sure if the baby could even talk yet. He was obviously well fed and tended, but his life had now taken a dramatic turn for the worst in the last fifteen minutes. Charlie checked him over and he didn't seem to have any cuts or abrasions that needed doctoring. "What's your name?" he repeated.

The child answered in a whisper so faint that Charlie barely heard him. "Adam."

"What? What is your name?"

The boy hugged Charlie's neck even tighter, afraid that his savior might just put him down and walk away. "Adam," he whispered.

"Well, Adam, you and I are going to try and find somebody who might take you and give you the care you need."

"Mommy?"

"No, Adam, Mommy isn't here anymore. Oh, Lord, help me with this boy," he prayed.

"Want Mommy!"

Charlie was holding Adam with his arms under the boy's legs and suddenly became aware of a wetness. Fearful that it was blood from a wound he missed, he laid him down on the ground for a closer inspection only to find the wetness was not from blood but from something entirely different.

"Oh, Lordy, you filled your britches. Where am I going to find changings?"

Charlie continued down the street with Adam in his arms. He was passing a general store just as a man was closing up, locking the door.

"Mister, I got a problem here. I was hoping you could sell me some changings."

"Sorry, young fellow, all able-bodied men are being called to the railyard because there's some kind of accident down there."

"I know. I just came from there. This child was a victim in one of the passenger cars, but I was able to get him out before it caught fire. Please. He needs just as much care as those who still need it."

The clerk hesitated but noting the bleeding from cuts on Charlie and the child, he unlocked the door. "All right. Come on in and let's get you fixed up."

Ten minutes later, Charlie had what he needed, plus some food that he thought would provide some nourishment as well as a used shirt and a pair of pants that looked like they might fit the child. Charlie checked his funds and found enough to cover the purchase, but didn't leave him much else.

"No need for that," said the shopkeeper, "seems you've done enough already."

"Thanks, Mister." He gathered up the supplies and stepped back out on the street. The clerk followed him out and re-locked the door.

"Good luck to you," they both said at the same time.

Charlie was in a strange town, known by no one, and unsure which direction to go when he heard a bell ringing. He turned in the direction of the sound and saw it was coming from the belfry of a church a block away. It was sounding an alarm calling people from the neighborhood. Charlie assumed it was for the accident and headed for the church.

People were coming from all directions to heed the call. A man in a long black coat, a starched white collar shirt and dress pants seemed to be in charge and was barking orders to congregants as they arrived. He had a gaunt look and was waving a Bible in one hand. Charlie assumed this was the minister of the church.

The pastor ordered some men to rush to the railyard and others to start assembling medical supplies. To the women he charged arranging the preparation of food for rescue workers. He called for the city fire department to make haste to the accident scene to extinguish the flames. Others were called upon to assemble barrels of water for whatever need might arise.

Seeing Charlie, he barked an order. "You, young fellow, give me the boy and get to the train wreck."

Charlie hesitated before replying, "I already been there, Preacher. I rescued this young boy from certain death and am lookin' for someone to take him. I'm just passing through town and can't care for him."

"Mrs. Butler," the reverend called to a woman, "come take this child. He's from the wreck."

From behind him, Charlie could hear the screams of a woman.

"Adam! Adam! Oh, God, please help me. Somebody's taken my baby off the train."

A heavy set woman rushed up to the church, closely followed by a policeman. She spotted the minister and rushed up to him.

Charlie was incredulous. He was certain the woman he thought was the mother was dead. Was she only holding the child for the real mother?

"Please, mister! Somebody's stolen my baby. A man snatched him off the train. I saw him from behind the tracks. I was thrown out of the window by the force of the accident. Please, please! Have you seen my Adam?"

Charlie stepped out from behind the minister. "Ma'am, I reckon this young'un must be belong to you."

The woman cried in relief and snatched the baby from Charlie's arms. "Arrest him, Constable," she cried. "That there's the man I saw run off with my baby. Arrest him for kidnapping."

The policeman grabbed Charlie and threw him to the ground. "Young fellow, you don't know the pain I can put on you. Snatching a baby from a mother's arms is the lowest kind of animal I can think of. Please resist so I can do to you what should be done to baby snatchers."

"Hold on, Officer," Charlie grunted. His face was buried in mud, and he found it hard to breathe. "I, I . . . thought the mother was dead . . . I brought him to the church . . . hoping somebody could take him. I . . . I ain't in no position . . . to take a baby on. Please, mister . . . I'm suffocating."

The distraught mother would have none of it. "Lies! I saw him walk off with my boy."

"Hold on, madam," replied the minister. "What he's saying must be true. He just told me he rescued the child from the wreck and brought him here hoping someone would take him because he couldn't care for him."

The policeman had his knee across Charlie's neck. "That true, young man?"

A second woman's voice came from behind the mother. Charlie looked up from his prone position in the mud and saw the mother who had broken her arm. She was holding it in a makeshift sling and it was obvious she was in a lot of pain. Blood was still oozing from several cuts on her face. Her twin girls peeked from behind her dress.

"Everything he's saying is true, Officer." She winced as she held her arm. "He not only rescued my girls from the train but came back and got me. As we were trying to get away, I saw him rush back into that burning car and come back out holding a baby. *That* baby!"

The policeman got up and helped Charlie back to a standing position.

"Oh! I am so sorry. I . . . I owe you my son's life," cried Adam's mother.

"I reckon I can see how you might think I was taking him. I saw no one around that looked like she was searching for someone and just figured you had died."

"Can someone please help me?" said the mother with the twins.

The minister rushed to her side and called for one of the women from the church to come assist her.

"Sorry if I treated you rough, young fellow," said the Constable.

"Mister, if you knew what I've been through lately, you'd know this ain't nothin'."

The policeman turned and headed back towards the railyard, the minister went back to barking orders to his parishioners and Adam's mother just stood in the middle of the street clutching him to her breast, leaving Charlie to wonder which direction he should go.

He was suddenly very tired. He had grown weary of travelling, he missed Grace, and he no longer cared about relatives living in Harrisburg. He looked up to get a bead on where the sun set in the sky, turned west and started walking.

He wanted no part of any more trains.

52

Grace

Her father's death could not have come at a worse time for Grace. The special bond she shared with Aaron was now broken. There were things she could discuss with him that she would never dream of talking about with others, not even her mother. She also felt her grandmother Lucinda had failed her in some way.

She was angry with Charlie for leaving to go with Buffalo Bill. She was angry with Mark Twain for not jumping into the water to save him from drowning. She was livid with rage at Duggie Hayes and all the misery he had caused her.

The incident with Isaac and his errant cousin was constantly on her mind. The final blow was the death of her father. How could he do this to her when he should have known she needed him so badly? She felt betrayed by everyone, and there was not anything that anyone could say that would ease the pain she felt.

Hannah tried, without success, to draw Grace out of the deep depression into which she had fallen. She sat at Grace's bedside many evenings trying to draw her out of the shell she had built around herself. Hattie tried as well, with no discernible effect.

Hannah brought in the circuit rider preacher, who rode through every couple of months, but neither could he penetrate Grace's sadness. The preacher's thumping his Bible and trying to cast out her demons only made her more cross. Rage, frustration, and helplessness covered her like a thick blanket on a hot summer afternoon.

Days went by when she never left her room except to go to the outdoor privy. Hannah was at least able to get some soup into her, but it wasn't enough as Grace lost a frightening amount of weight. Her cheeks became sunken, her dress hung like a shapeless sack, and the lack of nutrition was weakening her.

It was finally a visit from a world renowned woman that brought Grace out of her self-induced despair.

Being situated right on the banks of the Mississippi River, Port Byron, though a small community of just 700 people in 1908, boasted five bars serving the sailors, longshoremen, and gamblers. Alcohol often flowed more freely than water from the town pump. Bar fights, knifings, and the occasional murder sometimes haunted the tiny hamlet, keeping the part-time sheriff busy. The jail, such as it was, was a small building near the pier where steamships and longboats often tied off. It was often filled with five to ten men in the single cell . . . men who were drunk, disorderly, or otherwise in violation of the simple laws of the town.

It was into this occasional den of debauchery that a woman stepped from a steamship on a Monday morning one early summer afternoon. She was a large woman, standing almost six feet tall, weighing 175 pounds and dressed all in black. She strode down the pier self-confidently with a fierce look of determination. She gripped a hatchet in her right hand.

Carrie Nation had embarked on a journey down the river from Minneapolis heading to New Orleans and had just one purpose in her life . . . to rid the world of the demon alcohol. Carrie often made use of the hatchet in her quest to put an end to drunkenness. She was a self-appointed crusader, and oftentimes would find herself jailed for her actions.

Port Byron had been visited recently by John L. Sullivan and President Theodore Roosevelt, but those visits would pale in comparison to the destructive storm that was about to descend upon it.

Hannah had to go into town on that very morning to get supplies from the Port Byron Mercantile Company. She hitched up the horse to their buckboard and made the half-mile long trip. She convinced Grace that she needed help in loading the wagon. Anything to get the eighteen-year-old girl out of the house. Maybe the fresh air would help her spirits. Hannah would have to drive by the string of stores and saloons to reach the Mercantile and almost always would be greeted by hoots and catcalls from the men who hung out in front of the bars.

This morning, however, was an entirely different matter. Approaching the bar that seemed to always attract the more unsavory of riverboat characters, there was a great hoopla of men cursing and crashing sounds from within the saloon.

Inside stood a woman on fire with indignation as she took her hatchet to tables, chairs, the bar and anything else that stood in her way.

"By the mercy of God Almighty," Carrie Nation screamed, *"The drink of the devil, Satan, has stained the souls of all men!"*

She swung her axe in a mighty arc, and it glanced a blow off the bartender's hand, delivering a gash that started spouting blood.

"Good morning, destroyer of men's souls! Better to lose a hand than to let it serve alcohol. God will have his judgement on you and every evil man within the sound of my voice!"

The axe had imbedded itself in the wood of the bar, and Carrie had to pry it loose as men scattered in all directions.

"They Are Out Of The Way In Strong Drink. They Err In Vision, They Stumble In Judgement! Isaiah 28:7!"

Turning on a drunk cowering under a table, Carrie again slammed her axe down, splitting the wood down the middle and causing it to fall on both sides of the man.

"No drunkards shall inherit the Kingdom Of God! First Corinthians, Chapter 6, verse 10!"

The sot, scared that he was about to die, soiled his pants, drawing himself up into a fetal position.

Three of the men rushed Carrie, and their momentum carried all four of them through the swinging bar doors. She planted her feet, and the three lost their grip and fell over each other into the street right at the hind wheels of Hannah's wagon.

"Lord of mercy!" she cried. *"What is going on?"*

Carrie, having made her point inside the bar, gathered up the hems of her dress, leapt over the three men and jumped up onto the seat beside Hannah and Grace.

"Well, move it, Madam, afore they come after all three of us respectable women!"

Startled, Hannah laid the whip across the back of her horse, and the wagon lurched forward, tumbling Grace over backwards onto its bed.

Holding onto her hat, Carrie's eyes carried the look of a crazed woman. Hannah had a firm grip on the reins, trying to bring her horse under control. Grace was bouncing around behind, frantically grabbing for anything she could find to keep from tumbling out into the street. An overnight rain had turned it into a mire of wet sludge.

Mud was splattering upon all three of the women from the wheels of the wagon. Hannah's feet were firmly planted and kept hollering "Whoa!" until the horse came to a stop in front of the Mercantile.

Hannah twisted around in her seat to find a bruised Grace flat on her back. "You all right, Gracie?"

"I think so, Mama. *Who* is that woman?"

"Sorry, ladies, if I created an uncomfortable position for you. My name is Carrie Nation and I was making myself a nuisance to those drunkards in that saloon."

"*Carrie Nation?*" cried Grace. "*The* Carrie Nation?"

"Well, young lady, I don't think there are many more like me around."

"'Making yourself a nuisance is putting it mildly, Miss Nation," said Hannah. "Those men had murder in their hearts."

"Maybe so, Mama," said Grace, "but I haven't had that much fun in months."

"Welcome back from the world of sadness, Gracie."

Carrie turned and looked at Grace who was picking herself up from the buckboard. "Now what would a sweet, young lady like you have to be so sad about?"

"Come to the Mercantile with us, Mrs. Nation," said Hannah. "We'll tell you all about it."

The trio of women sat in three rocking chairs on the front porch of the store and Hannah, with a bit of prodding of Grace, told the story of Charlie's death, the episode with Duggie Hayes, the failed romance with Isaac Harmony, and finally the sadness of Aaron's passing.

"Well, I must say, Mrs. Reynolds, you and Grace have certainly weathered quite a storm of your own." She turned to Grace. "Now I want you to listen to me and listen to me well, Grace. We are now in the twentieth century, and women have to make their own happiness. You do not have to rely on a man to give you the satisfactions of life. I married a man who I thought would give me a good life. Unfortunately, he was an alcoholic and died a year after we married."

"Oh, I'm sorry, Mrs. Nation."

"Don't go feeling sorry for me. The rum took hold of a good man, but he brought his travails upon himself. I married a second time to a minister and a lawyer. It was during my marriage to Mr. Nation that I received the call from God to take up the temperance movement."

"Temperance?" queried Hannah. "Isn't that the crusade against alcohol?"

"Indeed, it is. I put on the armor of intolerance and carried my movement right into the dens of Hell where the destroyer of men's souls was being sold. I rejoiced when President William

McKinley was assassinated in '01 because he was a secret imbiber and got what he deserved."

Carrie leaned forward in her rocker and pointed a finger at Grace. "That is why, Grace, that you have to stand on your own two feet as a member of the fairer sex and realize that no man can make your happiness. Stay away from the bottle. Never let that poison touch your lips and do not let your lips touch those of any man who consumes any form of liquor, beer or wine. Do that and your life shall be one of your own making."

The blare of a horn from the steamship sounded from the pier, and Carrie got to her feet. "I must go or I will miss my ride. May I impose upon you one more time, Mrs. Reynolds to deliver me to the pier?"

"Of course. Gracie, I'm going to do my trading. Please take the buckboard with Mrs. Nation to the landing."

"Okay, Mama." She turned to Carrie. "We'll take a different route that will steer us around the main street saloons."

"Thank you, Grace. I believe I have made use of my hatchet enough for one day."

They climbed onto the wagon and set off for the pier. Carrie continued to encourage Grace to work herself out of depression and get on with her life. When they had gotten to the landing, Carrie got off, turned and reached up, grabbing Grace's hand in a firm grip.

"Heed my words, Miss Reynolds. You are a beautiful young woman and I am sure you will marry for love someday, but the peace within your heart is what shall carry you through your life. God will provide."

"Yes, ma'am." Grace watched the woman walk up the gangplank with a determined stride, her hatchet gripped in her right hand, seemingly ready to make use of it again in her quest.

Grace watched Carrie standing on the walkway of the ship as it pulled out of port. They waved to each other, and soon it was making its way around the bend and disappearing from sight.

The chance meeting was all that Grace needed to make a resolution to never again be bound to the will of a man.

At that very moment, on the opposite end of the state, Charlie crossed the Indiana/Illinois border.

53

Charlie

A rickety sign leaning up against a fence post brought a quicker pace to his steps.

INDIANA/ILLINOIS STATE BORDER

He wondered how Grace might have changed. He had been gone for over five years and he had grown about three inches and added several pounds to his lean frame. Somehow, whenever he tried to conjure up an image of Grace as she might look now, he could only see the thirteen-year-old girl swinging on the gate and just beginning to blossom into womanhood.

With each step taking him closer to Port Byron, he tried to imagine their reunion. He had no doubt she waited for him. His letters to her would surely let her know he still loved her and wanted to marry upon his return.

Charlie had given up trains. He had nothing but bad memories of them and vowed he would never hop another boxcar. He occasionally was able to hitch a ride on a hay wagon or buckboard headed in a westerly direction. He kept a close count of the dwindling money in the sock hanging from his neck. Whenever he got low, he stopped and offered to do chores or build fences. If he encountered a young woman who took an interest, he would do the work and be gone the next day.

Walking, riding, and his various stops along the way turned from days to weeks. He crossed northern Illinois with just one purpose: Grace May Reynolds.

He lost count of the number of towns he passed through. Frankfort, Joliet, Plainville, Yorktown, Paw Paw, Mendota. Not having a map, his trek began to drift northward until he got to the town of Franklin Grove. It was here that he stopped to assist a farmer in building a barn. The man was rather poor and couldn't afford to give Charlie much in the way of wages. He told him of a coal mine company further north near the town of Mt. Morris that was hiring workers.

While Charlie was anxious to conclude his journey, the need for money was paramount, and he decided to give it a try. He would work a week or two, giving him enough to finish his trek, and he could be in Port Byron by the end of October.

Three days later, he entered Ogle County and was in Mt. Morris by nightfall. He found an abandoned barn to sleep for the night and arose the next morning to seek out the coal mine company.

In short time he found the company and headed for a shack at the adit to the mine that had a sign that said simply *"Hiring"*.

A large man sat behind a desk, smoking a foul smelling cigar and motioned Charlie in as he stood in the doorway.

"Lookin' fer work?"

"Yes, sir, I am."

"Ever work a mine afore?"

"No, sir, but I'm strong and can give you a good day's work for a fair wage."

The man grunted and asked him his name.

He wrote it down on a piece of paper. "I pay you thirty-five cents a day for twelve hours of work and give it to you when you come up out of that cavern of hell. We don't provide no grub. You're on your own for that and your own clothes. It's filthy work, you risk your life because of frequent accidents, and you'll be bone tired at the end of a shift only to get up and do it again the next day. We have a bunk house with dirty mattresses that have been there for more'n ten years. You get hurt, I ain't paying you nothing for that day and you'll have to clear out so I can give your mattress to another man that *can* work. You probably won't last a whole day." He looked up at Charlie as he wafted a blue cloud of smoke into the air. "Can you live with that? If not, get the hell out of here and stop wasting my time."

"Yes, sir." Charlie was not put off by the man's demeanor. He needed money and could not turn down thirty-five cents. That was a pretty decent wage.

"All right. Don't say I didn't warn you. Go to the entrance of the mine and find Josh Lillard. He'll put you to work."

"Thank you, sir."

The man merely grumbled and went back to his paper work.

Charlie stepped back outside. A man about his own size approached him as he looked for the man called Lillard.

"They hiring in there?" he asked Charlie.

"Yeah, but that guy sure doesn't sound like he wants to hire anyone. He doesn't paint a pretty picture of life around here. Good luck."

"Yeah, I don't live here, but my family does. I brought my new wife over from Iowa to visit and introduce her to my relations."

"Well, good luck." Charlie offered a hand shake. "My name is Charlie Fisher."

"Pleased to meet you, Charlie. My name's Vern Marshall."

"Well, good luck again, Vern."

Charlie went to look for the man Josh Lillard who was standing by the entrance to the mine holding a clipboard. After Charlie introduced himself, Lillard asked how much experience he had in mining coal. When Charlie told him none at all, the man spit on the ground and growled, "'Nother one with no idee on what to do in that pit of hell. Mister, I got twelve-year-old boys that can pick out a ton every day. Then that idiot that's hirin' sends me greenhorns. Well, there's a hod coming up on the track. Climb aboard and it'll take you down."

Charlie's new acquaintance walked up just then, and he was instructed to follow the group of five men and young boy to the scuttle.

"Hi, Vern. Reckon you got hired on, too."

Vern fell into place beside Charlie. "Yeah, I ain't gonna be here but a month or so and then Bertha and I will head back to Iowa, down Leon way. You have a place to stay, Charlie?"

"No, I'm just stopping off for a week or so myself and then I'll push on to Port Byron, where my girl is waiting for me and we'll get married. I guess I'll just stay in the bunkhouse with the other men."

The group climbed aboard the scuttle as it rattled its way back into the mine. Torches were placed into the mine's walls every twenty feet, casting dim shadows along the track.

"Why don't you stay with me? My pa has plenty of room and always likes to meet new people. What do you say?"

"Sounds good. They didn't make the bunkhouse sound very inviting."

A man who appeared to be the boss of the gang started shouting over the noise of the hod car on its tracks. "Alright, most of you here are newbies so here's what's gonna happen. At the end of the track we get on an elevator down into the mine. At the bottom you'll find gas lamps and a pick. You're gonna give me at least a ton and a half of coal on your twelve-hour shift. You slack off and you ain't gonna be paid a dime. Toby there'll only be required to give me a ton since he's just a kid."

He paused long enough to spit a wad of chewing tobacco, splattering it off the wall. The car rambled to a stop before an elevator. "Everybody out. At the bottom of the shaft, you'll head into the mine about five hundred feet. This is called room and pillar mining. We carve coal out of rooms, and the only thing holding up the earth above you are pillars of coal. You accidentally disturb a pillar, you get several hundred feet of dirt, rock and coal down on your heads and you'll be shaking hands with the devil. I doubt the likes of this bunch will get much help from God."

Charlie was beginning to feel apprehension about his decision to mine coal, but kept quiet and just nodded his head in acknowledging the straw boss's admonitions.

The group of men and the boy Toby crowded onto the elevator. The boss slammed the gate down and pushed a button. The elevator lurched knocking down Charlie and one other man. The noise from the machine drowned out any complaints.

As they descended, Charlie shot a glance at Vern and could see he, too, was having doubts as to the wisdom of their choice of jobs. Vern gave a nod to Charlie in agreement to the unspoken fear they both felt knotted in the pit of their stomachs.

The elevator descended into the shaft for a full five minutes as it went down nearly 500 feet before coming to a second, teeth jolting stop. They all gratefully pushed against each other to get out when the straw boss opened the gate.

The man instructed them on how to wear the gas lamps attached to their helmets, told them to select a pick-axe and to follow him. As they threaded their way through several rooms, they saw the pillar supports of coal. A track with a second scuttle led them into a space that was smaller than the ones they had just passed through.

The straw boss showed them how to use their tool to knock out pieces of coal. He instructed Toby and one other man to gather up the pieces and carry them back to the hod. Charlie and Vern worked side-by-side as they knocked out large chunks of the fossil fuel.

Hour after hour, the men worked without speaking. The only sound was their heavy breathing, the clank of axe against coal, and thuds when the coal was thrown into the hod. They got five minute breaks every hour and were given fifteen minutes to stop mid-way through the shift to eat whatever they brought with them. Charlie, Vern and a few others didn't think of bringing something down with them so they had to go hungry or rely on the generosity of those who brought their lunch.

At the end of their shift, all the men wearily trudged back to the elevator to take the same noisy trip back to the top. As they stepped into the waning sunlight all the men and one boy couldn't even recognize each other as they were covered in black coal dust head to foot.

"C'mon, Charlie. Let's get out of here," exclaimed Vern. They collected their thirty-five cents from the paymaster and walked the mile back to the Marshall farm. They stopped by a large stream with a five-foot waterfall, shed their clothing and rinsed some of the grime from their bodies. Charlie had no change of clothes so he beat them against rocks, wrung them out and got back into them wet. It was not an ideal way to meet his new hosts but it would have to do.

Darkness had settled as Charlie was introduced to Vern's father and mother, Marion and Rebecca. He found Vern's mother to be a rather dour woman, not given to smiles and seemed a bit put out at having to set another place at the table. Marion, however, a man two inches shorter than his wife, was outgoing and engaged Charlie in conversation at dinner.

Vern introduced his new bride, Bertha, a very congenial young woman and not unpleasant to the eye. She warmly shook Charlie's hand and invited him to sit beside her at the table. Charlie was beat and could barely get his fork to his mouth as they dined on venison, cooked cabbage, and potatoes with a spoonful of very lumpy gravy.

After dinner, Vern set up Charlie in the hay loft of the barn and bid him goodnight. Charlie was asleep before Vern had gotten out the door. He slept soundly through the night, completely devoid of dreams.

The process went on for a week. Rise at dawn, eat a good breakfast, walk the mile to the coal mine and go through the same routine. Both Charlie and Vern were able to meet their quota of a ton and a half a day, often picking out chunks to make almost two tons. Each night was the same . . . dinner and bed.

At the end of their first week came the day that both Charlie and Vern would never forget.

54

Hattie

H attie had always been the meeker of the sisters living on the Reynolds farm. Whenever the two got into trouble, it was usually due to the actions of her younger sibling. She always felt she lived under the spell of Grace and her dominance of their sisterly bond.

Grace was the one who instigated their misadventures. Grace was the smarter of the two in school. Grace always seemed to be the one favored by Aaron when they were growing up. Grace had the special relationship with their grandmother, Lucinda.

So when she and Harmon fell in love and got married, Hattie felt she could finally move out of Grace's shadow.

It didn't help that she and Harmon moved into the Reynolds' home after her parents built a new cabin on the same property. Grace was still very much a part of her life, and Hattie found herself still at the receiving end of her younger sister's impulsive behavior.

After Aaron's death and Isaac Harmony's disgraceful conduct, Grace had withdrawn into her shell, and Hattie finally felt she had some breathing room. For some inexplicable reason, however, Grace regained her spontaneous nature after meeting Carrie Nation and felt she needed a new outlet for her fancies.

Grace's daily visit to the Harmon/Hattie household was taking its toll on the latter's nerves. She didn't like the feeling of inferiority, and it was stirring resentment. When she became pregnant with their first child, time was needed to devote herself to her impending motherhood. Grace threw herself into the notion that since she was going to be an aunt, she could also dictate how life would be better if Hattie would only see the good sense of her ideas. The baby should have its own room. The baby would be happier with a crib rather than a cradle. The baby, whether boy or girl, should bond with its new aunt right from its first day of drawing breath.

Grace said since she had learned many potions from Lucinda, that would keep the baby from the colic, help generate a better nutrient from mother's milk, and repel insects with a sachet of special herbs hanging over the sleeping baby.

Hattie no longer wished to be playing second fiddle and decided that the next time Grace intruded, she would tell her to leave her alone, that her help was not wanted or desired. She was heavy with child and irritable, just a few weeks away from birth. She wanted that remaining time to just be happy, to enjoy what she had always wanted . . . to be a mother.

On this day, Hattie glanced at the clock and could count the seconds before Grace would come through the back door, without bothering to knock. Grace's routine visit at precisely 10:30 in the morning, however, came and went.

Hattie lifted herself out of her chair and went to the door to peer out. No Grace. Here she was with an argument already rehearsed in her mind and nobody to whom she could give it vent. She stood at the back door for ten minutes waiting for her sister to appear, but Grace never showed. Something must be wrong, she thought, so she stepped off the porch and made her way back to the new cabin, some 300 feet away.

She went inside to find her mother standing at the stove preparing a bowl of potatoes. "Hello, Mother."

Hannah dropped a potato on the floor. "Oh, you startled me, Henrietta. What are you doing here?"

"Grace always shows up on our doorstep every morning at 10:30 sharp and this morning, she didn't. Is she all right? Did she take sick or something?"

"Why, no, honey. She left here a little after ten, and I haven't seen her since."

"I wonder where she could be."

"Well, I'm sure she will show up. I can never figure that girl out. She finally comes out of her depression and is back to her usual shenanigans. Maybe she went to visit Granny Lucinda's grave."

"Maybe. I oughta go look for her, Mama."

"You'll do no such thing," Hannah said, eyeing Hattie's stomach. "Grace can take care of herself. If there's anything we've learned about your sister, it's that. She's probably back at your house, wondering where *you* are."

"Okay, Mama. I'll bet that is where she is right now." Hattie turned and went back out the door. "Love you, Mama," she panted. The baby moved just then, bringing a fresh twinge of pain. "I think I'll go back and lie down."

After returning to the cabin she shared with Harmon, she lay on her back staring at the ceiling. She couldn't get comfortable in any position, so she got back up and went to the rear door and looked through the screen. "Where could she be? I'm getting worried."

Hattie decided that since the baby stopped moving and the pain had subsided, it wouldn't hurt to walk the path back up the mountain to where Granny Lucinda was buried. She grabbed a walking stick from the kitchen corner and started out.

As the trail gradually ascended to the top of the cliff that overlooked the Mississippi, she became more heated and was panting just as she reached the edge of an arroyo. Peering over the top into the gulch, she became woozy, made a misstep and tumbled over the brink. She half slid, half fell for about twenty feet and came to a stop against a briar bush, just before falling another fifty feet into the gully. She had clenched her eyes tightly against the pain she was feeling as the rocks, gravel and thorns tore at her skin. She opened her eyes and couldn't believe what she saw. Not three inches from her she looked at the unconscious face of her sister. Apparently, Grace had made the same misstep, and now they were both twenty feet down into the arroyo and another fifty feet from certain death if they hadn't been snagged by the same briar bush.

"*Grace!*" She reached over, and gently squeezed her shoulder dreading she would find her sister had died in the fall.

Grace moaned and slowly opened her eyes. She didn't realize where she was for the moment and gradually focused on the pained expression of her sister.

"Hattie?" She tried to sit up but couldn't get control of her arms which were covered in scratches and bruises. "What? What happened?"

"I came looking for you when you didn't show up this morning. I fell on the same place where you must have."

"I . . . I was just looking for some violets. Something to bring you when I visited this morning, but I . . . I fell." She glanced over the edge of ridge where they had both landed and fear gripped her. *"Oh, God!* What if . . . what if we hadn't been stopped by this briar?"

Hattie's face contorted with pain. "We have another problem, Gracie. The baby's coming."

Grace's eyes flew open in a panic and then calmed down immediately. "Okay, okay. Listen, Hat, nobody knows we're down here. Let's yell for help every once in a while. Let's move you, in the meantime, to a more comfortable position. If my little nephew is going to survive, we have to stay collected and do what we have to do. *Help!*"

Grace struggled to sit up and helped Hattie into a sitting position where she could deliver if nobody came to save them.

"Help!"

"The pains are coming closer together, Gracie."

"Lordy, what I wouldn't give for a pan of hot water right now! *Help!*"

Hattie tried to laugh at the thought of getting such a thing here but another spasm gripped her and she yelled out in pain.

"How far apart are they coming, Hattie?"

"About a minute apart. Oh, please, Lord," she prayed, "don't let anything happen to my baby boy."

"Boy? How do you know it's a boy?"

"I don't know. I just know. Oh, where's Harmon? Harmon has to be here. Where's my baby's daddy?"

"Calm down, Hattie! You can't panic now. You have a baby to think of."

"*Help!*"

Pain, again, contorted her face. "Oh, here he comes! Here he comes!"

Grace helped her lay flat on her back and lifted her dress. "Hold your legs up by the knees, Hattie. C'mon, we can do this."

Hattie obeyed and grunted again. "Oh, God, it hurts so much. He's coming out."

"Yes, he certainly is. Now just relax a moment and then push with every ounce of strength you've got."

Hattie obeyed again.

"*Help!*"

"He's coming, Hattie. I see his head. He's almost here. Come on, little one. One more push, Hattie."

With one mighty last heave, Hattie pushed and felt sudden relief.

The baby, covered in blood and the placenta, took his first breath of air and started wailing. He did *not* like being away out of the warm room from which he had just emerged.

Hattie's own tears were no longer of pain but of great joy. "Give him to me, Gracie. Give me my baby."

"Well, look here. It *is* a boy." She placed the crying newborn in Hattie's arms.

"Oh, he's beautiful, Gracie. He's absolutely beautiful."

"I think after this little adventure, you ought to name him Cliff," Grace said, peering over the edge into the chasm.

"Oh, no. Harmon and I decided that if it was a girl, we'd name her Rebecca, after Mama. If it was a boy, we decided it would be Harlan after Harmon's father." She moved aside her blouse and he started to suckle at her breast. "Harlan Aaron Lovell."

"He's a fine looking boy, Hat, but we have to find a way out of here. *Help!*"

Grace looked at the steep side of the gulch from where they both landed and knew she would never be able to make it to the top to go find help. "We'll just have to wait here until somebody misses us."

The sun had reached its zenith and was now inching its way across to the west. It cared not that its hot rays were giving great discomfort to two injured women and a newborn baby.

With the occasional *'Help!'* both sat and panted. Grace had taken off her own blouse and draped it over Harlan to keep the sun from burning him. She felt self-conscious because she had no undergarment, but embarrassment was the least of her predicaments right now. The sun continued to dip and had reached the crest of the opposite side of the gulch.

"Hattie! Don't move!"

The new mother looked up and saw a new fear in her sister's eyes. "*Why?*"

"Shh! Be very, very quiet. There is a rattler snaking its way towards you, not a foot away."

Hattie clutched Harlan closer to her breast, praying that he wouldn't start crying. Grace slowly picked up a rock and raised her arm over her head. If she sensed it would strike, she could only hope that her aim was true to the mark.

The rattler was about six inches from Hattie's left leg and raised its head to get a sense of this obstruction in its path. So far it had not given its warning rattle and seemed to sniff at Hattie's leg, its tongue flicking about and then slithering over. Harlan started to whimper at being held so tightly. Hattie locked eyes with Grace, who slowly shook her head in a warning.

Grace's arm twitched. If she missed, the snake would almost certainly strike at Hattie and, at this level, its fangs would sink into Harlan's exposed leg.

Grace hesitated for just a moment and was about to loft the rock when a rifle shot from above them found its mark, and the snake's head disappeared in a spray of blood, gristle and brain.

Grace was in the midst of a throw and couldn't stop as she threw the rock. Its path went straight through where the rattler's head used to be. It bounced off the edge and fell into the gully.

Grace and Hattie both looked up and saw Harmon slowly lowering his rifle, smoke still wafting out of the barrel. Hannah was standing there, too, peering over the edge.

"Stay right there," Harmon shouted down. "I have to go get a rope."

"Trust me on this one, Harmon," Grace yelled back, "we ain't goin' anywhere." She crossed her arms across her chest, reddening with shame when she remembered she had no shirt covering her.

Fifteen minutes later he was back with a rope which he tied around a tree and started to lower himself down. Grace had retrieved her shirt but didn't know if she could ever look at Harmon again knowing he had seen her half-naked.

He removed his shirt and fashioned it into a sling so Hannah could pull the baby up, doing so gently so it didn't swing into protruding bumbles on the hillside. Reaching the ledge, he allowed himself just a moment to hold his newborn son.

Thirty minutes later as the gathering dark put the arroyo in a gloom, Hattie, Grace and the new baby Harlan were at the top beside their rescuers.

A quick conversation told them that when Harmon got home from his work in the field and found Hattie missing, Hannah deduced that she had ignored her admonition and went looking for Grace. Knowing Grace liked to visit the grave of Granny Lucinda, they decided to take the trail to the top. Harmon thanked God he had brought along his rifle.

Hannah took her new grandson into her arms while Harmon picked up his wife and carried her. They started back down the trail.

It was a week before Grace gathered up her courage and went to call on the Lovells and their new baby. She avoided Harmon's eyes and had very little conversation with him. Hattie completely forgot her rebuke and welcomed her sister with open arms every time she stopped for a visit.

55

Charlie and Vern

C harlie had already decided that this would be his last day in the back breaking toil deep inside the earth, knocking out chunks of coal. He had enough money saved to make it the rest of the way to Port Byron. He gladly accepted the charity of Marion Marshall who waved off Charlie's offer to pay for his room and board.

"You've been a good friend over the past couple of weeks to my boy and his new bride. Consider your debt paid and perhaps you can do the same for someone else in this situation."

"Thank you, sir. I'll be back to stay the night and I'll leave at dawn tomorrow morning."

"God speed to you, son."

Vern fell into step beside Charlie as they made their morning trek to the mine. "We've only known you for a fortnight, my friend. I hope our paths cross again someday."

"I feel the same, Vern. You and Bertha have been good to me so I kind of feel a kinship to you."

When they got to the mine, they wearily climbed aboard the hod as it started its noisy way into the colliery. By the time they got to the elevator shaft, Charlie was more than a little happy that this would be his last trip to the bottom.

When it jolted to a stop the crew of five men and two young boys got out, picked up their tools and gas lamps and followed the track into the coal lined tunnel.

The straw boss instructed Charlie to go to a room that had just been started to be excavated and told Vern to work in the tunnel and clear the coal floor so more track could be laid. An hour passed as the men labored to get out the fuel.

One of the boys who was operating the hod slipped and fell. As he did so, he grabbed at the brake to catch his fall but, in doing so, hit the release and it started rolling forward. A separate hod just behind ran into the first one and the momentum of the two pushed them down the track at a speed they weren't designed to do.

As both hods gathered speed, men were jumping out of the way to keep from getting run over. Vern tried to stop the car but was powerless against its weight and force. The scuttle was up to more than ten miles an hour when it came to the end of the rail and flew through the air, slamming into one of the pillars holding up the tunnel sending flying chunks in every direction. The second car followed and it, too, hit the column knocking down the remaining pieces of the column of coal.

Charlie's room was just beyond the decimated pillar, and he turned to hear a loud rumbling as the ceiling started to crumble onto the floor. Dust, coal and screams of men pierced the air as the ceiling continued to fall. In the span of ten seconds, the room where Charlie, two other men and the boy Toby were sealed behind a wall, their only way out.

The only light in the room from their gas lamps did little to penetrate through the thickness of dust. When the rumble of falling coal finally ceased, they could do little to catch their breath. Every intake of air only brought minute particles of coal dust, sending all of them into coughing spasms.

As the dust began to settle Charlie called out to the others. "Everybody all right?"

He got responses only from Toby and one other man. Charlie aimed his lamp towards the blocked tunnel and saw a leg twitching under the mass of coal. He quickly crawled to the man and started digging at the lumps of coal. He had worked his way up to the man's hip when it stopped its spasms and was still. He knew the man had to be dead under all that crushing weight.

"Fellas, it won't be long before our air runs out and all for we know, nobody on the other side of that blockage lived through it. It's up to us to save ourselves."

Toby understood and joined Charlie in pulling away coal pieces. He was lifting another piece when a new rumbling started. Charlie looked up and saw a half ton piece of coal tearing loose from the wall that was about to fall on top of the boy.

He grabbed Toby's shirt and pulled him back just as the coal fell right in the spot where the boy had been kneeling. They spider-crawled backwards away from the blockage as a fresh blanket of dust fell settled on top of them.

"Thanks, Charlie. You saved my life."

"Make me a promise, Toby. If we get out of here, don't you ever come back. Ain't worth it."

"You kiddin'? My ma would have me hide tacked to the barn door if I ever tried to set foot down here again."

"Alright. Let's go again but keep an eye on that ceiling."

The other man in the room made a groaning noise. Charlie aimed his light to see a large head wound that lacerated his scalp. The fellow then passed out.

"Looks like you and me, Toby. We gonna get out of here, it's you and me."

The two of them began to claw at the debris to clear out the tunnel when again they heard a new rumble. A piece of the ceiling fell loose. Charlie yelled and tried to push Toby away again, but it happened too fast and both man and boy were struck on their heads. A large cut was opened on Charlie's scalp and Toby, while thrown clear, was knocked out. Another piece then fell and although Charlie raised up his arms in protection he was still buried under two hundred pounds of coal. The second mass of rock and dirt also knocked him unconscious.

The only thing that saved Charlie from suffocation was a dome created by his arms around his head, making a pocket of air. A sliver of an airway helped, so that air from the room could still get in through to keep him alive for a while longer.

On the other side of the blockage between room and tunnel, a dazed Vern raised himself up to a sitting position and tried to make sense of what had just happened. The moans and shouts of others in the tunnel brought his focus back to his surroundings. Seeing the blocked corridor, he jumped up and started digging with his hands to get to the room where he knew his new friend Charlie had been working.

He realized that he was probably dead, but he worked with a frenzy anyway pulling chunks of coal out of the way. He yelled back to others to come and help but none came, and he knew it was going to be only him attempting a rescue.

"Charlie! Can you hear me, Charlie?" He paused to listen but there was only silence coming from the room on the other side of five tons of rock, dirt and coal.

He worked furiously for thirty minutes, pausing several times to call out Charlie's name. He was half way through the snarled mass when he thought he heard a muffled moan. Vern cocked his ear but the noise of others behind him in their own injuries kept him from hearing anything further. He redoubled his efforts and fifteen minutes later, he heard a muted cry for help.

In the room, Toby had regained consciousness and realized Charlie was buried under the mass of coal. The boy started his own rescue attempt, but the blow to his head had caused a concussion and he soon passed out again.

Charlie also woke up from his blackout. He tried to assess his surroundings. He could see the sliver of light coming from the room, but was afraid that if he tried to move his arms it would only trigger another collapse of coal. He decided that if he was going to die, he would die fighting and attempted to claw at the obstruction over his head. There was no maneuvering his arms to get an advantage to helping himself and he stopped struggling.

He prepared himself to die in this black tomb. He thought of his family, his brothers and sisters. "I love each and every one of you." He tried to remember their names but his head wound had him confused and could only think of Skillet, Buffalo Bill and Orville. Those names didn't sound right to him and his head hurt too much to continue.

The one name he did remember was the one that brought him peace. "Grace. Little Bit. I love you. I'm sorry. I never should have left you." At that point, he sighed and passed out.

Vern worked feverishly at the mound of coal before him. He heard no more sounds from the room but that didn't stop him. He had to stop periodically to work on the pile of coal growing behind him.

Charlie came to again and thought he could hear somebody grunting. "Toby? Toby, boy . . . is that you?"

Silence.

"*Charlie? Can you hear me, Charlie?*"

"*Vern?* Is that you, Vern?"

Vern finally opened up a small hole into the room. He yelled into the gap. "*Charlie? Can you hear me, Charlie?*"

He then heard a muted reply. "*Vern?* Is that you, Vern?"

Scrabbling at a quickened pace, Vern widened the gap between the tunnel and the room. He finally created a wide enough space that he could crawl through. He crept right over the top of Charlie, loosening up bits of coal that fell onto Charlie's face and in his mouth.

Charlie spit out the dust. His mouth was so dry that he could barely whisper. "Watch it, Vern! You're right on top of me."

Vern pulled himself through and turned to dig at the debris on top of Charlie. He pulled off two huge chunks and could see Charlie's face in the dim light of his hat lamp.

"Boy, am I glad to see you," he whispered through cracked lips. "I thought I was a goner for sure."

Vern pulled the rest of the coal off his friend and helped him into a sitting position. "Anything broken, Charlie? You okay?"

"I've got me a terrible headache, but I think I'll live. Where's Toby?"

Vern scooted over to the unconscious boy and felt his pulse. "He's alive, Charlie, but we still gotta get him and you out of here."

"There's another fella over there that needs help, too."

Vern crawled over to the man and saw two lifeless eyes staring up into the darkness. "Sorry, I think he's dead."

"Let's get out of here, Vern. You go on through the hole and I'll get Toby up and you can pull him through."

Once Toby was safely through the hole, Charlie had to dig a bit more to widen the hole because he had twenty pounds on Vern and couldn't make it. Finally able to crawl through, Charlie stood up on wobbly knees. "Can you carry Toby back to the elevator?"

"Yeah, he don't weigh much. How come they let kids like this work down here? It ain't right."

Making their way past more bodies in the tunnel, the trio got to the elevator and got inside. Vern hit the switch and the lift lurched into an agonizing screech of metal. Charlie collapsed to the floor as it ascended to the top.

They were met by a cluster of men who had rushed in to assist in any rescue of miners that might still be alive. One of them took Toby and, throwing the boy over his shoulder, led the way back to the entrance of the mine.

Stepping into sunlight, Charlie and Vern both stood and thanked their Maker they were alive. Someone gave them blankets and guided them to a table where a doctor was waiting to treat those who made it out.

"Water," Charlie croaked. A woman, probably the wife of one of those still below, handed him a dipper of tepid water. He didn't think he had ever tasted anything so sweet.

"Take care of Toby, Doc, before you get to us. He's in a bad way."

The doctor attended to the boy, washed the laceration on his scalp and clamped a towel over it to stem the bleeding. Charlie looked over as Toby's eyes open. Charlie nodded and Toby mouthed the words, "Thank you" before passing out again.

Just at that moment, a buckboard pulled up to the table. Vern looked up and saw Bertha jump down and run to hug him. "Oh, I was scared to death. I heard about the mine collapse and all the way down here, I didn't know if you was alive or dead."

"Darlin', take us home."

Three days later Charlie felt he was back to good enough health that he would continue his way to Port Byron. Vern and Bertha offered Charlie the use of a horse and told him they would stop by in Port Byron on their way back to Iowa to retrieve the animal.

Charlie climbed onto the horse, reached down and took Vern's hand and shook it. "Vern, no more coal mining. Okay?"

Bertha chimed in, "Oh, don't worry, he won't. I'll see to it."

Charlie pulled on the reins of the pinto and headed west.

56

Grace

Harlan lay sleeping peacefully in Grace's arms as Hattie was taking a nap for some much needed rest. The doctor had come by and found the baby to be quite healthy despite his traumatic birth just two weeks earlier.

Battered and bruised from head to toe, the sisters had also received the blessing of the physician to resume their lives. Grace was quite pleased to be declared Harlan's godmother. She only hoped she would find somebody who could give her the children as precious as the one she was now holding.

As happened often during times of peace and quiet she looked back on the twists and turns of her life since Charlie left over five years ago: his death, Duggie Hayes, winning the horse race, Isaac's betrayal, the birth of Harlan. Those incidents could not even begin to address the pain of losing her father. The darkness in her soul compounded mightily but the chance meeting of Carrie Nation was the catalyst for casting out her inner demons giving her a new resolve to start life anew.

Harlan's eyes flickered briefly, but seeing the comforting face of his aunt lulled him back to his dreams.

Yes, life was going to be okay. She just knew it.

A day later Hannah went to her flour bin only to discover it full of weevils. Twenty pounds of the white powder had to be thrown out and left her with no ingredients for the bread baking she had planned for the day.

Grace was coming in the back door with an armful of wood and dumped them into the bin behind the stove.

"Mama, if you have nothing else for me, I'd like to go and see if Hattie needs any help."

"Yes, as a matter of fact, I do have something. I am completely out of flour and want you to run into the Mercantile and get some for me. Here's a dollar. That should be enough for twenty-five pounds. Make sure you check it closely. I just threw out nearly that much because of weevils."

"Alright, Mama. I should be back afore noon."

Grace took the money and went to saddle Champion for the ride into Port Byron. Mounting the horse, she clucked a language she had made up just for her sorrel. Champ knew what to do and they started down the path towards town.

Grace stopped at the end of the lane to sit for a moment and study the gate that was half hanging off its post. "Daddy would have fixed that by now, Champ. You know that the last time I ever saw Charlie alive was right here. I remember swinging on it while he rode off to take up with Buffalo Bill." She sighed and reached down to smooth out Champion's mane. "Did you know he called me his Little Bit? I hated that at first, but I grew to love it as an endearment. I'd do anything to have him hold my hand right now and say it to me again." A tear formed in her eye. "**Anything!**"

She clucked again, and Champion took the path towards town.

As she turned onto the dirt road that Port Byron had named Main Street she passed by two men who were standing behind a tree.

Isaac Harmony nudged his cousin and nodded towards Grace. She passed them by, unnoticed, as they skirted along the town's businesses, staying out of her sight.

"Cousin," said Duggie Hayes, "this is our chance to get even for all the embarrassments she's placed on us. I got me an idea. Follow me around to the back."

Grace rode up to the front of the Mercantile, got off Champion, tied his reins to the post and went inside.

The cousins went to the back door of the store. Duggie pulled a dirty rag from his pocket and put a match to it. The flames flickered and the cloth caught hold. He opened the back door and threw it in and quietly shut the door. "Come on. Let's get out of here afore somebody sees us."

They edged around the backs of two stores, crossed back to Main Street over to the river side. They sat down on the bank and waited so they could watch the results of their arson and savor their revenge.

Inside the store, Grace went to the counter where the merchant stood taking inventory of his canned goods. "Good morning, Mr. Thomas." The rotund man turned and returned her greeting.

"Mama needs twenty-five pounds of flour, but I need to check it for weevils."

"I can guarantee you, Gracie that it is weevil free, but you're certainly welcome to go through it." He measured out what he thought the weight would be and placed it on the scales. "How's that new baby doing up to your place?"

"Right as rain. He's even gained a pound or two since being borned."

Ezekiel measured off another scoop of flour, and the scales read just a shade over 25 pounds. "That be all for you, Gracie?"

"Long as I'm here, you got any mail for the Reynolds."

"Let me check. That reminds me. I found a letter addressed to you that must have fallen behind the sorting table. Let me see if I can find it for you."

While she waited, Grace browsed through the store and stopped to look at some pretty dresses stacked on a ledge behind the counter. She pulled out a gingham print and sniffed her nose.

"You smell something, Mr. Thomas?"

"Here's that letter, Gracie. It looks like it might have been under that table for a spell. What did you say just now?"

Grace reached out and took the letter. "I said, 'Do you smell something?' "

Ezekiel turned and saw smoke coming from under the door that led to his storage room out back. "Oh, Lordy. Something's on fire back there."

Grace threw the letter on the counter without looking at it and followed him to the door. When he opened it, the supply of fresh oxygen caused the room to explode and flames belched out, singeing the hair on their arms.

"Gracie, grab anything you can find, and let's try and beat back the flames before it takes the whole store."

She looked around and grabbed the gingham dress she was going to try on, handing it to Ezekiel. He took the dress and stepped into the room, swinging the dress as he made his way into the flames. Grace retreated into the store, grabbed another from the pile of dresses and rushed back. Smoke was now billowing out and she caught a lungful, sending her into a spasm of coughing. She took a deep breath and stepped into the room.

The smoke was so thick that she couldn't see Mr. Thomas, but she had no trouble seeing the flames. She started swinging the dress trying to beat out the blaze.

She quickly became disoriented, and bumped into a wall of shelves. One of them collapsed and an iron fell, striking her on the head.

She collapsed to the floor, out cold, as the fire inched its way closer to where she had fallen.

57
Charlie

As Charlie reined in the pinto at the gate leading to the Reynolds farm, he saw a rider on a horse a half mile distant. He gave it no further thought and nudged the pony up to the farm. He stopped at the cabin, not knowing that it was now occupied by Hattie and her husband, Harmon. He dismounted, went onto the porch and knocked on the door.

Harmon answered the knock and saw a bearded Charlie standing at the door. "Can I help you, Mister?"

"Oh, I'm sorry. I was looking for Grace Reynolds. Don't she live here anymore?"

"Grace is my sister-in-law. Who might you be?"

"I'm Charlie Fisher."

"*Charlie Fisher?* But . . . but that can't be . . . you're dead."

Charlie, a bit taken aback. "Now do I look like a dead man to you?"

"I'm flabbergasted. Grace and the rest of the family thought you passed on . . . some sort of a drowning incident back in '03."

"I've been sending Grace letters, so how could she think I was dead?"

"Well, she ain't gotten them."

"Where is she, might I ask?"

"I just saw her head into town less'n ten minutes ago."

Charlie remembered the rider he saw. "I must have just missed her. Mebbe I can catch up."

"Sure wish I could see the look on her face when you do. You ride fast enough, you can catch her by the time she gets there. I don't know where she was going but there's not that many places in town so you can prob'ly find her soon enough."

"Thanks. What's your name?"

"Harmon. Harmon Lovell. I married Henrietta a couple of years ago."

"Well, son of a gun. Hattie's married! *I have* been gone awhile. See you later, Harmon." Charlie mounted and wheeled the horse around and took off at a gallop back to the road.

Harmon stood watching for a minute and turned to go back in the house. He called out to his wife. "Henrietta, you ain't gonna believe who just came to our front door."

Charlie was getting excited now. It was more than five years since he'd laid eyes on Grace, and he wondered how much she had changed. He rubbed the whiskers on his chin and thought she might be a bit surprised herself.

Dead, he thought to himself. How could she not have gotten his letters?

Charlie galloped onto Main Street, and the first people he saw were Hayes and another man sitting on the river side of the road. He couldn't believe his eyes. His sworn enemy had turned into a hulk. He must have grown eight inches and put on a hundred pounds from the last time he saw him. Hayes instantly recognized the rider on the pinto.

"No. It can't be. It *can't* be!"

"Who's that, Duggie?"

"Fisher. Charlie Fisher. Back from the dead."

Charlie glared at his former friend and the tall good looking man standing beside him. Contempt boiled up inside of him, and he was about to rein his horse in but thought better of it. He had to find Grace. He recognized Champion standing in front of the Port Byron Mercantile but what alarmed him was seeing smoke coming out of the front door.

Others had noticed it, too, and they all started running towards the store. One man shouted to start a bucket brigade from the river to the store. Some leaped into action to find any receptacles they could find to carry water.

Charlie pushed the pinto into a full gallop and was off the horse before even reaching the front of the store. He rushed over and untied Champ's reins to give the horse a chance to get away from the fire. He ran into the store calling Grace's name.

Looking around he saw no one inside. Maybe she had gotten out the back. No. Impossible. Flames and smoke came pouring out of the back room.

"Grace! Gracie? Where are you?"

He ran to the storage room and putting his arm over his face, ran into the wall of fire. He stumbled over a body and fell to the floor. Reaching around to the person he could tell it was a man who had been overcome by the smoke. He jumped up and pulled at his leg, dragging him back into the main part of the store. Two men had come in and were holding rags over their faces.

"Get this man out of here!" Charlie yelled at them. Turning, he went back inside. He got on his knees to stay as low as he could to the floor and started feeling around. He couldn't see through the smoke. *"Gracie! Gracie! Where are you? Call out!"*

The crackling blaze made it hard to hear, but he thought he might have heard a moan from just in front of him. The heat was becoming more intense as he felt his way around the floor. His hand came down on Grace's arm. He put his face in as close as he could, and the flames that were creeping towards her cast their light on the most beautiful woman he had ever seen, even more than Clementine. She had red hair. It must be Grace.

He crawled around, put his arm under her and drug her back to the storage room door. Somehow it had swung shut on him. He reached up to grab the handle but it was too hot to the touch. Both of their bodies were up against the door keeping it from swinging inwards.

Another lungful of smoke had Charlie coughing hard. He pulled her back away from the door, took the gingham dress that she still had grasped in her hand and reached up to turn the knob, swinging it open.

He dragged her through the door, inch by inch. He stood up to take her in his arms and carry her out when the flames in the storage room ignited a drum of coal oil. The blast slammed against their backs, propelling them through the front glass window. They landed in the dirt road bleeding from several cuts. Their lungs gasped for fresh air. They laid there for a minute trying to catch their breath. Slowly, Grace regained consciousness.

Her eyes fluttered open, and she stared into the face of a bearded man who was grinning widely at her. She tried to focus on his features but thought she had to be dreaming. Maybe she was dead and this was Heaven.

"Good morning, Little Bit. It's been a while."

"Who . . . who . . . what?" Grace couldn't find the words as she tried to make sense of the man in front of her. No one ever called her Little Bit. Only Charlie could call her that.

Charlie reached up and wiped some of the grime from her face, brushing her red hair back behind her ears.

"Told you I would be back, Little Bit. I always keep my promises."

"Charlie?"

Epilogue

Charles Henry Fisher married Grace May Reynolds on March 14, 1910 and the ceremony was attended by Hannah Rebecca Reynolds and Henrietta and Harmon Lovell. There may have been others in the wedding party, but their names have been lost to the ravages of time.

They had four children, just as her grandmother had said she would: Early Ernest, Charles Henry V, Harvey Harold, and Iva Lorraine. Early, also known as Earl, sired no children during his marriage to Helen Killian. Charles V married Blanche Marie Marshall and sired Gary Lee (author of this story) and Sheryl Rae. Harvey married Marilyn Rogers and they had one child, Marilyn Jean. Iva Lorraine never married and lived with her parents until their deaths. She then lived with her brother Earl until his death, and then with my parents until her own demise.

Charlie died on March 11, 1962 just three days shy of their 52nd wedding anniversary. Grace passed away on September 8, 1969. All four of their children are deceased.

Grace was a direct descendent of John Alden, of *Mayflower* fame, although I am certain she was never aware of it.

This story is entirely fictional with just a few grains of truth in it. The incident of a boy cutting Grace's braids off in school is true. Charlie was, indeed, a musician but gave up the life as one because of Grace. "I don't want him around all those women," is a direct quote handed down from my father, Charles V. Also, Grace laid claim that John L. Sullivan was, indeed, her great uncle. Lucinda Buzzard Reynolds was a full-blooded Lakota Native American.

There is no record of any of the incidents mentioned in the story actually happening to Grace or Charlie except those listed above.

Buffalo Bill Cody did, indeed, travel overseas for a series of shows featuring his Wild West program. Mark Twain had visited New Orleans many times. The Wright Brothers fame is well known. The incident involving the *General Slocum* exploding on the East River is a well-documented account.

Vern Marshall and Bertha Mae Blatt were my maternal grandparents. I thought it would be interesting to intertwine their stories well before their children (my parents) would meet, marry and sire me.

I hope you enjoyed the story.

Charlie, 1940

Grace, 1945

50th Wedding Anniversary, March 14, 1960